BETWEEN THE LIVING AND THE DEAD

This Large Print Book carries the
Seal of Approval of N.A.V.H.

A DAN RHODES MYSTERY

BETWEEN THE LIVING AND THE DEAD

BILL CRIDER

THORNDIKE PRESS
A part of Gale, Cengage Learning

GALE
CENGAGE Learning·

Farmington Hills, Mich • San Francisco • New York • Waterville, Maine
Meriden, Conn • Mason, Ohio • Chicago

GALE
CENGAGE Learning®

LIBRARY OF CONGRESS CATALOGING-IN-PUBLICATION DATA

Names: Crider, Bill, 1941–
Title: Between the living and the dead / by Bill Crider.
Description: Large print edition. | Waterville, Maine : Thorndike Press, 2016. | ©2015 | Series: Thorndike Press large print mystery | Series: A Dan Rhodes mystery
Identifiers: LCCN 2015037204 | ISBN 9781410484215 (hardcover) | ISBN 1410484211 (hardcover)
Subjects: LCSH: Rhodes, Dan (Fictitious character)—Fiction. | Sheriffs—Fiction. | Texas—Fiction. | Large type books. | GSAFD: Mystery fiction.
Classification: LCC PS3553.R497 B48 2016 | DDC 813/.54—dc23
LC record available at http://lccn.loc.gov/2015037204

Published in 2016 by arrangement with St. Martin's Press, LLC

Printed in Mexico
1 2 3 4 5 6 7 20 19 18 17 16

*This one's for Seepy Benton,
always an inspiration.*

I look for ghosts; but none will force
Their way to me: 'tis falsely said
That there was ever intercourse
Between the living and the dead.
— WILLIAM WORDSWORTH,
"THE AFFLICTION OF MARGARET"

CHAPTER 1

Sheriff Dan Rhodes had a feeling he was in trouble when Seepy Benton announced that he had a summer job.

"You've given up teaching math?" Rhodes asked.

"No," Benton said. "I've just decided not to teach summer school."

Seepy Benton, or Dr. C. P. Benton as he was known to his students, taught math at the community college branch in Clearview. He also considered himself an official member of the Blacklin County Sheriff's Department because he'd gone through a law enforcement academy for the local citizens.

"I thought you liked teaching," Rhodes said.

"I do," Benton said. "It's the best job in the world. I just thought I needed a change, some time to expand and grow."

Rhodes glanced at Benton's waistline. "I'd

say you're off to a good start."

They were sitting at Rhodes's desk in the county jail early on a warm Tuesday evening in late May. Rhodes had been called to help Alton Boyd, the county animal control officer, deal with a dispute between a couple of neighbors about some dogs. Diane Kelley had accused one Theodore Hertel of stealing four of her dogs. Mr. Hertel claimed that the dogs came over to his house all the time and ate the food intended for his own dogs and that he didn't want four more mangy hounds hanging around, mooching food, and giving his dogs fleas. He'd called Boyd to pick up the dogs, and when Boyd arrived, Ms. Kelley had shown up and asserted her claim. Boyd had called Rhodes, and between the two of them, they'd straightened things out. Rhodes had stopped by the jail to fill out the paperwork, and Benton had found him there, though Rhodes suspected he'd dropped by hoping to find Deputy Ruth Grady, whom he'd recently started dating. She was on patrol, however, so Benton had settled for Rhodes.

Benton ignored the remark about his waist, which was just as well, Rhodes thought. To tell the truth, Benton was looking better than usual. His beard was neatly trimmed, and so was the half circle of hair

10

that had formerly been rather shaggy. His old straw hat looked as disreputable as ever, though, as it rested on his knees. Benton had a hand on the brim to keep it from slipping to the floor.

"Don't you want to hear about the job?" Benton asked.

Here it comes, Rhodes thought. "Does it involve investigating?"

Benton looked surprised. "How did you know?"

Rhodes hadn't known, but he'd been afraid something like this was going to happen. Benton thought of himself as a fine criminal investigator, and he was probably going to set himself up as a private eye. Just what Blacklin County needed.

"Well?" Benton said when Rhodes didn't say anything more.

Rhodes gave in. "You'll be sort of like Sam Spade?"

"Oh," Benton said. "I thought you'd guessed it, but you're wrong. I'm not going to be a private eye. Try again."

Rhodes was relieved. At least he didn't have to worry about Benton nosing into his investigations and trying to solve crimes. He hoped.

"I can't think of any other kind of investigator," he said. "You'll have to tell me what kind you're going to be."

"A paranormal investigator," Benton said.

Rhodes started to say that while Benton wasn't normal, he didn't appear to be paranormal, but he knew that wasn't what Benton had meant. What he had meant sounded to Rhodes as if it might be even more trouble than if Benton had decided to become Sam Spade.

"You're going to be a what?" Rhodes asked.

"Paranormal investigator. I'm going to open my own office. Clearview Paranormal Investigations. Or CP Investigations. Get it?"

Rhodes got it, but he didn't want it.

"You gonna be a ghost hunter?" Hack Jensen asked from across the room.

Hack was the dispatcher. He was tall and thin, with a little mustache like the kind worn by characters in 1940s movies.

"Well, you could call it that," Benton said. "I'll have to hire a couple of assistants, of course. I can't do everything alone."

"Who did you have in mind as an assistant?" Rhodes asked, thinking that it had better not be Ruth Grady.

"Harry Harris, for one," Benton said. "He's interested in the paranormal."

Rhodes didn't say anything, but Benton

12

must have noticed something in his look.

"All that other stuff is over and done with," Benton said. "I think Harry and the dean got it all straightened out."

That "other stuff" was something Rhodes and Benton had discovered in the course of an earlier investigation. Harris had somehow found a way to fake his evaluations in ProfessoRater, an online tool for students. There was also the little matter of his not having reported a dead body he'd seen.

"You think he'll be reliable?" Rhodes asked.

"Sure. He's made mistakes, but he's repented and been scolded by the dean. And by you, too, I believe. Now he just wants to hunt ghosts."

"We had us a ghost right here in the jail once," Hack said.

"No, we didn't," Rhodes said. He looked at Benton.

"Did so," Hack said.

Rhodes wasn't going to get into that kind of argument. "Some of the inmates thought we had a ghost," he told Benton, "but there wasn't one. We don't need you to perform an exorcism or anything."

"I won't be doing exorcisms," Benton said, "but I could locate the ghost for you."

"There wasn't any ghost," Rhodes said.

"It was purely imaginary. Like all ghosts."

"That's what you'd like us to believe," Hack said.

"Only because it's true."

"If you say so. I remember we looked up jailhouse ghosts on the Internet. Couldn't find much information, though, just something about some jail in Australia or somewhere."

"I remember that," Lawton said, coming in from the cellblock. Lawton was the jailer, and he was Hack's opposite in appearance, rounder and smoother-faced, though almost as old. "I was hopin' we had us a real ghost, but I never saw it. You oughta take another look on the Internet, Hack. When we had us that ghost, or thought we did, it was before the Google. Might find more stuff now."

Hack was already at the keyboard of his computer before Lawton finished talking.

"Lord a-mighty," Hack said after a few key taps. "Look at this."

Lawton looked over his shoulder. "Who'd've thought it? Look at this, Sheriff."

Rhodes wasn't inclined to get up. "Just tell me."

"I typed in 'jailhouse ghost' just like I did the other time," Hack said. "Guess how many hits it got."

14

Rhodes wasn't inclined to guess any more than he was inclined to get up. He'd already used up his daily capacity for guesses when he'd guessed about Benton's job. "Just tell me."

"It's a mighty big number," Lawton said, and Rhodes knew he was in for it. Those two couldn't resist delaying any kind of real answer for as long as they thought they could get away with it.

"Sure is," Hack said. "A great big one. I don't think you'd ever guess it, even if you was to try."

"Just tell me," Rhodes said.

"Bigger than the population of Clearview," Lawton said. "Bigger than the whole county. You reckon it's bigger than the population of Houston?"

"Nope," Hack said. "Not that big."

"How many people live in Houston, anyway?" Lawton asked.

"I don't know," Hack said, "but it's a whole lot. I could look it up on the computer."

"It's over two million," Benton said before Hack could click the keys. "So how many hits did you get?"

Rhodes grinned. Lawton and Hack might not tell him, but they wouldn't play their little game with Benton.

"It's less than two million," Hack said.

Or maybe they would.

"It's over a million, though," Lawton said.

"One million four hundred and ten thousand," Hack said, giving in. "About. And you know how long it took to get that many hits?"

"Not long," Benton said.

"Three-tenths of a second," Lawton said.

Hack turned away from the computer and gave Lawton a look. "I'm the one who did the Googlin'."

"I'm the one suggested it," Lawton said.

"Never mind," Rhodes said. Those two would argue for the rest of the day if he let them. "That's a lot of jailhouse ghosts."

"Some of those hits are repeats," Benton said. "Maybe most of them. Those don't count."

"Still a lot of 'em, no matter how many repeats," Hack said, turning back to the computer. "Wonder if our ghost is in there."

"We didn't have a ghost," Rhodes said.

"Maybe you did," Benton said. "Maybe you still do. Why not let me check it out? I have some equipment out in my car."

"You need equipment to hunt ghosts?" Hack asked. "What kind?"

"More than you might think," Benton said. "That's why I'll need assistants. I can't

16

carry all of it. You wouldn't be interested in a second job, would you?"

Hack laughed. "Not me. It's all I can do to hold down this one. Lawton, now, he could use some work. Get him on his feet, get him some exercise."

"What?" Lawton said. "Exercise? I'm the one keeps this place clean while you sit in that chair and play solitaire on the computer. If anybody around here needs exercise, it's you."

Rhodes cut in again before the argument could start.

"The county won't let them take second jobs," he told Benton. "You'll have to look somewhere else for your pack mules. Now tell us about the equipment."

"Bet it's just like *Ghostbusters*," Hack said. "Ecto-goggles, ecto-containment unit. All that stuff."

"And a slime blower," Rhodes said. "Can't forget the slime blower."

"That's not exactly what I have," Benton said.

"Next you'll tell us you don't have clients who look like that Sigourney Weaver did thirty years ago," Hack said.

"You seen her lately?" Lawton asked. "Looks just the same. I think she's some kind of secret servant to Gozer the Gozerian her ownself."

"If Seepy got hired by somebody looked like that, he'd be in trouble with Deputy Grady, anyway," Hack said. "Best to stick to clients that look like me and you."

"Getting back to the equipment," Benton said.

"Yeah," Lawton said. "If you ain't got ecto-goggles, what do you have?"

"Well," Benton said, "to start with I have a couple of really good flashlights."

"Heck, ever'body has a flashlight," Hack said. "What else?"

"I have a digital recorder, the thermal scanner, the motion sensor, and the EMF meter."

"Hold on," Hack said. "What's that last one again?"

"The EMF meter," Benton told him. "It detects electromagnetic fields."

"Ghosts are magnetic?"

"It's not the same thing," Benton said. "It's complicated, but let's just say that there are electromagnetic fields all around us. The presence of a ghost can disturb the field. The EMF meter I have is a combination meter and thermometer, since ghosts can cause a sudden temperature drop in a room or a building."

"Kinda like the PKE meter the Ghostbusters had," Lawton said.

"A little," Benton said. "If there are ghosts around, they might register on it some way or another."

Rhodes resisted the temptation to say there was no such thing as ghosts. It seemed obvious to him, but it was equally obvious that Benton was serious about all this.

"We don't want to disturb the customers back in the cellblock," Rhodes said, "and I really don't want to get that ghost rumor started again. I think we'll take a pass on the ghost hunt."

"You've always been a killjoy," Hack said.

Rhodes nodded. "True, but somebody has to be the voice of reason. That's why they pay me the big bucks."

"You're not a believer, are you," Benton said.

"He's hardheaded, all right," Hack said.

"I used to be," Benton said, "until I started reading Stuart Hameroff. He's a professor at Arizona State, and he uses quantum physics to explain that life after death might be possible."

"Let me guess," Rhodes said. "It's complicated."

"Not really," Benton said. "The idea is that there are structures called microtubules in our brain cells and that our consciousness —"

"Never mind," Rhodes said, holding up a hand to stop the flow of words.

"Microtubules?" Lawton said.

"That's right," Benton said. "You see —"

"Never mind," Lawton said. "I need to stick to simple stuff, like Casper, the Friendly Ghost. Him, I can understand."

"Figures," Hack said. "Him bein' in a comic book and all. That's about your speed."

"I guess you know all about microtubes and such," Lawton said.

"Microtubules," Hack said.

"Whatever. I guess you know all about 'em."

"More'n some people I could name. Know as much about Casper as you do, too."

"Bet you can't sing the theme song."

"How much?"

"Can't bet money." Lawton indicated Rhodes. "It's illegal, and the sheriff's sittin' right there. Anyway, I'd win."

"Not a chance," Hack said, and he launched into an off-key rendition of the theme song from the cartoons. After a couple of bars, Lawton joined in.

Rhodes looked at Benton. "See what you've done?"

20

Benton stood up. "Time for me to make my exit."

"Me, too," Rhodes said. "I could use a good night's sleep."

"I hope you get it," Benton said, "and that you don't have that theme song stuck in your head. Like I do, now."

Rhodes was well into his good night's sleep when the phone beside the bed started to ring.

"Don't answer it," Rhodes's wife, Ivy, said, her voice thick with sleep.

"I have to," Rhodes said, turning on the light on the nightstand. "It might be an emergency."

Ivy rolled over onto her back and put her arm over her eyes. "It's always an emergency."

Rhodes grinned and answered the phone. It was Hack, calling from the jail.

"Got a little problem," Hack said. "Deputy Grady can use some backup."

Ruth Grady was sensible and level-headed. If she said she needed backup, she had a good reason.

"Who else is on duty?" Rhodes asked.

"Don't matter," Hack said. "They're all too far off. This is on the north side of town, where Ruth was patrollin'."

Rhodes sighed. "What's the problem?"

"You ain't gonna believe it," Hack said.

"Just tell me," Rhodes said.

"You don't put much stock in co-incidences."

"Just tell me," Rhodes said again.

"Much less the other thing," Hack said.

"Hack," Rhodes said. "It's late, and I was asleep. Now tell me what the problem is."

"Well," Hack said, "It seems like there's somethin' goin' on at the haunted house."

CHAPTER 2

Rhodes held the phone away from his ear and looked at it. Ruth Grady was dating Seepy Benton. Rhodes hoped there was no connection between this call and Seepy's new enterprise. He put it back to his ear and said, "Does this have anything to do with Seepy Benton?"

"Not as far as I know," Hack said, "but then I don't know very far."

Rhodes sighed and said he'd look into it. He hung up the phone and got dressed as quickly and as quietly as he could, but Yancey, the little Pomeranian, woke up and came into the bathroom to see what was going on. The dog was too sleepy even to make a single yip, and because he wasn't the one who had to go check out a haunted house, he just watched Rhodes for a couple of seconds, then went back into the spare bedroom to get cozy in his doggy bed.

The two cats, Sam and Jerry, were a bit

more curious, but not much. Rhodes had thought cats were nocturnal animals, but as far as he could tell, Sam and Jerry enjoyed sleeping just as much at night as they did during the day, and during the day they really enjoyed it. Or appeared to, since that was about all they did.

Sam was solid black, and Jerry was black and white. They purred and rubbed against Rhodes's legs when he went into the kitchen to get himself a drink of water from the refrigerator before leaving. They didn't purr and rub for long, however. They'd lost interest in him and lain back down on the floor by the time Rhodes put his empty water glass on the counter. They were both asleep by the refrigerator, and it was as if he'd never been there.

Rhodes got his Kel-Tec PF-9 and ankle holster out of the gun safe in the room where Yancey was sleeping. Yancey didn't bother to wake up again. The PF-9 was a lightweight pistol with a polymer body that carried seven 9 mm cartridges. Rhodes figured it would provide enough firepower to take down any ghosts he was likely to encounter.

Rhodes left the house by the front door. He didn't want to go through the back and wake up Speedo, who might start barking and arouse the neighbors, who wouldn't be pleased.

The county car was in the driveway. Rhodes got in and backed into the street. Turning north, he saw heavy black clouds banked in the sky, blocking the stars. A late-spring norther was on the way, and he hoped it would bring some rain. It seemed as if it hardly ever rained anymore.

A flash of lightning ran down the clouds, and a few seconds later Rhodes heard a dim rumble of thunder. Just the right kind of weather for investigating strange doings at a haunted house.

Rhodes supposed that nearly every small town had a haunted house. There was one in the nearby town of Obert, and Rhodes had experienced a little trouble there a few years back. Not from ghosts, however, and he wasn't expecting to run into any ghosts tonight, either. Or this morning. The clock on the dashboard said it was a little after midnight.

Clearview's haunted house was only a couple of blocks from the local cemetery, which was probably one reason it was considered to be the home of ghosts. Another reason was that it had been abandoned for forty years or more. It had belonged to a high school teacher named

Ralph Moore, who had died one evening of a sudden heart attack. Because he'd died on the weekend and had few friends, his body hadn't been discovered until he failed to show up for school on Monday morning. A good many rumors had circulated afterward, all of them gruesome and all of them untrue, as far as Rhodes knew. One story said that the teacher hadn't had a heart attack but that he'd been killed and mutilated with an ax. Another said that his pet dog had eaten part of his body to avoid starvation.

The stories were magnified in some cases because Moore had died on a Halloween weekend, and trick-or-treaters had horrified each other for years afterward with tales of how they'd stood on Moore's front porch ringing the doorbell while the dog had been munching on his body parts inside the house.

Another thing that added spice to the stories was the fact that Moore was supposedly an unpleasant character. In an era when teachers felt free to deal out corporal punishment, Moore, at least according to rumors, had dealt out more than his share and enjoyed doing it. He'd been known to sit on his porch with a pellet gun and shoot at dogs and cats that wandered into his yard. And even at the occasional youngster who happened by.

There were other stories, but Rhodes didn't remember them. Once, not long after he'd first been elected sheriff, he'd looked into the musty old reports on Moore's death, just out of curiosity. There hadn't been much of an investigation, but the sheriff at the time hadn't thought there needed to be one. As it happened, Moore didn't even have a pet dog. He had a small aquarium with a few fish, but they hadn't escaped to feed on him. He hadn't been mutilated, either. The only marks on the body were a few bruises that had probably resulted from Moore's having fallen when he had the heart attack.

Not that anybody would believe the facts. The rumors were a lot more fun.

As for the stories about his pellet gun and his doling out of spankings at school, no record of those things remained.

Moore's only kin had lived in some other state. Rhodes couldn't remember which one. Colorado, maybe. Or Wyoming. Somewhere out west, anyway. They hadn't wanted the house, but they hadn't wanted to sell it, either. They'd never come to see it or remove any of Moore's things. The half block of property it sat on had little value to them or to anyone, but as far as Rhodes knew someone was still paying the taxes on it to keep it from being sold at auction on the courthouse steps. So the old house had stood there, surrounded by its wrought-iron fence, deserted, while people speculated about it and told stories of strange noises and spectral faces at the windows or lights moving past them.

Over the years the stories had become fewer and less often told, until now the house just crumbled away on a lot that was so overgrown with trees and weeds that most people who drove past it probably didn't give it a glance. Some of them might not even have known the house was there, but every now and then someone would notice something amiss, and the sheriff's office would get a call.

Like the one tonight. Hack hadn't been too clear about what the problem was, and Rhodes wasn't sure whether that was because of Hack's typical behavior or because Ruth Grady hadn't known exactly what it was and hadn't been able to tell him. "Disturbance" was all the information Rhodes had been able to get out of Hack. Rhodes was a little suspicious because of Ruth's involvement with Seepy Benton, and the old Moore house was clearly the kind of place that Benton would like to prowl through in his new capacity as a paranormal investigator. If there was anywhere in Clearview that was likely to have a few ghosts, the Moore house was the place.

Rhodes saw Ruth's county car from several blocks away. It was parked at the curb in front of the Moore house, its light bar flashing. Rhodes pulled to a stop behind it, turned on his own light bar, and got out.

The house sat well back from the street. The lot took up most of the block, so no other houses were very close. Across the street was the city water tower, and it had the entire block to itself. The other houses Rhodes could see down the street were all dark. The people inside were getting a good night's sleep.

Rhodes saw the entrance to the cemetery a couple of blocks away. He'd had an adventure or two there, but he hoped that wouldn't be the case this time.

Although the thick clouds were still some distance away, a few drops of rain hit Rhodes in the face. Ruth Grady got out of her car and met him. She was short and stocky, and she was wearing a hat. This was one of the times Rhodes wished that he didn't look so silly in a hat. It would at least keep the rain out of his face. It would also cover up the spot on the back of his head where his hair had thinned, but that didn't matter so much in the rain.

Ruth held a big tactical LED flashlight in one hand, but she hadn't turned it on.

"What do we have here?" Rhodes asked her.

"I'm not sure," Ruth said. "Somebody who was driving by called it in to Hack. The number was blocked, so he doesn't know who it was. The caller said there were flashing lights in the house, and some gunshots."

"Hack said there was a disturbance," Rhodes told her.

"People get disturbed by gunshots."

Lightning lit up the sky to the north and gave the clouds a momentary glow.

"People are suggestible, too," Rhodes said. "Haunted house, thunder, lightning reflecting off the window glass."

"What window glass?" Ruth asked.

Rhodes looked at the house. It was old, nearly a hundred years old, he thought. Two stories tall, with a covered porch on both floors, at least on the front. Rhodes couldn't see any window glass. The wrought-iron fence was covered with vines and bushes, and trees grew around most of the house, concealing some of the windows. The ones that Rhodes could see all had screens over them. The screens must have been rusted, but Rhodes couldn't tell that in the darkness.

"Your friend Seepy Benton isn't in there, is he?" Rhodes asked.

"So you've heard about his new job," Ruth said.

"I have. You think he's in there?"

"He hasn't started looking for ghosts yet," Ruth said.

She sounded doubtful, but Rhodes decided to let it pass. "Have you heard any gunshots since you got here? Seen any flashes of light?"

"No. It's been quiet. Except for the thunder."

As she said that, thunder crashed practically overhead, and lightning crackled. The wind started to blow, whipping the trees around the house. An aluminum can bounced and clattered along the street.

"Littering," Ruth said. "Class C misdemeanor."

"Probably not for just a can," Rhodes said. "I'll go pick it up."

As he started for the can, rain began to fall in big drops.

"Forget the can," Rhodes said, changing direction. "We need to get under cover."

At one time the gate in the wrought-iron

31

fence had been chained and locked, but both chain and lock had long since disappeared. The gate gave a shrill *skreeek* when Rhodes pushed it open, and he was reminded of an old movie he'd once seen on late-night TV, back in the days when they still showed old movies at odd hours. *Cry of the Banshee* was the title, and it had starred Vincent Price, which would surprise absolutely no one who'd watched a lot of those old movies. As Rhodes remembered it, things hadn't ended well for Price.

Rhodes had to break several vines to get the gate open. If there was anyone in the house, they had to find another way in.

The sidewalk was overgrown with grass, with only a few patches of concrete to be seen. Rhodes jogged to the porch and up the three steps to get under the roof. Ruth was right behind him. She had drawn her service revolver and held it in her right hand. The flashlight was in her left. The wind blew rain onto the porch, and they moved closer to the door. Soggy leaves tumbled around their feet.

"Better watch your step," Rhodes said. "Some of the flooring could be rotten."

Ruth turned on her flashlight and shined the beam over the porch floor.

"Looks pretty solid," she said. "They used

good wood in these old houses."

"Be careful anyway," Rhodes said. "Check the door."

Ruth turned the light on the door. There was no screen. The top third of the door had three windows. Two of them still had glass in them. On the bottom of the door, the white paint was flaked and peeling. There was no doorknob. Old doorknobs were collectible, and someone had removed it.

Rhodes reached out and gave the door a push. It didn't move. He pushed harder. The glass rattled in the panes, but the door still didn't move.

"Stuck," Rhodes said. "I don't think anyone got into the house this way, at least not tonight. We'll have to check the back."

"I'll go," Ruth said. "I have the flashlight."

Rhodes was pretty sure that "I have the flashlight" meant "You're too old and decrepit to be wandering around in the dark because you might get hurt." Or maybe it meant "If you hadn't been in such a hurry to get under cover, you'd have gotten your own flashlight out of your car."

It wasn't something Rhodes wanted to think about too much. Anyway, Ruth was better equipped than he was to enter a house where gunshots might have been fired. She had her revolver, and her duty belt held a collapsible baton, pepper spray, and handcuffs. All Rhodes had was his pistol. He bent over and removed it from the ankle holster.

He straightened, glad that he could do it without his bones creaking, and said, "We'll both go. You don't want to go in the house without backup."

"What if someone comes out the front door?" Ruth asked.

Rhodes touched the door. "It would take a while to get this thing open. If anybody's in there, we'll get them before they can get out. As much noise as we've made out here, I'd be surprised if anybody was still in there."

Ruth didn't say anything. Rhodes listened for sounds inside, but all he could hear was the wind in the trees and the pattering of the rain against the house.

"Rain's slowing down," Rhodes said.

"Okay," Ruth said. "Let's go."

"You first," Rhodes said.

Ruth was already on her way down the steps, the flashlight beam floating over the drenched weeds as she made her way around the house. Rhodes followed, the cold rain soaking his already wet shirt and getting through his shoes to soak his socks as well.

The back of the house was different from the front. The fence was still standing, but the wide gate was off its hinges and lying in the weeds. An old rusted-out Dodge pickup stood there as if it were planted, sunk into the ground almost up to the wheel hubs. The tires, practically indestructible, still clung to the rims, and they'd be around for a long time to come. The truck's hood was up, and Rhodes suspected that the engine was gone. The skinny hackberry tree growing up through the engine compartment was a clue.

The tracks through the crushed weeds were a clue to something else.

"Somebody's been here and gone," Ruth said, shining the light along the tracks. "Not too long ago, either."

So maybe there had been someone in the house after all, and even though it was clear that a vehicle had left the backyard, they couldn't be sure that there wasn't someone still inside.

The back door was missing a top hinge, and it hung open at a slant. Ruth directed the flashlight beam into the interior. Rhodes couldn't see anything other than what appeared to be an empty room. They approached it with caution, keeping well apart from each other. When they were closer, Ruth was able to illuminate more of the room. It was small, probably an enclosed porch.

Ruth went up the steps, stood at the top, and let the beam roam over the inside, which looked completely bare. She glanced at Rhodes, who nodded. He was pretty sure that anybody who'd been inside was long gone, if not before he and Ruth had arrived, then shortly after the squealing of the gate and the pushing on the front door. It wouldn't to do take chances, however.

Ruth stepped inside the doorway and walked through the small room to stand on one side of a door leading into another room. Rhodes followed and stood on the opposite side of the door, all too aware of the way his clammy clothing stuck to his body.

"Me first," Rhodes whispered. "Put the light on the ceiling."

Ruth turned the flashlight up toward the ceiling of the larger room, giving it some partial illumination. Rhodes went through the door with his pistol at the ready. He saw no one, and no one shot him, so he told Ruth to come on through.

She did and moved the light around the

room, which had obviously been a kitchen. The old cabinet doors were all open, and some of them had fallen into the floor. So had a couple of drawers. The cabinets and drawers were empty except for some scraps of browned newspaper that had been used as shelf liner. The stove and sink were gone. The refrigerator was still there, being too old for anyone to steal. Its door was missing. It could have been removed as a safety measure, or maybe someone had thought of a use for it and taken it. Spiderwebs hung from the cabinet doors and in the windows.

The floor was covered with cracked and buckling linoleum. The linoleum was covered with dirt and littered with trash: a few fast-food sacks, soft drink cups and cans, and a couple of candy wrappers. Transients might have spent a night in the house from time to time. Or maybe someone else had. The story about the house being haunted was usually enough to keep people away.

The place had the musty smell that all old deserted houses did, but Rhodes detected another odor in the air, too.

"You smell that?" he whispered.

Ruth nodded. "Gunpowder."

Just as she spoke, one of the fast-food bags rustled and something scampered across the floor, rustling through other bags as it ran.

Ruth didn't move, but Rhodes twitched. He thought it was a testimony to his own iron nerves that he didn't blast away at it with the Kel-Tec.

"Mouse," he said.

"I know," Ruth said. "Probably a lot of them in here."

"Beats staying outside in the rain," Rhodes said, thinking that the mouse didn't know how lucky it was not to have been blown away by a volley of 9 mm slugs.

Three doorways led out of the kitchen, one to the front of the house and to what Rhodes supposed had been the sitting room, one on the left to what must have been a dining room, and the other to what had probably been a bedroom.

Rhodes inclined his head to his left and said, "Door number one?" He nodded toward the one that opened into the sitting room and said, "Or door number two? Or," nodding to his right, "door number three?"

Ruth moved toward door number two, which was the one the mouse had fled through. Rhodes thought that was a less than excellent choice, but maybe the mouse had moved on. Ruth waited on one side of the door until Rhodes had positioned himself on the other side.

They stood there and listened. Rhodes

heard the trees brushing against the sides of the house and the wind rattling the window-panes and whining through cracks in the walls. The rain had stoppped.

Rhodes didn't think anyone was in the house with them. He hadn't heard the sounds of anyone moving, and nobody had tried a shot at the flashlight. Or at the mouse. They had to follow procedure, though.

"Let's do it the same way," he said, and Ruth directed the flashlight beam upward again.

Rhodes slipped around the door and into the dark room, sweeping his pistol side to side, but there was no one to shoot at, and the mouse was either gone or in hiding. The room was empty of furniture, but something lay in the middle of the floor. Rhodes had a bad feeling that he knew what it was.

"Come on in," he said, and Ruth entered the room, shining the flashlight around. The beam stopped when it came to the lump in the floor, which wasn't a lump at all.

It was a man. He was quite still, and Rhodes was sure he was dead. Ruth turned the light on the man's face, and Rhodes sighed.

"You know who he is?" Ruth asked.

"Yeah," Rhodes said. "I do."

"You don't seem surprised to find him like this."

"I'm not," Rhodes said.

CHAPTER 3

Rhodes used his cell phone to call Hack and request an ambulance and the justice of the peace. Hack was naturally curious, but Rhodes didn't give him a chance to ask any questions. The cell phone was fully charged, but the battery held only so much juice.

"I'll send 'em," Hack said, and Rhodes could tell the dispatcher's feelings were hurt.

"I'll tell you about it later," Rhodes said. "We're busy right now."

"Right," Hack said, and broke the connection.

The ambulance was just a formality, as the man lying on the dirty floor was dead. There was no doubt about that. The JP would make the declaration, and the EMTs would remove the body. That's what he was now. The body. It didn't matter that Rhodes had seen bodies before, and it didn't matter that the dead man hadn't been an upstanding citizen. Now he was just the body. There was something sad about that, every single time.

"We have ten or fifteen minutes," Rhodes told Ruth, shaking off his brief melancholy. "I'll take some photos. You should probably do the same."

Both of them used their cell phones to take pictures of the crime scene and then e-mailed them to the sheriff's department. Rhodes didn't think they'd be of any help, but it was procedure.

"We should check the rest of the house," he said when they were finished with the photography.

"You want the upstairs or the downstairs?" Ruth asked.

"I'll go up," Rhodes said. "You stay down here. Don't let anybody mess up the crime scene any more than you have to. I'll get the front door open so they can come in that way."

"What about a flashlight? We could use some gloves, too."

"I'll get them from the car," Rhodes said. The cell phone had a flashlight, but he preferred the real thing, and they needed the latex gloves to handle any evidence they picked up.

He went into the little entry hall in front of the sitting room. It took a good bit of tugging to get the door open, but he finally managed it. He jogged out to his car. The rain had stopped, but Rhodes's socks still felt squishy inside his shoes, and the wind pressed his cold, wet clothes against him. He got the gloves and flashlight from his car. When he returned to the house, he pushed the door shut again, but wet leaves had already blown inside. Rhodes didn't think anyone was likely to complain.

The stairway to the second floor was in the hall, and Rhodes focused the flashlight on it.

"Watch out for mice up there," Ruth said.

"Nobody likes a smart aleck," Rhodes said.

He handed her a pair of latex gloves, and she put them on. He put on his own pair of gloves and gave the stairs another look. The steps were dusty and dirty, but they appeared to be solid. Old houses like this one were built of wood that easily held its own through the years and were much sturdier than the ones being built now.

Rhodes didn't think anyone had used the steps in a while, but he went up to make a quick search of the four upstairs bedrooms, just to be sure. He found that they were all much the same, small, square rooms with a few strips of wallpaper hanging off the walls or lying on the floor. A good bit of the old woven backing still clung to the wall.

The rooms contained little of the furniture that had once been in them — a couple of dressers with all the drawers pulled out and broken and an armoire with shattered mirrors on the doors. Rhodes figured those things had been too heavy for anyone to carry down. No mice jumped out of the furniture to surprise him, for which he was grateful. He didn't want to gun down a mouse.

He went into a narrow hallway and looked at the stairs to the attic. They were even dirtier than the ones to the second floor. No one had used them for years, maybe decades. He might have gone ahead to check the attic in spite of the evidence of its disuse, but he heard the ambulance arrive. By the time he got down the stairs, the JP was there, too.

Ruth had the EMTs and the JP waiting on the porch, and Rhodes told the JP to come in first. His name was Wade Franklin, and he was a tall slab of a man wearing a long robe with pajama bottoms visible below the hem and a pair of run-down house shoes. He didn't look thrilled about being called out so early in the morning, so Rhodes didn't comment on the color of the pajamas.

"Sorry to have to wake you up," Rhodes said as they went into the hall.

"Just part of the job," Franklin said. "What do we have here?"

Rhodes stopped him at the door to the sitting room and pointed inside. "A man named Neil Foshee. He's from Railville."

"That's over the county line. Why'd he have to come and get killed in our county?"

"He does some business here," Rhodes said. "With his cousins."

"I don't think I know him. What kind of business?"

"Meth," Rhodes said. "We just shut him and his cousins down not long ago. They're all out on bail."

"Looks like this one will be staying out," Franklin said. "I'd better have a look at him."

"I don't want to prejudice your findings, but it looks to me like he's been shot."

"Shine a light on him," Franklin said.

Rhodes did. Foshee lay on his back, still as a plank, eyes wide open and staring at the ceiling. Two red blotches stained the front of his blue shirt.

"Looks dead to me," Franklin said. "I'll check to be sure if you don't think I'll mess up your crime scene."

"Just don't touch anything else," Rhodes said.

"I know better," Franklin said, taking three careful steps into the room and bending down over Foshee's body. In a couple of seconds he straightened and walked back to join Rhodes. "He's dead, all right. I'll get the paperwork done."

"Thanks," Rhodes said.

They went back to the porch. Franklin left, and Rhodes asked the EMTs to wait a few minutes while he and Ruth went back inside and looked over the body. Ruth held the flashlight, and they saw nothing nearby. Rhodes knelt down and checked the shirt pockets. They were empty. He patted the pants pockets and heard some clinking. He reached into the pockets and came out with some change and keys.

"No cell phone?" Ruth asked.

"Back pocket, maybe," Rhodes said. He rolled Foshee over. "Nope. Just a wallet."

"Some people have gotten smart about cell phones," Ruth said. "Too smart to leave a helpful video on one for you to find it."

Rhodes stood up. "Sometimes you can find one, though. Even I did."

"With a little help."

"From your friend Seepy," Rhodes said. "I admit it, but I've learned a little bit about cell phones since then. I even know that if Foshee had a phone, it was probably a prepaid one that he bought at Walmart or from some guy at a flea market."

"A burner," Ruth said.

"A burner?"

"That's what we streetwise cops call prepaid phones. Burners."

"You might have been hanging around Buddy too long," Rhodes said. "He's the one who likes cop talk."

"Just trying to clue you in."

"I'll try to remember the term," Rhodes said.

"They don't really burn them," Ruth said.

"I know. They just buy a dozen or so and throw one away every couple of weeks."

"Right. So it's like they burn them. I guess. You can even buy burner phone numbers now. Before long cell phones won't be much use for catching crooks."

"Not unless we stay smarter than they are," Rhodes said. "Look around. Foshee must have had a weapon, too."

They looked but couldn't find anything else.

"Killer probably took it with him," Ruth said.

"Probably," Rhodes said. "We'd better call in the EMTs."

Ruth went to tell them they could come in and get the body. Rhodes heard her warning them to be careful of touching anything, but he thought it was probably unnecessary. The room looked to be clean of any clues. He'd have someone go over it carefully in daylight, but he wasn't expecting to find anything. If there had been any bullet casings, they'd have seen them already. The killer had used a revolver, or he'd picked up the brass. Maybe the trash in the kitchen would provide some clues, but Rhodes knew even that was unlikely. They'd never find the prepaid phone, either. The burner. It would be at the bottom of a creek by now or smashed up with a hammer and thrown in a trash pile.

If life were fair, Neil Foshee would've written a dying message in his own blood on the dirty floor of the sitting room and made things easy for them, unless the message was like the ones in books and movies and too cryptic to be figured out by anybody but some genius private investigator. Blacklin County lacked genius private investigators, and for that matter it lacked private investigators of any kind. Rhodes considered that a good thing.

Neil Foshee might have looked at it another way. He might have thought that if life were fair, nobody would have shot him, but considering his life choices up to this point, it was almost inevitable that he'd come to a bad end, like Vincent Price in *Cry of the Banshee.*

The EMTs came in, laughing at some joke or other one of them had told. Death didn't bother them. They'd seen too much of it. Auto accidents, heart attacks, bad falls, lots more. To them Foshee was just another body.

Rhodes wondered if there was anyone to mourn Foshee. Maybe his former girlfriend Vicki Patton would, but Rhodes didn't think she'd have any reason to. Foshee had thrown her out of his pickup at a roadside park, leaving her without any clothes or even her purse. She'd been the one who'd helped Rhodes find the meth house where Foshee and his cousins were cooking up a batch of chemical mischief, and Rhodes hoped she hadn't seen him since then. He'd have to ask Ivy about it. Ivy had become friends with Vicki after Rhodes had introduced them. It had been an awkward introduction, since Vicki had been wearing nothing more than a raincoat at the time. Rhodes grinned at the memory. It wasn't often that he got to take a naked woman home with him and surprise his wife.

Foshee wouldn't be doing any grinning, not anymore. The EMTs loaded him into a body bag and hauled him out. That was the end of the story for him.

Except it wasn't, not really. His death would affect other people, and somebody would have to pay for it. Rhodes didn't know who or how, but he knew that the story of a death like Foshee's didn't end when the body bag was zipped up.

"It's kind of creepy, isn't it," Ruth said when the EMTs were gone.

"What's creepy?" Rhodes asked.

"This house is supposed to be haunted, and a man was killed here tonight. Do you think there'll be another ghost to keep the first one company?"

"I don't even think there was a first one," Rhodes said.

"Maybe not," Ruth said. "What do we do now?"

"I'm going to call the jail and tell Hack to get in touch with the sheriff's office over in Railville and let somebody there get in touch with Foshee's next of kin. You're going to stay here and look around for clues."

"It's a little dark for that."

"You don't have to look too hard. Mainly I want you here in case somebody decides to come back and check what happened."

"What about the trash in the kitchen?"

"When you finish your shift, put up some tape. I'll get someone to go through it tomorrow. For now, concentrate on this room."

"What about ghosts?"

"I wouldn't worry about them."

"Okay. It's not them I'm worried about anyway," Ruth said.

"What are you worried about, then?"

"Mice."

Rhodes wished he hadn't flinched at the mouse. "I think you can handle the mice."

"What if they gang up on me?" Ruth asked.

"Maybe it's Hack you've been hanging around for too long," Rhodes said. "Instead of Buddy, I mean."

"Now you've hurt my feelings."

"Time for me to leave, then," Rhodes said.

When Rhodes called Hack, the dispatcher tried to pump him for information about what had happened at the Moore house, but Rhodes gave him only Foshee's name and condition.

"Who killed him?" Hack asked.

"He didn't give us a name," Rhodes said.

"Have I mentioned that you're gettin' sarcastic lately?" Hack asked. " 'Cause if I haven't, I should've. You need to watch that. It's not like you. You ever get yourself checked out for that low T problem?"

"I don't have a low T problem."

"How do you know you don't if you ain't been checked out?"

"I just know. My problem is that somebody woke me up from my good night's sleep."

"Not my fault people go and get killed when you're asleep. You oughtn't take it out on me."

"You're right," Rhodes said, tiring of the argument. "When Andy Shelby comes in this morning, tell him to get out to the Moore house. Ruth will fill him in, and he can finish working the crime scene."

"Yes, sir. Anything else you want me to do while I'm at it?"

"When Buddy comes in tomorrow, you have him look for Earl and Louie Foshee. They should be easy enough to find. We probably have their address there in the office. We need to ask them some questions."

"Yes, sir. Anything else?"

"Neil Foshee was living in Railville, so call the sheriff over in Bates County and tell him what's happened. If there's a next of kin there, he'll know, and he can do the notification."

"You want me to wake up the sheriff in the next county?"

"Wouldn't be a good idea. He's not as easygoing as I am. He might come over here and shoot you."

"This ain't his jurisdiction."

"Never mind," Rhodes said. Nobody ever got his sarcasm. "Don't call the sheriff. Just call the department."

"Okay. What else?"

"Just don't wake me up again," Rhodes said.

"I promise not to," Hack said. "Not tonight, anyway."

"It's morning already," Rhodes said.

"There you go, then," Hack said.

Driving home, Rhodes considered what might have happened to Neil Foshee. Drug deal gone bad? That was certainly possible, considering Foshee's propensity to sell meth that his cousins Earl and Louie cooked up. Someone getting revenge for something Foshee had done? Also a good possibility, since Foshee was the kind of man who'd force a woman to take her clothes off and get out of his car in a roadside park. Rhodes didn't think that Vicki Patton would kill anybody, but if there was anything he'd learned during his years as a sheriff, it was that anybody would do just about anything, given the right circumstances. Or the wrong ones.

Two questions nagged at Rhodes. Why was Foshee in the Moore house and how did he get there? The tracks in the backyard would need some study. If Foshee had come with someone, who was it? If Foshee had arrived in his own vehicle, who'd taken it away?

The set of keys in Foshee's pocket had included a key to a car or pickup, but that didn't necessarily mean someone else couldn't have had a key. For that matter, Foshee could have walked to the house from somewhere else.

Rhodes decided not to worry about things for now. There would be plenty of time for that after the investigation got started, and that wouldn't be until tomorrow. As for right now, Rhodes would just try to get a little sleep.

Rhodes tried to be quiet going into his house, but Yancey came yipping out of the dark as soon as Rhodes opened the door.

"Good boy," Rhodes said. "No burglar's going to get past you."

Rhodes didn't really believe that. He was just trying to contribute to Yancey's self-cofidence. In reality, if a burglar came through the door, Yancey would cower under the bed and not make a sound.

"You'd better be quiet or you'll wake up Ivy," Rhodes said, as Yancey continued to caper.

"He's already done that," Ivy said, coming out of the bedroom. She wore a long green gown and looked as fresh and awake as if she'd been up for hours. Rhodes could never understand how she managed it.

"You look a little bedraggled," she said. "Did somebody beat you up?"

It was a logical question, Rhodes supposed. He'd occasionally found himself in physical confrontations.

"It was raining," Rhodes said. "I'm sorry we woke you. I hoped I could slip in without Yancey getting excited."

"Have you ever managed that before?"

"I can't remember," Rhodes said as Yancey danced around his feet and yipped.

"I can," Ivy said. "None. That's how many."

"You could be right. This time I thought I might get lucky."

Ivy cocked her head and looked at him. "You thought you might get lucky?"

"I meant about Yancey."

"Well, you never know about getting lucky," Ivy said. "Are you coming to bed?"

Rhodes grinned. Low T, indeed. "I'll race you," he said.

CHAPTER 4

Rhodes hadn't gotten a lot of sleep, so he was a bit bleary-eyed the next morning. He and Ivy sat on the steps into the backyard while Rhodes threw a squeaky ball for Speedo and Yancey. Speedo, a border collie, was considerably bigger than Yancey, but that didn't matter to Yancey, who had the advantage of being somewhat more agile and could occasionally slip in under Speedo's jaws before they could clamp down on the ball.

"I need to tell you something about last night," Rhodes said as Yancey ran across the yard with Speedo in pursuit. "We found a body in the old Ralph Moore house. It was Neil Foshee."

"He's the man who dumped Vicki at the roadside park," Ivy said.

"That's the one."

"I'm sorry he's dead, but he wasn't much of a human being."

Yancey came up and wanted Rhodes to take the ball, but he wouldn't let it go when Rhodes reached for it. Speedo stood close by, watching, ready to take off if Rhodes managed to get the ball and throw it again.

Rhodes got the ball and threw it all the way across the yard. The two dogs whirled and took off after it.

"Has Vicki seen him lately?" Rhodes asked.

"If she has," Ivy said, "she hasn't told me. Not that she would. She knows I wouldn't approve."

The telephone rang inside the house. A landline. Rhodes liked having it.

"I'll get it," Ivy said, standing up. "You stay here with the dogs."

Rhodes thought that was a good idea. Yancey had the ball again and brought it over to Rhodes.

Ivy came to the door to tell Rhodes about the call. "Hack says it's an emergency."

"It's always an emergency," Rhodes said.

"He sounds excited."

That was unusual. Hack was hardly ever excited.

"Come on, Yancey," Rhodes said, standing up. "Time to go back inside."

Yancey wasn't interested. He ran across the yard with the squeaky ball, trying to get

Speedo to chase him. Speedo looked at Rhodes as if to say, "Want me to round him up for you?"

Rhodes chased down Yancey himself and grabbed him up. He took the ball out of his mouth. It was easier to get it from him than from Speedo because Yancey couldn't get it into his mouth and always had a precarious hold on it.

Yancey wriggled like a landed fish and tried to grab the ball, but Rhodes threw it to Speedo, who bit and made it squeak. The sound made Yancey wriggle even more.

"That was mean," Ivy said. "Are you going to talk to Hack or not?"

"We're coming," Rhodes said, carrying Yancey across the yard and into the house. He was careful not to set the little dog down until the door was safely closed.

Yancey ran to the door and whined.

"You're lucky you get to live inside," Rhodes told him. "Speedo has to stay out there in the yard in a Styrofoam igloo, and you get the run of the house."

Yancey didn't seem to care about being lucky. He ignored Rhodes and continued to whine at the door. Rhodes left him there and went into the kitchen. Ivy handed him the phone.

" 'Bout time," Hack said when Rhodes

spoke. "We got a situation."

"Don't we always?" Rhodes said.

"Not like this," Hack said, and instead of digressing, he went right into it. "We got a wild bull on the loose from the vet's and headin' for the Walmart. You need to get out there right now."

"That's Alton's job," Rhodes said.

As the animal control officer for the county, Alton Boyd was the one in charge of things like bulls. However, it seemed that Rhodes was called to help him out all too often, having been involved with capturing both alligators and donkeys.

"Alton needs some backup. Before you say send somebody else, you got Andy doing a crime scene, and Duke's off in another part of the county. Alton's got Dr. Stanton and his assistant, but they ain't enough."

Dr. David Stanton was a veterinarian, fairly new in town. He had a new building a half mile or so down the highway from the Walmart. Rhodes wasn't sure who his assistant was.

"If that bull gets to Walmart, much less gets in the buildin', there's gonna be big trouble," Hack said. "You better get on out there."

"I'm on the way," Rhodes said.

■ ■ ■ ■

The Clearview Super Walmart was located out on the highway that led to Railville. Rhodes arrived at the entrance to the parking area and looked around. It was a little early for there to be much of a crowd, only about an hour after sunup, but there were a few cars in the lot near the entrance to the building. There was always someone shopping at Walmart, no matter what time it was. A couple of motor homes were parked at one edge of the lot. They weren't likely to belong to customers but to people who'd pulled in for the night. Walmart seemed to welcome travelers, whether they were customers or not.

Looking down the highway, Rhodes saw the bull. It was a reddish color, maybe a Brangus. Rhodes wasn't entirely sure. Whatever it was, it was well over a ton of beef on the hoof, and it was ambling along the side of the highway with several people in hot pursuit. One of them was Alton Boyd. Another was Dr. Stanton. Rhodes didn't recognize the others.

Boyd was hazing the bull with a lariat, trying to turn it back in the direction of the veterinary clinic. He might as well have been a housefly for all the good he was doing. The bull kept its eyes straight ahead and kept on coming toward the Walmart.

Rhodes pulled into the parking lot and got out of the county car. He wasn't sure if he could keep the bull out of the lot, but he could try. A bull in a parking lot wasn't as bad as a bull in a china shop, but if the bull got in among the cars, it could cause a lot of damage, even to as few cars as there were. Just a good head butt would crumple the sides, and the bull had a pair of horns that could puncture metal. A person who got unlucky could also get punctured, but at the moment Rhodes was the only person in the lot. He hoped he wouldn't get unlucky.

Another car parked beside Rhodes, and Jennifer Loam got out. She was blond, smart, and, ever since leaving the local newspaper, the owner of a Web site called *A Clear View of Clearview.* She was also the site's reporter, photographer, and webmaster. In her spare time she sold ads. She was dating Andy Shelby, who had promised Rhodes more than once that he wasn't feeding her news tips. Yet here she was. Someone had passed the word. Since Andy was working the crime scene at the Moore house, Rhodes suspected Hack.

"Hey, Sheriff," Jennifer said. "It's always

something, isn't it?"

Rhodes checked to see if she had her little video camera running. She didn't, but it was right there, ready to go.

"It's always something, for sure," he said. "You'd better stay clear of the bull. You don't want to get gored."

"That's not in my job description," she said. "I'm just here to watch and learn."

Rhodes didn't think there would be much learning going on.

"And to take some great video, of course," Jennifer continued. "If anybody gets gored, maybe I can sell it to a network or become an Internet sensation."

Rhodes hoped she was kidding, but he didn't ask. He turned his attention to the bull, which was only about thirty yards away now. It had begun to run, and it outdistanced the pursuers. Alton Boyd had dropped to the back of the pack. Too many cheap cigars.

A couple of cars on both sides of the road had stopped, and people were recording the chase with their phone cameras. If Jennifer didn't get anything good, someone else might.

"What's your plan?" Jennifer asked Rhodes, turning her camera on him.

"I don't have one," Rhodes said. "I've

never been on a roundup before."

"It's only one cow," Jennifer said.

"It's a bull," Rhodes said. "There's a difference."

"I know that. Here he comes."

Rhodes looked. Sure enough, the bull was almost at the entrance, and Rhodes still didn't have a plan. He didn't have a rope, not that he'd have been able to lasso the bull even if he had one. If Alton Boyd could catch up, maybe he could do it, but even if he could, the bull might just drag him along with it.

Rhodes walked almost to where the entrance met the highway, prepared to stop the bull somehow. He'd wave his arms and yell, but what he hoped was that the bull wouldn't turn. It didn't have any reason to. It could just keep on going straight, which would make a lot more sense. Not that bulls had an abundance of sense. This one especially. If it had any sense, it wouldn't be running down the highway.

For the first time, Rhodes wondered how the bull had gotten there and why it was on the loose. If Dr. Stanton was involved, the bull might have come from his clinic. Maybe someone had been unloading it and it had escaped. Not that it mattered. It was here now, and they needed to get it corralled.

Too bad there wasn't a corral handy.

Rhodes heard the bull snorting as it approached. The men following it had dropped back a bit, but Alton Boyd was making an attempt to regain his lost ground. He wore cowboy boots and ran awkwardly, but he was catching up.

"Don't scare him," Rhodes called out. "He might turn."

Too late. Boyd was twirling his lasso in a wide loop above his head as he ran. It appeared that he was going to attempt to rope the bull and stop it before it went any farther, and Rhodes was afraid things wouldn't go according to plan.

They didn't.

Or maybe they did, since Rhodes didn't know what Boyd's plan had been. If it had been to lasso the bull, he succeeded.

It was what happened next that Rhodes suspected hadn't been a part of any plan, or if it had been, then Boyd hadn't thought it through. He was strong, stronger than a lot of people Rhodes knew, but he wasn't strong enough to stop a running bull. Hardly anybody was, except maybe Hercules, and Boyd was no Hercules. Years ago Rhodes had seen a series of badly dubbed Italian movies on television that went under the general title of *Sons of Hercules*. Boyd wasn't one of them, either.

He tried, Rhodes had to give him credit for that. He dug in the heels of his boots and leaned back as the rope tightened, but the bull didn't even slow down. Boyd was jerked forward and onto his stomach. It was like a scene from some old B Western. Rhodes had seen a few of those, too.

"Oh, boy!" Jennifer said.

Boyd was dragged along the side of the road for a few yards, churning up dust and gravel as he tried to dig in his heels. He released the rope. When he did, the bull did just what Rhodes had feared he might and swerved right into the entrance to the parking lot.

Rhodes was right in his way. If he'd had a red cape, Rhodes might have waved it and danced lightly aside. Lacking the cape, he jumped awkwardly to his left and almost fell down.

"Oh, boy!" Jennifer said.

Rhodes didn't have time to worry about how he was going to look in the now sure to be viral video. He had to do something to stop the bull, which was headed straight for the entrance to Walmart. Two men who had just left the store took one look, turned around, and ran back inside so fast that the automatic doors barely had time to open for them.

The opening and closing of the doors seemed to have confused the bull, and he slowed down. Rhodes went after him, though he had no idea what he'd do if he caught up with him. He could grab the rope, but the idea of getting pulled across the Walmart parking lot and getting asphalt burns all over his body didn't appeal to him. Jennifer Loam would love it, but Rhodes didn't feel any obligation to get her video any extra hits.

The automatic doors opened again, and a woman came out pushing a cart. Obviously no one had warned her about the bull, because when she saw him, she pushed the shopping cart away from her and went back into the store, leaving whatever she'd bought to the mercy of the bull.

The bull slowed even more and looked at the cart.

"Maybe the two of us could stop him," Alton Boyd said.

He was standing right behind Rhodes, who hadn't heard him come up.

"I think it would take more than two of us," Rhodes said.

"He's just walking now," Boyd said. "We could do it."

"Not worth the risk," Rhodes said, keeping a wary eye on the bull, which was meandering over to the shopping cart. It was full of white plastic bags that held the bounty of the woman's shopping trip. Rhodes wondered what was in them.

The bull must have wondered, too, because it stopped and stuck its head into the cart. Rhodes heard it snuffling as it moved its head around the bags.

"Cereal," Boyd said. "Sugar cereal. A bull would go for that. Let's get hold of that rope while he's not moving."

Rhodes wondered what they'd do if the bull started to move again, but by that time the men who'd been chasing it had all caught up.

"We can *all* grab the rope," Rhodes said, looking around at them. "That way we'll have a chance of controlling him."

He didn't know whether that was true or not. There were six men, eight with him and Boyd. The bull still outweighed them by a good margin.

"We gotta be quiet and move slow," Boyd said. "Don't scare him."

The men all crept along with Rhodes and Boyd in the lead. The bull paid them no attention at all. He was munching on something in the cart. Maybe a nice box of Frosted Flakes. Rhodes got as close as he could without touching the bull and took hold of the rope. Boyd and the others followed his lead. The bull kept on munching.

"Now what?" Rhodes asked. "Dr. Stanton?"

The veterinarian was next to Boyd in the line of men holding the rope. He said, "We just hang on. Rafe Steadman should be here any minute."

"What does Rafe have to do with it?" Rhodes asked.

"It's Rafe's bull. He should be bringing his trailer."

Rhodes looked back toward the highway and saw a Ford F-150 turning into the parking lot, pulling a slat-sided trailer behind it.

"There he is," Rhodes said.

"All we have to do now is get the bull into the trailer," Stanton said.

"Sounds easy enough," someone said.

Somebody chuckled at that. Rhodes was skeptical, too, but it was worth a try. They didn't have anything else. He watched as Steadman pulled the trailer around and started to back it toward them.

The bull must have heard something, too, because he raised his head from the shopping cart and turned to look. He wasn't disturbed. He went back to crunching whatever he'd found in the cart.

Steadman stopped the truck at an angle to the shopping cart, got out, and came around to the back of the trailer. He was a tall, skinny man, dressed in jeans and a Western shirt. He wore a gray Western hat. He opened the gate and pulled out a ramp from beneath the trailer.

When the bull heard the gate being opened, it looked around again. This time it didn't like what it saw. It shook its head, scattering something that looked to Rhodes like mini wheat squares, and snorted. It moved forward, shoving the cart aside, and jerking the rope.

The men all dug in their heels, but it didn't do any good. The bull pulled them right along, and half of them fell down, letting go of the rope as they did so and allowing the bull to move even faster. It was headed toward the motor homes, some of the occupants of which had come out to watch the fun. When they saw the bull heading in their direction, they all started to go back inside except for one small boy wearing a T-shirt and shorts. He must have liked the bull, because he started to run toward it. A woman turned back from the motor home and yelled at him. The bull snorted and lowered its head.

Rhodes and Boyd were still hanging on to

the rope, but they were the only ones. They ran to keep up with the bull, but they couldn't stop it.

Rhodes knew he had to do something. He'd been to the Clearview summer rodeo every year for a long time, and one of the events that he remembered was the bulldogging. A horseback rider would chase a steer, a steer much smaller than the bull, lean out of the saddle, grab the bull's horns, and come out of the saddle to wrestle it to the ground.

Wrestling the bull to the ground was out of the question, but Rhodes thought he might at least be able to get its attention and distract it from the child, who now appeared frozen in place. His mouth was open, and maybe he was screaming. Rhodes couldn't hear him because of the roaring of his own blood in his ears.

Rhodes released the rope, ran forward, and took the bull by the horns.

CHAPTER 5

Twisting the head of a steer when you're coming off a horse isn't easy. Twisting a bull's head when you're running alongside of it is next to impossible, or at least it was for Rhodes. The bull snorted and flipped its head, and Rhodes felt himself being lifted off the ground. He somehow hung on and kept twisting. The bull didn't fall. It didn't stumble. It didn't even slow down. It did, however, turn slightly to the left, which was the side Rhodes was hanging on to.

Encouraged, Rhodes tried to dig in his heels. He couldn't, but the bull did turn a bit more to the left.

Rhodes wondered if Alton Boyd was still hanging on to the rope. He didn't dare look back, and for that matter he couldn't really see what was ahead of him. Everything was pretty much a blur at the moment.

After a couple of seconds Rhodes realized that someone was on the right side of the bull, running along and flapping a cowboy hat at it. Steadman, Rhodes thought. He was trying to help Rhodes turn the bull away from the mobile homes, and they were succeeding.

The bull sped up, and Rhodes felt his feet skidding along the ground. He was no longer doing much to turn the bull. He was just hanging on for the ride. He thought about letting go, but he knew that wouldn't be a good idea. Hanging on to the bull was bound to be better than bouncing off an asphalt parking lot.

Steadman kept pace with the bull, swinging the hat. The bull flipped its head again as if trying to get rid of a particularly annoying insect. Rhodes felt his legs fly out almost parallel to the surface of the parking lot. He wondered what would happen if the bull just kept going like that battery-powered bunny in the TV commercials. Would the bull and Rhodes wind up in Mexico? Or maybe Canada, depending on the direction the bull took? Surely the bull would run down before that happened.

Rhodes saw something in front of them. He tried to focus. It was the trailer, and now he heard yelling on his left. Several of the bull's former pursuers were there, waving their arms and jumping around as if they were on a trampoline.

Rhodes thought at first that they wanted to warn him about something, but then it occurred to him that they were trying to guide the bull into the trailer. With Steadman on one side and the men on the other, they'd formed a sort of corridor. If Rhodes could guide the bull down the middle and keep him from running over anybody, it might even work.

Rhodes didn't like to think about what might happen once he and the bull got into the trailer, assuming that they would. The trailer was big enough to hold the bull, and there would be plenty of room for Rhodes, too, but not if the bull decided to crush him against the side.

Before Rhodes could think too much about that, it was too late for him to worry. The bull slowed, but not enough for Rhodes to take the chance of letting go, and then they were at the trailer. This was the critical moment. If the bull turned quickly, someone was going to get trampled, and if it didn't go straight into the trailer, Rhodes was going to get raked off by the side.

The bull didn't turn. It ran up the middle of the ramp and into the trailer, coming to an abrupt stop just in time to avoid smashing into the front of it. The bull stood there trembling, its hot hide quivering. Rhodes let go of the horns and scrambled as quickly as he could up the board sides of the trailer.

He flipped over the top and climbed down. He was drenched with sweat and doing a little trembling of his own, but he was all in one piece. Standing beside the trailer, he took a deep breath and let it out slowly. Only then did he hear the applause and cheers. He turned to look at the entrance to Walmart. It seemed as if all the employees and customers had come out to watch the fun, and they'd seen the chase and Rhodes being flung about by the bull. It must have seemed like a scene in a movie to them.

Alton Boyd came up, grabbed Rhodes's hand, and started to pump it.

"I never seen anything like it," Boyd said. "You're a real hero, Sheriff, riskin' your own life to save that little kid. Sage Barton couldn't've done it any better."

"All I did was get bounced around by a bull," Rhodes said, "and don't bring Sage Barton into it."

Sage Barton wasn't real. He was a character created by two women named Claudia and Jan, who'd been to a writing workshop in Blacklin County a few years back. They'd since written a series of very successful thrillers featuring Sage Barton, a character so daring, so dynamic, so unlike Rhodes that he didn't see how anybody could ever confuse the two. Recently Seepy Benton had started telling people that it was no coincidence that Sage Barton had the initials S. B. and that it was clear that it wasn't Rhodes but some other daring and dynamic Clearview resident who was the inspiration for the character.

"Old Sage's got nothing you ain't got," Boyd told Rhodes, "that's all I got to say."

"If there was any hero," Rhodes said, "it was the woman with the shopping cart. She's the one who stopped the bull."

Boyd looked toward the cart. "She's gonna have a hard time gettin' all that bull drool off her groceries. Maybe she can get a refund."

Boyd moved away as Dr. Stanton came up.

"Thanks for the help, Sheriff," Stanton said. "Steadman's bull really didn't want to get his booster shot. He got away from us before we had him penned. We'll have some extra help at the clinic when Steadman gets him back there."

"I can send Alton Boyd along if you need him," Rhodes said.

"He'll have to come along and get his rope back anyway," Stanton said. "You were really good with that bull. I heard they were going to make a movie about Sage Barton. You ought to try out for the part."

"I think the movie deal fell through," Rhodes said, "and Sage Barton and I don't have anything in common."

Stanton nodded to Jennifer Loam, who was headed in their direction. "Whatever you say, but if you change your mind, I think there'll be some great video to use as your screen test."

Rhodes sighed as Stanton walked away. He had put out a hand to push himself away from the trailer when Jennifer Loam said, "Hold it right there, Sheriff."

"What?" Rhodes asked.

"Some people want to thank you," Jennifer told him.

A young woman and man walked up. A small boy walked between them, holding their hands.

"These are the Carrolls," Jennifer said. "Elaine and Tom. Their son is Charlie."

"Hi, Charlie," Rhodes said.

"You saved our son, Sheriff," Tom Carroll said. "We can't thank you enough."

"He's right," Elaine Carroll said. She let go of Charlie's hand and gave Rhodes a hug. "We'll never forget this. You're our hero."

"Hero," Charlie said. "Hero."

"Just trying to stop the bull," Rhodes said.

"It was much more than that," Elaine said, stepping away. "A whole lot more. Our son could've been trampled if you hadn't grabbed that bull. I've never seen anything so brave."

"Hero," Charlie said.

Rhodes shifted his feet and looked to Jennifer to rescue him. She didn't, however, because she was too busy taking video. The Carrolls continued to thank him and eventually left. Rhodes tried to leave, too, but Jennifer stopped him.

"Just stand there for a second," she said.

"Why?" Rhodes asked.

Jennifer bent over and located a small rock on the asphalt. She straightened and tossed it at the trailer. It smacked against one of the boards and bounced off.

"Smile, Sheriff," she said.

Rhodes didn't smile. He turned and looked at the trailer, where the bull was glaring at him through the slatted boards. Rhodes turned back to Jennifer, who was working the camera again.

"I'm beginning to understand why so many law enforcement officers don't like video cameras," Rhodes said.

Jennifer continued to video him as Steadman started his pickup and pulled the trailer out of the lot. People had returned to the store or gotten in their cars. The fun was over.

"I'm going back to the office now," Rhodes said, as Jennifer lowered the camera.

"You are?"

"That's what I said."

"I know what you said, but isn't there something else you need to do first?"

"What would that be?" Rhodes asked.

"Well," Jennifer said, "there's the haunted house."

"Who told you?" Rhodes asked. "Andy or Hack?"

"We journalists never reveal our sources."

Rhodes thought about asking whether someone who had a Web site was a legitimate journalist, but he decided it wasn't worth starting an argument. Jennifer had been a fine reporter when she'd worked for the *Clearview Herald,* and she hadn't changed anything but the medium by which she delivered her stories.

"Anyway," Jennifer continued, "I didn't hear it from either of them. I went by the jail this morning to check on last night's reports and read all about it."

"Ruth's already done her report?"

Jennifer nodded. "It's a good one, too.

Now tell me who killed Neil Foshee and I'll go write it up."

"I don't know yet," Rhodes said.

"But you will."

"I will, but it might take a while."

"You're going over there before you go anywhere else, aren't you?"

Rhodes admitted it.

"I'm going, too," Jennifer said.

Rhodes didn't mind that she hadn't asked if she could go. She was free to do whatever she wanted as long as she didn't intrude on the crime scene.

"I'll see you there," he said.

The old house looked even shabbier in the daylight. The paint was peeling, the roof needed to be replaced, and weeds covering the yard looked even worse in the daylight. The vines tangled in the wrought-iron fence were so thick in places that the fence seemed to have disappeared. Water from the previous night's rain still dripped off the trees and the eaves of the house. Andy's county car was parked in front, and Rhodes pulled in behind it. Jennifer stopped behind him.

They both got out of their cars, and Rhodes reminded her that she wasn't to go into the yard. "It's a crime scene now," he said.

He pointed to the yellow tape that Ruth had put up all along the fence. It showed up well against all the green foliage. The tape also encircled the house itself, though of course it wouldn't stop anybody who wanted to sneak in.

"I'll stay out front here and take some pictures," Jennifer said.

"Some video, too, I'm sure."

"Naturally."

Rhodes didn't have anything to say to that. He slipped under the tape and opened the gate, which gave off an unearthly shriek. Rhodes wondered if Seepy Benton would think the fence was possessed by a ghost. Rhodes hoped not. He went on through the opening into the yard, noticing that the sidewalk was not only overgrown with grass and weeds but was cracked and uneven. He and Ruth were lucky they hadn't fallen down last night. He didn't look back to see if Jennifer was taking video of him approaching the house. He was afraid he'd trip and embarrass himself, so he kept his eyes down.

Instead of going up on the porch, he went around to the back of the house. Rainwater that still clung to the taller weeds soaked the bottoms of his pants legs, but he ignored it. He found Andy Shelby bent over and looking at the tire tracks in the crushed weeds in the backyard. It was shady and cool there because of all the trees. Some of them had rotten limbs, but they all looked sturdy enough not to topple over for a while.

"Found any clues yet?" Rhodes asked.

The deputy was young and eager, and he looked so good in his Western hat that Rhodes felt a slight twinge of envy. In fact, Andy looked as good in the hat as Raylan Givens on *Justified,* which only made the twinge a little sharper.

Andy straightened. "Morning, Sheriff. I haven't found much. These tracks are so messed up that there must have been cars in here more often than just last night."

Rhodes remembered the fast-food sacks in the house. "Probably so. Any way to tell the fresher tracks?"

"It's easy to see where some weeds were broken off last night," Andy said, "but how many cars were involved is another story. More than one, I'd say, but that's just a guess. They came through where the gate used to be. Once they got in the yard, there wasn't a lot of room to manuever because of the trees, but you can see that some of them were able to turn around and drive out without backing up. Not that knowing that does us any good."

"Maybe not, but at least it's something we know. What about inside the house?"

"There are some hamburger wrappers that should have some greasy fingerprints on them, but since they're greasy, they're likely to be smeared. Maybe some of the other stuff will have some better ones. Something for Mika to work on."

Mika Blackfield was the newest member of the sheriff's department. Rhodes had talked the county commissioners into hiring someone to do the forensics work that had mostly fallen to Ruth Grady in the past, to the detriment of her ability to go on patrol. Mika had a law enforcement degree, and she'd been looking for work since moving to Clearview with her husband, Todd, who was a pharmacist at Walmart. Rhodes hoped that he hadn't come outside to witness the episode with the bull.

Mika wasn't a full-time member of the department, but she was on call and could come in just about anytime. She and Todd didn't have any children yet, though they were hoping that would change.

"Anything besides the fast-food remains?" Rhodes asked.

"Traces of something that looks like

marijuana and something that might be meth," Andy said. "More stuff for Mika. That's all, though. No shell casings or anything like that."

Rhodes thought it over, then said, "It's possible somebody's been dealing drugs here for a while."

"Looks like it," Andy said, "and that somebody would be Neil Foshee."

He was probably right. Foshee's cousins were the ones who cooked the meth, and it wouldn't be much of a surprise if they had a marijuana operation going, too. There were plenty of places in the county where they could cultivate it. Rhodes had broken up a big operation a few years ago.

"Why do you think he was killed?" Andy asked. "Drug deal gone wrong?"

"Could be," Rhodes said, "but it's too early to go that far without speculating. We need to get more information."

"How are we going to do that?"

"We'll start talking to people. Maybe somebody will tell us what we need to know, and if that doesn't work out, we'll find what we need some other way."

"You sound awfully sure of that."

A big drop of water fell from one of the trees and plopped down on Rhodes's bare head. He wiped a hand across it and said,

"It's always worked out that way before."

"Then maybe it will again," Andy said. "You want me to go around and talk to people at the closest houses to see if they saw anything last night?"

"Take your evidence by the jail first and come back. Ask about the last few weeks, not just last night."

"Got it," Andy said. "You see that old pickup over there?"

He was referring to the rusted-out heap with the hackberry tree growing up through the engine compartment.

"Hard to miss," Rhodes said.

"That thing's older than I am," Andy said. He gave Rhodes an appraising look. "It might even be older than you are. This place has been deserted a long time. I heard it's supposed to be haunted."

"So they tell me," Rhodes said.

Andy took off his hat and shook off a drop of water. Rhodes envied him again.

"Most people probably stay away from it if it's haunted," Andy said as he settled the hat back on his head. "Makes it a good place for drug deals."

"You didn't run into any ghosts while you were in there, did you?"

"Nope. They don't come out in the daytime, do they?"

85

Rhodes shook his head. "I'm not sure what they do. How about mice? See any of those?"

Andy grinned, and Rhodes suspected that Ruth had made some sort of comment to him.

"I think mice are like ghosts," Andy said. "They only come out at night."

"Maybe so," Rhodes said. "Are you about through here?"

"I want to look around inside some more. Probably another hour and I'll be done."

"Don't forget to ask the neighbors if they've seen or heard anything unusual lately, not just last night." Rhodes didn't think they'd get any information, but he liked to be as thorough as possible. "By the way, Jennifer Loam's out front, taking pictures."

Andy looked alarmed. "I hope you don't think I told her about this."

"I know you didn't. She heard about it from Ruth."

"Yeah, I was there. Ruth thinks Seepy Benton needs to look this place over. You know about his new business?"

"Clearview Paranomal Investigations," Rhodes said.

"Right. If there are any ghosts here, he can find them. Maybe they saw the murder

86

and can tell us who did it."

Rhodes laughed. "That would sure save us a lot of work."

"Are you going to let Benton look it over? See what he can find?"

"You think he'd find anything?"

"You never can tell," Andy said. "It might be worth a try."

"Probably not," Rhodes said. "Besides, the results might be skewed because of what happened last night."

"How's that?" Andy asked.

"There might be a brand-new ghost haunting the place now."

Andy took off his hat and held it in front of him in both hands as if out of respect for the dead. "You're right, but that would be even better."

"How could it be better?"

"We wouldn't have to question the other ghosts. We'd just ask Foshee's ghost who shot him."

"If it were only that easy," Rhodes said.

CHAPTER 6

Rhodes was on his way back to the jail when Hack called him on the radio.

"You need to stop by the mayor's office," Hack said.

"He's in his office?" Rhodes asked.

"That's what his secretary said."

The city of Clearview contracted its policing services out to the county, but the mayor, Clifford Clement, liked to think of himself as Rhodes's boss. Rhodes didn't feel that way. He was paid by the county, and the county was paid by the city, so Rhodes thought of the county commissioners as being his employers.

Clement's position as mayor was purely a part-time job, and not a well-paying one, either. Clement didn't need the money, having achieved success in life the old-fashioned way, by selling mutual funds and managing other people's money. Rhodes thought that Clement liked being the mayor because it gave him the opportunity to order the city employees around. Or try to.

Clement usually spent the mornings at his place of business or on the local golf course and came into his office in the afternoons if there was anything that needed his attention, which is why Rhodes was surprised to hear that he was in the office this early in the day.

Clement didn't like Rhodes very much because he'd been a suspect in a murder investigation at one time. Rhodes had told him there was nothing personal in the investigation, but Clement still resented it.

"Did his secretary mention what the mayor wanted with me?" Rhodes asked Hack.

"I meant to say administrative assistant," Hack said.

"That's okay," Rhodes said. "Alice wouldn't mind being called a secretary."

Alice King was the mayor's secretary, or administrative assistant, and Rhodes suspected that she did most of the work that got done in the office.

"Whatever you want to call her, you need to go by there," Hack said.

"I'm on my way," Rhodes said. "Anything else?"

"Nothing you need to worry about," Hack

said, which immediately caused Rhodes to worry.

"Tell me," he said.

"Well, Miz Loomis has called three times."

"Turn signals," Rhodes said.

"You got it. Hard to believe, but some people just won't use 'em."

"She give you their plate numbers?"

"Always does."

"You told her we'd send them all a citation, first thing?"

"Just like I always do. One of these days, she's gonna catch on though."

"We'll cross that bridge when we have to. What else?"

"That's about it."

"You're sure?"

"Nothin' to tell," Hack said. "Just that Seepy Benton's been by here."

Now they were getting down to it. "What did he want?"

"He was just askin' if I knew what you might think about somethin'."

"What specifically did he want to know about?"

"That haunted house. The one where the murder was. The murder you wouldn't tell me about last night. That one."

If there was anything Hack knew how to do, it was to hold a grudge.

"I knew you'd find out all about it when Ruth came in."

"Sure. She's not like some people I could name. She doesn't keep everything to herself. She'll let people know what's goin' on."

"We're drifting off the subject here," Rhodes said.

"What subject was that?"

"Seepy Benton and the haunted house."

"Well, you know about his new business, that ghost stuff. He wanted to know if I thought you'd let him in the house."

"What did you tell him?"

"What do you think I told him?"

"Hack," Rhodes said.

"Okay. I told him that you were a hard man and had a mean streak, that's what. Maybe not in those exact words, but I let him know you wouldn't let him in there."

"Good," Rhodes said.

"He's gonna come at you anyway. He swears he can find a ghost if there's one in there." Hack paused. "Mice, too. He said he's good with mice."

Ruth had been talking, all right, but Rhodes wasn't going to give Hack the satisfaction of commenting on the mice.

"Seepy will have to find me before he can come at me," Rhodes said. "You'd better not tell him where I am."

"Me?" Hack said with an attempt to sound both innocent and hurt. "You know I'd never do a thing like that."

"Right," Rhodes said. "I'm sorry I mentioned it."

"You ought to be," Hack said.

The Clearview city hall was in sore need of repair and had been for years, but so far the city hadn't been able to come up with the money to do anything about it without raising taxes, and nobody on the city council wanted to do that. They were afraid they'd be lynched by the citizens if they did. The damage wasn't visible from the outside of the structure, however, and the old building looked quite respectable. Rhodes went in and walked down the deserted hallway to the mayor's office. The door to the outer room was open, and Alice King sat at the desk.

Alice had been a year behind Rhodes in high school, and she'd always been full of spunk. She was a cheerleader, and she still looked as if she might leap out from behind the desk at any moment and lead some shadowy crowd in a rousing round of "Go, team, go!"

"Hey, Sheriff," she said as he walked in, as perky as if she were at cheerleader practice. "How's your day been so far? Great, I hope."

Rhodes wondered if she'd think getting bounced around the Walmart parking lot by a sweaty bull qualified as great. He wasn't going to find out, though, because he lied and said, "It sure has, Alice, and how's yours been?"

"Fine as frog hair," she said. "Are you here to see His Honor?"

"That's right. Hack tells me you called."

"That Hack," Alice said. "He's a sight. Told me to ask you about mice, for some reason. You have a mouse problem, Sheriff?"

Rhodes wondered if it was legal for the sheriff to shoot his own staff. If it wasn't, it ought to be.

"No," he said. "Not a problem. I have two cats."

"I just love cats," Alice said. "Especially the calico ones. Is either one of yours a calico?"

"No, they're mostly black."

"I like black ones, too, but mine's a calico. She's a real mess."

She might have gone into more detail about what a mess her cat was, but the door to the inner office opened, and Clifford Clement poked his head out. He was losing his gray hair and kept it cut short to disguise the loss as much as possible. He had a short, neatly trimmed beard, which Rhodes thought he'd likely grown to compensate for the hair loss.

"I thought I heard you out here, Sheriff," Clement said. "Come on in."

He went back into his office. Rhodes looked at Alice, who shrugged, and went on through the door.

"Close it," Clement said.

He was already seated behind his desk and made no move to get up and shake Rhodes's hand, which didn't bother Rhodes at all. Rhodes closed the door and sat in the visitor's chair without being asked.

"Hack said you wanted to see me," Rhodes said.

Clement nodded. "That's right."

"What for?"

"It's about something that happened last night."

"How did you find out about that?"

Clement started to speak, hesitated, then said, "From the Web site that young trouble-maker has."

Rhodes didn't consider Jennifer Loam a troublemaker, but he could see how the stories she used might irritate the mayor. The stories were calculated to get people to the Web site and drive up the count so Jennifer could sell advertising, not to please the city officials. Also, Jennifer was friendly to Rhodes. Clement wouldn't approve of that, either.

"What did you want to know about the man who was killed?" Rhodes asked.

"He was just a drug dealer, wasn't he?"

Rhodes didn't like the word "just" in that context or the direction in which the conversation seemed to be headed.

"He hadn't been convicted yet," Rhodes said. "Now he never will be."

Clement looked surprised. "He won't?"

"We don't convict dead men."

Clement recovered his composure. "Of course not, but he would've been if he hadn't been killed." Clement's tone left no room for doubt. "People like that are a black eye on our town. Trash, that's all they are. It's a waste of city and county funds to spend too much time investigating what happened to him. We have too many of his kind around here. One less is good news."

Rhodes was liking the conversation less and less. "We investigate every crime, especially something like this. It doesn't matter if the dead man's a drug dealer or a mayor."

Clement's eyes snapped. "What's that supposed to mean?"

"Nothing," Rhodes said, "except that we owe it to the county and the city to do the best job we can, and if somebody's been killed, we owe it to the victim and his family to find the killer. It doesn't matter who the victim is."

"You don't owe anything to a dead man," Clement said, "and as far as the family goes, those Foshees are a plague on this county. They're nothing but trouble. We don't owe them anything at all."

"Let me see if I have this right," Rhodes said. "A man's been killed, and you want me to slough off the investigation."

"I didn't say that."

"You implied it."

"Maybe you just inferred it."

There were times when Rhodes thought that everyone in the world had changed into Hack and Lawton, but maybe it was his own fault. Maybe he brought out the worst in people. He stood up.

"I don't want to argue with you, Mr. Mayor," he said. "I'm going to investigate this crime just like any other one. If you think it over, I know you'll figure out that you want it done that way."

"You'd better keep things on the quiet," Clement said. "I don't want the reputation of this town spoiled by some meth dealer's death getting splattered all over the Internet."

"I don't think Jennifer Loam has many readers outside the county," Rhodes said, though he didn't really know. "You don't have a thing to worry about."

Clement did look worried, though, and it made Rhodes wonder why. It wasn't just the town's reputation that was bothering him.

"I'd better not see any sensationalism about this on that site," Clement said.

"I don't have anything to do with it," Rhodes said, "and I'm sure you wouldn't want to interfere with the freedom of the press. Or is that just something I'm inferring?"

"Don't get smart," Clement said.

Rhodes grinned. "I don't think there's any danger of that happening."

Clement snorted, and Rhodes left him there.

Alice King smiled a perky smile at Rhodes when he came back into the outer office.

"Did you two have a nice talk?" she asked.

"Just peachy," Rhodes said.

"That's great. You have a great day, now."

"You, too," Rhodes said, and got out of there.

When he got back to the county car, Rhodes got Hack on the radio and asked if he'd heard anything from Buddy about the Foshee boys.

"He's out around Milsby somewhere, lookin' for 'em," Hack said. "They gave an address out there when they bonded out."

Milsby had once been a little town, but there wasn't much left of it now. The meth lab that the Foshees were running had been in a deserted house in that area.

"Tell him to call for backup if he locates them," Rhodes said.

"He's not gonna try to arrest 'em," Hack said. "Just bring 'em in for questioning."

"Earl and Louie don't take kindly to being asked to come in for questioning."

"Since they're out on bond," Hack said, "they wouldn't want to mess up and get thrown back in the pokey."

"You're giving them credit for more of a thought process than they're likely to go through."

"Yeah, I guess so. They're both about two tacos short of a number four dinner at the Jolly Tamale. I'll let Buddy know. You gonna be his backup if he needs it?"

"Give me a call," Rhodes said. "I'll be at Ace's Auto Parts."

"You got car trouble?"

"I have to question a suspect," Rhodes said. He signed off and racked the mic before Hack could ask him anything else.

Although Vicki Patton lived in Railville, she'd found a job in Clearview after getting to know Ivy. She knew a little about cars, and while Ace Gable had been hesitant about hiring someone from out of town, she'd proved to be an asset to his store, which was located in a little strip center just up the highway from Walmart.

Ace's was the biggest store in the center. The sign out front just said ACE'S. It had once said ACE'S AUTO PARTS, but there had been too much trouble with people painting out part of the *P* in the sign. Because whoever had been altering the sign had never been caught, Ace had a slight grudge against Rhodes for a while. He'd pretty much gotten over it since Vicki, who had used Rhodes as a reference, had turned out to be such a good employee.

Rhodes parked outside the store. An old gray Pontiac Bonneville with the hood up was parked in the space next to him. Now that Pontiacs weren't being made any longer, the Bonneville might become a collector's item. Ace was helping a man remove the car's battery. The man was Bob Strother, who had retired from his job with the gas company back when there had been a gas company in Clearview.

"We'll just take 'er in and put her on the tester," Ace said, taking the battery by the handle provided by the manufacturer. "If she's a bad 'un, we can fix you up. If she just needs charging, it won't cost you a thing."

Ace was a big man, taller than Rhodes, and had arms muscled like a weight lifter's. His short-sleeved black polo shirt with ACE'S stenciled in red over his heart showed off his biceps. On his right biceps he had a tattoo of an ace of spades with a flash of lightning running diagonally across it. On his left was a Big Daddy Roth Rat Fink tattoo. Both biceps bulged as Ace lifted the battery out of the car as if it didn't weigh any more than a small box of corn flakes. He also wore a black baseball cap with ACE'S AUTO PARTS in red across the front. He'd moved to Clearview about five years previously to open his parts store, and it had been a success from the beginning.

"I bet it's bad," Strother said. "If I hadn't got a jump start from my neighbor this morning, I'd still be stuck at home."

Rhodes got out of the county car, and Ace said, "Hey, Sheriff. What brings you back out this way? We don't have any bulls for you to wrangle."

"You see the video?" Rhodes asked.

"Nope, heard it from a customer who said he was there when it happened."

Strother laughed. "You been riding bulls, Sheriff? Maybe you oughta enter the rodeo this summer."

"No, thanks," Rhodes said. "I've had enough of bulls to last me a while."

Ace didn't seem to notice he had a car battery dangling from his hand. "If it's not about bulls, what's it about? Whatever it is, I'm innocent."

Strother laughed again. He was easy to please.

"I need to talk to one of your employees," Rhodes said.

Ace's eyes narrowed. "Which one?"

"Ms. Patton."

"Vicki?" Ace was immediately defensive. "What's she supposed to have done?"

"Not a thing. I just need to ask her about someone she used to know."

Ace's eyes narrowed. "Who would that be?"

Ace seemed a bit overprotective for an

employer, and Rhodes wondered if he had any rules against the boss fraternizing with the help.

"She can tell you that later if she wants to," Rhodes said. "I won't keep her long."

For just a second Rhodes thought that Ace might throw the battery at him, but then the big man relaxed and said, "Okay. She's at the counter. It's about time for her break anyway. Come on, Bob. Let's me and you see about this battery."

Strother and Ace went into the store, and Rhodes followed. Vicki was indeed behind the high counter, which held two big electronic cash registers and a couple of computer monitors. The auto parts were arrayed on racks that lined the big room in back of the counter, whereas the room Rhodes was in held racks of items that customers could pick up for themselves, things like car wax, bulbs for various lights, fuses, polishing cloths, motor oil, bucket seat covers, floor mats, and just about anything else a person might need for a car or truck. And plenty of things that nobody would ever need, which probably sold just as well as or better than the rest of the merchandise.

Ace and Strother walked along the counter to the back of the store where the battery tester was, Ace giving Vicki a grin as he passed by, and Rhodes went up to the counter.

"Hey, Sheriff," Vicki said. "You need some auto parts today?"

Vicki had red hair, freckles, brown eyes, and a nice smile. Rhodes could see why Ace might be interested in her.

"I wish that was it," Rhodes said. "Ace told me it was about time for your break. Can we go outside and talk?"

Vicki looked uncertain. "I shouldn't leave the counter."

"It's okay, Vicki," Ace called from the back of the store. "I'll watch the counter."

Rhodes wasn't surprised that Ace had been listening, but he was a little surprised that his hearing was so good.

"I'll be right back," Vicki said.

"Take your time," Ace said. "It's not like we're covered up with customers right now."

Vicki walked to the front of the counter, pushed up a hinged section, and stood by the door. Rhodes joined her, and they went outside. No one was on the walk, so it was as good a place to talk as any.

"What's this about?" Vicki asked.

"Neil Foshee," Rhodes told her. "It's not good news."

"Couldn't be good news if it was about him," Vicki said. "He get arrested again?"

"No," Rhodes said. "Somebody killed him."

CHAPTER 7

Vicki's eyes widened at Rhodes's words. "Neil's dead?"

Rhodes nodded. Vicki didn't seem to be unhappy about it.

"Who did it?" she asked after a second or two.

"I was hoping you might be able to help me with that," Rhodes said. "Maybe you know someone who might want to kill him."

"I didn't go out with him that much," Vicki said. "Just a few times. You know what he did to me. If I could've killed him then, I might've done it myself, but I'm over that now."

"I didn't think you did it. Did he ever mention any enemies to you, people he didn't like or who didn't like him?"

"Everybody liked him," Vicki said. "He was Mr. Personality, and he had the stuff that made them feel good."

"You didn't know that at first."

"No, and I liked him then. He was fun to be around. He seemed nice, and he was a good dancer. He wasn't nice at all when I found out about him and said I was going to tell the law."

That was when Foshee had taken her clothes and left her at the roadside park. She was right. He wasn't nice at all.

"Had he called you since he got out of jail? Made any threats?"

Vicki looked through the store window. Ace was behind the counter now, talking to Strother, but he was looking out at Rhodes and Vicki. The sun was getting high, and Rhodes was uncomfortably aware of the thin spot in his hair. He was going to have to get a hat or a cap or a toupee. Maybe Ace would give him a baseball cap.

Vicki turned back to Rhodes and lowered her eyes to look at the sidewalk. "I'd've told you if he called."

"I know. Something's happened, though. You want to tell me what it is?"

"It's nothing." Vicki still wasn't looking at Rhodes. She stared at the engine of Strother's old Pontiac. "Just . . . he came here a couple of days ago. He was looking for a muffler for his truck, or that's what he said. He claimed he didn't know I was working here. He said some things to me that were pretty bad."

"If he threatened you, you should've called the jail. He was violating his probation by visiting you."

"He was a customer," Vicki said, looking out at the highway.

Yeah, right, Rhodes thought. "Did he buy anything?"

"No, and he didn't stay long. Ace . . . Mr. Gable came up to the front before Neil could buy anything. Neil left."

Rhodes didn't blame Foshee for leaving. A man the size of Ace wasn't anybody to mess around with.

"Ace thinks a lot of you," Rhodes said. "You've been a big help here at the store."

Vicki finally turned her eyes on Rhodes again. "I'm pretty good with auto parts. My daddy likes to work on cars, and sometimes he'd let me help when I was little."

"Did Ace say anything to Foshee when he was in the store?"

Vicki grinned. "He told him to get out and never come back. He told him that if he did, he'd break him in two." She paused. "He could do it, too."

Rhodes didn't doubt it. Ace was big enough to snap Foshee like a stick if he wanted to. Rhodes didn't have a list of suspects, but if he'd had one, Ace would have moved to the top of it.

"Ace . . . Mr. Gable . . . wouldn't have broken Neil in two, though," Vicki said. "He's not like that. He wouldn't hurt anybody."

Rhodes thought about the way Ace had looked at him when he'd mentioned talking to Vicki about someone she used to know. At that moment, Ace had looked like a man who'd hurt somebody.

"Does Ace know you used to date Foshee?"

Vicki nodded. "I told him about it. I didn't tell him about the roadside park, though. That's too embarrassing."

It was a bit embarrassing to Rhodes as well, so he changed the subject. "When you were dating Foshee, did he ever get into any arguments or fights with anybody?"

"No, never. I told you, everybody seemed to like him. I wish I could help you find out who killed him, but I can't think of anybody who'd want to do that."

"That's okay," Rhodes said. "I had to check. You like Ace, don't you."

"He's real nice."

"Have you been dating him?"

"Not yet." Vicki smiled. "He's going to buy me dinner tomorrow night, though."

"I hope he takes you somewhere nice,"

Rhodes said. "I have to ask you one more thing. Where were you last night?"

"Home. I watched a movie on TV. One of those pirate things with Johnny Depp."

Rhodes thought the last good pirate movie had starred Geena Davis.

"How was it?"

"It was okay. It was number three or four. The first one was the best."

"The sequels are never as good," he said, but he thought it was too bad that Geena Davis had never made a sequel to hers. "Let's go back inside."

When they went back into the store, Ace was running Strother's credit card. A new battery sat on the counter beside the cash register.

"Old one's dead as a doornail," Strother said, taking the credit card that Ace handed him and putting it in his billfold. "This new one's got a five-year guarantee on it, though. Ought to last at least that long."

"Good luck," Rhodes said. He'd never had a car battery that lasted that long.

"I'll go out and help you put it in the car," Ace said. "That is, if Vicki and the sheriff are finished talking."

"We are," Rhodes said. "I'll watch you install the battery. Might learn something."

He thanked Vicki for her help and followed Strother and Ace outside. Ace had brought a wire brush and some kind of cleaner for the connections on the battery cable. He set the battery on the little platform where it belonged, and when he'd removed the corrosion from the connections, he hooked the battery up.

"Give it a try," he told Strother.

Strother got in the car and started it. He leaned out the window and said, "Works great."

"You have any trouble, you come on back," Ace told him, and slammed down the hood.

Strother drove out of the parking lot and onto the highway, leaving Ace and Rhodes on the walk.

"You find out what you wanted to know from Vicki?" Ace asked.

"She couldn't help me," Rhodes said. It was time to tell Ace what he'd been asking about. "I had some questions about Neil Foshee."

Ace's jaw muscles tensed. "That drug-dealing son of a bitch better not come back here to my store again."

"He won't," Rhodes said. "Somebody killed him last night."

Ace gave him a nasty grin. "Too bad."

Rhodes didn't say anything, and after a

few seconds Ace said, "Wait a minute. You don't think I did it, do you?"

"The thought did cross my mind," Rhodes told him.

"Well, it can uncross it. I didn't like him, but I didn't kill him."

"Where were you last night?"

Ace took off his cap, slapped it against his thigh, and put it back on. He didn't offer to give Rhodes one, and this didn't seem like the time to ask.

"I don't know where I was," Ace said. "Where I always am, I guess. It was Tuesday, so I closed the doors at six. Took me a while to get things taken care of, but I finished around six thirty. Then I went home. Watched a little TV. The Astros game."

"They win?"

"They never win," Ace said.

"Nobody watched with you?"

"I'm a single man, Sheriff. Nobody to vouch for me besides my cat."

Rhodes would've figured Ace for a dog man, which proved once more that he should never make assumptions.

"Cats can keep a secret," he said.

"You got that right," Ace said, "not that I have any secrets. I was right there at home, and Leroy would tell you that if he could."

"Leroy being the cat."

"Who'd you think I was talking about?"

"Never mind. You're taking Vicki out for dinner tomorrow night?"

"She told you, huh? Well, I am. That doesn't mean I killed a guy."

"You didn't like him, though."

"Hell," Ace said, "nobody did."

Rhodes was just pulling out of the parking lot when he got a call from Hack.

"Buddy says to tell you he's got 'em cornered."

"Got who cornered?" Rhodes asked.

"Louie and Earl. That's who you had him lookin' for, remember?"

"He wasn't supposed to corner them," Rhodes said. "We just wanted to talk to them."

"Buddy knows that. They ain't really cornered. They just won't come out of their house or let him in it. Seems like they don't want to talk to him."

"Where are they?"

"Out at Milsby. You know where Miz Wilkie lives, I guess."

Rhodes knew. Mrs. Wilkie had set her cap for him at one time, but she'd eventually given up on him. She was now working for Mikey Burns, one of the county commissioners, as his admistrative assistant. He was the one who had her interest now.

"I know where she lives," Rhodes said.

"Figgered you did. Down the road from her place there's the Collins place. Nobody's lived there for a year or two, and the Foshees have moved in. Don't know if they own it, but they're there. So is Buddy, but he's just parked out front. He tried to talk to them, but he didn't get anywhere. I told him to wait till you got there before he tries again."

"Be sure he waits. You never know what those Foshees might do. I'll go right now."

"I'll tell him, but I can't promise he won't do anything. I ain't his boss."

"Just tell him," Rhodes said.

"You sure are gettin' snippy these days," Hack said. "I ever mention that?"

"Not in the last ten minutes," Rhodes said.

Buddy was standing outside his county car, leaning against the passenger side, when Rhodes came to a stop behind him.

"Sure hot today," Buddy said when Rhodes got out and joined him.

"Be summer soon," Rhodes said. "Then it'll be hot. This is just warm."

"I guess," Buddy said. He indicated the house with his thumb. "Louie and Earl are holed up in there. I went to the door, but they said they wouldn't talk to me unless I had a warrant. I told 'em I just wanted to talk, but they turned up the radio real loud and made out like they couldn't hear me."

Rhodes heard some sounds coming from the house. They weren't what he'd have called music, but he was a few years behind the curve when it came to what was popular.

"Who is that?" he asked.

"Pharrell Williams?" Buddy said. "John Legend? I don't know. Justin Timberlake?"

Buddy liked to pretend that he wasn't quite as far behind as Rhodes was, but he was close.

"We could ask," Rhodes said.

"Good idea. Maybe they'll talk to us when they see you."

The yard was surrounded by a chain-link fence. It must have been a strong one, because the yard hadn't been rooted up by the feral hogs that roamed the countryside in Blacklin County, and all over Texas for that matter. Rhodes pushed the gate open. It didn't squeal like the gate at the Moore house. He and Buddy walked up a narrow concrete walk to the house. The yard had been mowed within the last week or two, and the previous night's rain had greened it up some. The house could've used some paint, but it didn't look too bad, considering that it had been vacant for a while. The driveway on the side of the yard led around to the back of the house, where the Foshees' vehicles would be parked.

"You better knock," Buddy said. "They don't like me much."

They didn't like Rhodes, either, as he knew from past experience, but he knocked on the edge of the screen door anyway. It banged against the door frame, and in a little while the inner door opened. Louie Foshee looked out through the screen.

Louie was a big man, about thirty. Not as big as Ace Gable, but big enough. Unlike Ace, however, he didn't look like a body builder. Or at least not like a body builder who went to the gym. He looked like a man who'd built his body with extra helpings of meat and potatoes with cobbler and ice cream for dessert. He wasn't soft, though. His belly looked hard as a bowling ball under his untucked blue shirt. He had a wide face like a frog's, and his eyes bugged out a bit, too.

"What you want, Sheriff?" he asked. He had to yell to be heard over the music. "I already told your deputy that we wouldn't talk to him without a warrant."

Rhodes cupped his ear with his hand. "I can't hear you!"

Louie repeated what he'd said about the warrant.

"I still can't hear you," Rhodes said

Louie gave him a disgusted look and turned to the room behind him. "Turn down the damn music!" he yelled.

It took a few seconds, but then the music was muted. Rhodes would've preferred not to hear it at all, but it wasn't loud enough to interfere with conversation now.

"We need to talk," he said.

Louie gave him another look. "I been trying to tell you that I ain't talking to you without a warrant. You got one?"

"We don't need a warrant to talk," Rhodes said. "You're out on bond right now, and I can call the judge and get the bond revoked if I have to. Then I'll take you to the jail where we can talk without any noise bothering me."

"You can't do that."

He had a point. It would take a lot more to get the bond revoked than Rhodes telling the judge that Louie wouldn't talk to him. He'd need much stronger grounds than that, but he didn't think that Louie was as sure about it as he tried to sound.

"You never know what a judge might do," Rhodes said, "but I can give it a try. Is it worth the hassle to you if he goes along with me?"

Louie thought it over. "Maybe not. You can't come in, though."

Rhodes wondered what Louie was hiding. Meth? A gun? Both? Neither?

"That's okay," Rhodes said. "You can come out here. Tell Earl to come, too."

Louie looked puzzled. Rhodes didn't think it would take much to puzzle Louie. "How you know he's here?"

Rhodes cupped his hand behind his ear again. "Who turned down the music?"

"Oh. Yeah." Louie turned back to the room again. "Earl! Come on. We're gonna talk to the sheriff."

"Don't want to," Earl yelled from somewhere in the house.

"Don't matter what you want. You come on."

Louie waited at the door until Earl came along. Earl was a couple of years younger than Louie, and almost as big. He was in a bit better shape, too, but he had the same wide face. Both of them had their dark hair cut in mullets straight out of the seventies. Rhodes wondered who their role models were. Rod Stewart? At least Rod Stewart could sing better than whoever had been on the radio.

"What's this about?" Louie asked, coming out the door. "Me and Earl been behaving ourselves just like we're supposed to. If it's about this house, we're renting it all legal. Terry Collins owns it. Inherited it from his uncle. Lives over in Railville. You can ask him."

"Yeah," Earl said. "You can ask him."

"This isn't about the house," Rhodes said. "You two look fully recovered since the last time we met."

The last time had been at the meth lab, where Louie and Earl had sustained a bit of damage from buckshot fired by Rhodes and Andy Shelby.

"Next time you might be the one gets hurt," Louie said. "What're you here for?"

"It's about your cousin Neil. He's been living here with you, hasn't he?"

"Yeah, but we haven't seen him lately," Louie said. "You seen him lately, Earl?"

Earl gave his head a vigorous shake. "Not me. No, sir. Haven't seen him lately. Old Neil. Wonder what he's up to?"

Earl and Louie were a lot of things, but they weren't good liars. Rhodes had known a few good liars in his time, and some bad ones, too. Earl and Louie were among the worst. They'd seen Neil lately, and they knew what he was up to. Or what he wasn't up to.

"Neil got us in trouble, making meth and like that," Louie said. "We let him live here 'cause he needs a place, but we don't hang with him anymore outside the house. Ain't that right, Earl."

"Right as rain," Earl said, nodding so fast that he looked like a bobblehead doll. "We don't associate with him outside the house. He's a troublemaker."

"Not anymore," Buddy said. "He's dead."

Louie and Earl opened their mouths and looked at each other with wide eyes. Rhodes had never seen two worse attempts at appearing surprised.

"We don't believe you," Louie said after recovering from his mock shock.

"It's true," Rhodes said. "Sad story. Killed by a wild hog."

"Neil wasn't killed by no hog," Earl said. "That's not so."

"Sure it is," Rhodes said. "Out in the woods last night. Wild hog got him down and ran those tusks right through him."

Earl was getting red-faced. He clenched his fists. "Did not."

"You be quiet, Earl," Louie said.

"But he's lying," Earl said. "Neil wasn't killed by no hog."

119

"That's right," Rhodes said. If he could get Earl worked up, there was no telling what he might reveal. "I was just joking. He wasn't killed by a wild hog. He was run over by a bus out on the highway. He was walking and texting. He never saw it coming."

Earl had little eyes like Louie's. He narrowed them to mere slits. "You're a liar."

"Earl," Louie said. "You hush right now."

Earl shook his head wildly. His mullet flew around on the back of his neck. "I ain't gonna hush. He's lying about Neil. Neil wasn't killed by no hog nor run over by no bus. Somebody shot him, and when a man's got shot, it's up to his family to take care of it, not some sheriff." He looked Buddy up and down. "Or some skinny little deputy."

"So you did know that Neil was dead," Rhodes said. "That's better."

"Not the part about the skinny little deputy," Buddy said. "That's not better. I don't like that one bit."

"Maybe we need to go inside, sit down, and talk this out," Rhodes said. "We can start with you two telling me how you knew Neil was shot and go on from there."

Earl stared at him.

"I told you to hush, dumbass," Louie said. "You never listen."

"I ain't no dumbass," Earl said. "He was

lying about Neil. People ought not to lie about somebody who's dead."

"Yeah, that's right," Louie said, "but now we have to go inside and talk. You go on, Earl."

Earl didn't move, so Louie gave him a little push. Earl opened the screen and went through. Louie went in right behind him. As soon as he was inside, he slammed the inner door before Rhodes and Buddy had a chance to move. Rhodes heard a dead bolt snick into place.

"They can't do that," Buddy said, although it was plain that they had.

Rhodes heard footsteps. It sounded as if Earl and Louie were running through the house.

"They're headed out the back," he said, and Buddy took off.

Rhodes ran after him, catching up just as he turned the corner of the house. He heard a door slam and reached out for Buddy's shoulder.

"Slow down," Rhodes said. "We don't want to run into anything we aren't ready for."

"Right," Buddy said, pulling his service revolver, a big .44 magnum. Rhodes felt a little inadequate as he got the little Kel-Tec from the ankle holster.

A couple of car doors slammed and an engine started.

"Let's get back there," Rhodes said. "Be careful."

When they got to the back of the house, they saw an old green pickup, black smoke coming from the tailpipe. Rhodes didn't know where Earl and Louie had gotten the pickup. Their cars had been shot up pretty badly in the raid on the meth house, but they'd probably made enough money to buy the old truck. There was no second vehicle, which meant that either Neil didn't have one or it was missing.

Rhodes ran to the driveway and stood in the middle of it and pointed the Kel-Tec straight in front of him. He hoped Louie and Earl had enough sense not to run over him or get shot trying, and they did. Instead of trying to get out on the driveway, they turned around and headed out across the backyard. The chain-link fence didn't slow them down much. The pickup hit a post and smashed it down, along with a swath of the fence, and they struck out across the pasture, bouncing across ruts almost like a pickup in a cartoon and running over small mesquite bushes without regard to puncturing the tires.

"Want me to shoot out the tires?" Buddy asked.

The way the pickup was bouncing around, Rhodes thought he'd be lucky to come within twenty yards of it. Or unlucky enough to hit Louie or Earl.

"Better not," Rhodes said.

"They'll get away."

Letting them get away was better than shooting them by accident. They knew a lot more than they were telling, and Rhodes thought Earl would crack for sure in about ten minutes. Louie might take a little longer.

"We'll just have to catch them," Rhodes said. He put the Kel-Tec back into its holster. "Come on."

He walked across the downed fence and into the pasture.

"On foot?" Buddy called from behind him.

"It's the only way to go," Rhodes said.

CHAPTER 8

Rhodes jogged along in the pasture. It was tough going because the feral pigs had been rooting up the ground, leaving chunks of earth and shallow holes. The ground was soft because of last night's rain shower, and mud stuck to Rhodes's shoes. It was hot, too. Besides not wearing a hat, he didn't wear boots. He preferred rubber-soled shoes. If he wasn't the only sheriff in Texas who didn't wear a hat, he was surely the only one who didn't wear either a hat or boots. Boots would have made it a little easier to walk across the rough, sandy ground. They wouldn't have provided much protection against the thorny mesquite bushes that grew all around, however. Neither did his short-sleeved shirt. Rhodes just had to avoid them.

About a quarter of a mile in front of him, the pasture turned into woods. Louie and Earl could either drive along the edge of the trees and try to find a way back to a road without running into a fence they couldn't knock over, or they could park the truck and try to get away in the woods. Rhodes was betting they'd take to the woods. Finding them in there wasn't a sure bet, but it was still better than shooting at them.

Rhodes's shirt was sticking to his back before he got halfway to the woods, but he'd been right about Louie and Earl. They stopped the truck and bailed out. Earl, who'd been driving, ran into the woods on the left, and Louie went into the trees on the right.

"You take Louie," Rhodes said to Buddy, who was panting along beside him. "Don't spend all day looking for him. If he gets away, we'll get him some other time. And no shooting."

"What if he shoots first?" Buddy asked.

Rhodes hadn't seen either of the Foshees with a gun, but that didn't mean they didn't have one. "If he doesn't kill you, then you can shoot."

"That's not real encouraging," Buddy said.

Rhodes stepped on a soft spot and almost fell, but he caught his balance in time and stumbled for a few steps.

"You okay?" Buddy asked.

"I'm fine," Rhodes said. "Just clumsy."

When they came to the pickup, Rhodes was tempted to stop and search it, but Earl already had a good head start on him. Rhodes kept going. As he passed the front of the truck, he saw Buddy disappear into the trees on his right.

Rhodes entered the woods. It was a bit cooler in the shade, but there wasn't a hint of a breeze. Rhodes didn't hurry. He didn't want to try running, what with all the sticks, leaves, and broken limbs on the ground. There was also the danger of snakes. Copperheads weren't unusual in the spring, especially in the woods, and there might be a rattlesnake or two around.

Rhodes got out his pistol. Snakes weren't usually aggressive, but if you stepped on one or got too close to it and agitated it, you'd be in big trouble. If you were of the non-boot-wearing persuasion, you could be in even bigger trouble, so it paid to be careful. Rhodes was careful. He didn't like snakes. He thought for a second of Bud Turley, a man who hadn't been careful. Rhodes wished he'd warned Buddy about snakes, but Buddy had lived in Blacklin County for most of his life. He'd be careful. So would Louie and Earl.

Rhodes started walking. Besides snakes,

there was the threat of poison oak and poison ivy. Rhodes didn't need to spend the next few weeks itching like a dog with the mange, so he tried to avoid contact with anything green, just to be on the safe side.

There was another threat, too, the feral pigs who'd torn up the pasture. The pigs usually came out at night, but in the daytime they'd lie up in some concealed shady spot in the woods to wait for darkness so they could begin their plundering. They were wreaking havoc all over the county, all over the state, and almost all over the country.

Some commissioner in Harris County, which included Houston, had gotten permission to trap the feral pigs in several parks, have them butchered, and give the meat to the food bank. Rhodes thought that was an excellent plan. If they had enough traps, they could feed the whole county forever because the pigs could reproduce faster than they could be trapped. Better not to think about the pigs, though.

Every so often Rhodes stopped to look for signs of Earl's passage through the woods. He saw some crushed plants and knew he was on the right track, but he couldn't hear anything other than birds twittering. Mockingbirds, he thought. They made so many different sounds that Rhodes couldn't know for sure. Birdsong identification wasn't one of his strong points.

Aside from the birds, everything was quiet. Rhodes walked slowly, and now and then he looked up into the trees. He'd learned the hard way that most people didn't look up, so it was easy to hide if you could climb a tree. Earl didn't look like a climber, but you could never be sure about someone like him. He might be more agile than he appeared. However, Rhodes didn't see Earl. He didn't even see any birds. They were all hiding from him among the new green leaves the trees were putting out.

Earl didn't seem to Rhodes like someone who could be quiet for very long, any more than he seemed like a climber. He appeared to be more like the kind who'd crash through the woods like a hippo, so Rhodes assumed that he was either resting or had been able to run so fast that he'd already gotten away. If he'd gotten away, there was no need for Rhodes to be in a hurry. He continued to ease along, hoping that he was still on the right track.

He was. Somewhere ahead of him he heard a commotion, then a yell, then something that sounded like a stampede.

It didn't take a genius to figure out what had happened. Earl had been unlucky and had stumbled across a passel of hogs. The hogs hadn't been pleased, which wasn't much of a surprise. A passel of hogs aroused from a nice daytime nap was rarely a happy passel.

The noise got louder. The hogs, and probably Earl, were headed in Rhodes's direction.

Rhodes didn't think Earl could outrun the hogs. He stuck his pistol in his belt. The Kel-Tec would be about as much use against stampeding hogs as a fly swatter. He looked around for a tree with low branches that would support his weight. He'd been a great climber of trees when he was a boy, but he was long past boyhood, and the last time he'd climbed a tree, somebody had taken a shot at him.

Better to climb than to be trampled, however. Rhodes grabbed a sturdy limb on an elm tree and pulled himself up. He got a leg over the limb and with only a little straining managed to get himself uncomfortably seated on it. His legs dangled down only a couple of feet off the ground, but they were high enough to avoid trouble if he raised them.

He'd barely gotten situated when he saw Earl coming with at least a dozen hogs squealing along in a thundering pursuit.

Earl was sprinting for all he was worth, dodging trees and limbs as best he could. When he couldn't dodge or duck a limb, he just let it slap him in the face and body.

The hogs churned up dirt and leaves and sticks, and some piglets came squealing along behind the adults as fast as their little trotters could carry them.

Earl dodged the trunk of the tree where Rhodes was sitting, probably not even noticing that Rhodes was there. He had other things on his mind. The hogs passed right under Rhodes's raised feet, snorting and snuffling.

Earl had a good head start, but Rhodes didn't think he could make it back to his pickup. Hogs could run ten miles an hour or so, and Earl didn't look to be able to run ten miles at all. It turned out not to matter how fast he could run because about ten yards past the tree Earl's feet got tangled up with a broken limb that lay in his path, and he fell sprawling. He slid a little way on his face and stomach and then lay still.

The hogs didn't slow down. They charged right over Earl as if they didn't even know he was lying there. Not all of them trampled him, of course. Some of them passed on either side of him, but a good number of them rumbled right over him. One of the piglets stopped for just a second to look at what was left of him and then ran on after the others. Rhodes had no idea how far they'd go before they stopped, and it didn't matter. What mattered was Earl.

Rhodes climbed down from the tree and went to where Earl lay flat on his face in the leaves. His clothes were ripped, and there was a good deal of blood. The back of Earl's head looked a bit mashed. Rhodes didn't think any of the hogs had gotten their tusks into Earl, but their hooves had done plenty of damage. Earl's shirt was ripped, and so were his pants. There were cuts on his back and legs. Hog hooves could be sharp.

Rhodes knelt down, turned Earl's head to the side, and felt the carotid artery. He found a pulse. It wasn't strong, but it was there.

Rhodes reached in his back pocket for his cell phone and was glad to find it hadn't fallen out while he was climbing the tree. He called 911 and gave the best directions he could to the place where Earl was lying. He hoped that the low-slung ambulance could get across the pasture and that the paramedics could get into the woods and find him and Earl.

When he'd completed the call, he pulled the Kel-Tec from his belt and fired four shots into the ground near a tree. That ought to bring Buddy, who might be on the way already if he'd heard Earl's yells.

Rhodes didn't think it would be a good idea for him and Buddy to try to move Earl, but they might have to if the paramedics couldn't find them. Earl was too heavy for two people to try to move anyway. The paramedics would have a stretcher, and four people could carry Earl out of the woods. Even with four, it wouldn't be easy.

Rhodes walked over to a hickory tree and leaned back against the trunk. If any nuts had ever fallen from the tree, they were gone now. Hogs would have eaten them.

After Rhodes had been standing under the tree for about ten minutes, he heard someone coming through the trees. He was still holding the Kel-Tec, just in case, and stood quietly, concealed by the trunk of the hickory tree.

Buddy walked right past the tree and stopped when he saw Earl lying on the ground.

"He's alive," Rhodes said.

Buddy twitched, but he didn't panic. He turned around and said, "You sure are sneaky, Sheriff."

"I don't mean to be," Rhodes said, and returned the pistol to its place.

"It's okay," Buddy said. "Good thing I'm not the nervous type." He looked down at Earl. "What'd you do to Earl?"

"Wasn't me," Rhodes said. "Hogs."

Buddy kicked a clod of dirt. "Should've known that, the way the ground's torn up. He alive?"

"For now. What about Louie?"

"Louie?" Buddy gave a short laugh. "I haven't seen hide nor hair of him. That scutter might be in Dallas or Houston or Timbuktu by now for all I know."

"We'll get him," Rhodes said.

"Maybe he'll come visit Earl in the hospital."

"And maybe I'll win the lottery this week."

"You buy a ticket?" Buddy asked.

"Nope."

"Didn't think so. You don't hold with gambling, since you put those eight-liners out of business."

"Didn't think much of it before that, either," Rhodes said. "Those eight-liners weren't legal anyway, not the way they were being run."

"I know that," Buddy said. "Just pulling your leg."

Just as Rhodes suspected. Everybody, including Buddy, had been hanging around Hack and Lawton too much.

Buddy looked away from Rhodes, back in the direction of the pasture. "You hear that?"

Rhodes listened and nodded.

"Guess it's the ambulance," Buddy said.

Rhodes wished he could believe that, but he didn't. "I don't think so. I think Louie's doubled back and gotten his truck started."

"Dang. You want me to go after him?"

"No use," Rhodes said. "He'll be long gone by the time you could get there."

"Now he sure enough'll be headed to Dallas or Houston."

"Or Timbuktu," Rhodes said.

"Yeah. That's in Africa, right?"

"Wherever it is, we'll get him."

"That's what you told me before," Buddy said.

"I still mean it," Rhodes said, pulling out his cell phone. He called Lawton and told him to put out a BOLO on Louie.

"You get the license number of the truck?" Hack asked.

"I didn't think I'd need it," Rhodes said.

"You ever a Boy Scout?"

" 'Be Prepared.' I know."

"Knowin' ain't doin'," Hack said. "We can get a license number from the records, though. Take a little longer, but not much since Mika's here."

Hack was impressed with Mika's computer skills, among other things. He'd been suspicious of having a female deputy when Ruth Grady had joined the department, but he'd been won over quickly. He thought highly of Ruth, and he'd admired Mika's skills from the first.

"She's workin' on some fingerprints," Hack said, "but she can take time to get that plate number. What happened to Earl?"

"He tried to run away," Rhodes said. "Went in the woods and some hogs trampled him."

"He gonna be okay?"

"Not sure."

"You gonna tell me what happened?"

"Later," Rhodes said, and silenced the phone.

"I hear the amublance now," Buddy said. "Was them all along."

"Good. I hope Earl will be all right."

Buddy didn't seem to concerned about Earl. "I hope we catch up with Louie."

"We'll get him."

"You keep on saying that," Buddy said.

"I keep on meaning it," Rhodes said.

CHAPTER 9

The paramedics had a stretcher, and they managed to get Earl to the ambulance. It wasn't easy, but Rhodes and Buddy helped by pushing limbs out of the way and spelling one or the other of the paramedics on the stretcher handles now and then.

The paramedics got him loaded into the ambulance. Rhodes and Buddy watched it drive across the pasture, and Rhodes felt sorry for Earl. Bad enough to get run over by hogs, but even worse to have to be bounced across a rough field in an ambulance. Earl hadn't regained consciousness, however, so at least he didn't know he was being treated roughly.

"What now?" Buddy asked.

"We'll search the truck," Rhodes said. "We might find a clue."

"I hope so," Buddy said. "I don't believe I've found a clue in a long time. I'm more of a man of action."

"Right," Rhodes said, "but even a man of action needs a break now and then. Let's take a look."

They didn't find anything in the truck, however, though there were bullet holes in the windshield and back window, and the glass spiderwebbed away from them.

"Wonder how that got there," Buddy said.

"Somebody took a shot at the pickup," Rhodes said.

"Yeah, but who?"

"Probably whoever killed Neil."

Rhodes got out his phone and called Hack to tell him to send Cal Autry out with a wrecker to pick up the truck.

"Tell him it's out in the pasture, down by the woods," Rhodes said.

"Somebody wreck it?"

"Abandoned it," Rhodes said, and ended the call.

"Do we search the house now?" Buddy asked.

"That's the plan," Rhodes said.

The first thing they discovered in the house was that the Foshees were better housekeepers than Rhodes would've expected. The house wasn't immaculate, but there weren't dirty clothes strewn everywhere, just a sock on the living room floor and a couple of shirts lying across the back of a sofa. There weren't even any dirty dishes in the sink. The house had three bedrooms, and all three beds were made, which was even more surprising than the lack of dirty dishes. The bathrooms were clean, too.

"Guess they haven't been mixing up any meth around here," Buddy said when they'd finished looking around the rooms.

"They're not that stupid," Rhodes said. "They always find somewhere else to do that."

"You think they're still doing it, even while they're out on bond?"

"Sure. That's all they know. They don't use it themselves, though. Let's check the closets."

The closets were neat enough, too, but there were a few things that shouldn't have been there, like the sack full of unused burner phones and the bag of diet pills and cold pills.

"They might make the meth somewhere else, but they have some of the ingredients here," Buddy said, just before he found another bag containing lithium batteries and drain cleaner. "There's enough evidence in these closets to revoke their bonds right now."

"They forfeited their bonds when they

ran," Rhodes said. "I wish we could find something that would point to a reason for killing Neil."

"That would be too easy," Buddy said. "Take all the sport out of it."

Rhodes wasn't interested in sport. He wanted to wrap things up quickly, but he had a feeling it wouldn't work out like that. They searched the rest of the house without finding anything of note. Rhodes had thought they might find some firearms, since the Foshees believed in being well armed, but nothing had turned up. The Foshees might not be geniuses, considering the meth ingredients in the house, but they weren't fools, either. They could argue that the cold pills were there in case they got sick, though the quantity was obviously suspicious. They could make a case for the batteries and the drain cleaner, too. A weak case, but a case nevertheless. As for the phones, there was nothing illegal about owning as many phones as you wanted. Weapons would have been a different story. The Foshees couldn't talk their way out of firearms possession while out on bond.

As they walked back to the county cars, Buddy asked Rhodes where he thought Louie had gone. "And don't say Timbuktu."

"Where do you think he went?" Rhodes asked.

"I'd go to Houston if I wanted to stay in the state," Buddy said. "A man could change his name down there and never be found. They got over two million people living down there. Easy to hide. Climate's bad, though. Traffic's even worse than the climate."

"I don't think Louie's in Houston," Rhodes said. "I think he's still right around here somewhere. The Foshees are big on family, and he'll be worried about Earl. He'll want to know who killed Neil."

"He won't know what happened to Earl. He won't even know we caught him."

"We'll make it easy for him to find out. It'll be in the paper and on the Internet."

"You think Louie can read or use the Internet?"

"He might be smarter than we think," Rhodes said.

Rhodes was on his way to the Dairy Queen to get some lunch when Hack called.

"Andy Shelby's got somethin' for you," Hack said.

"What does he have?" Rhodes asked.

"Wouldn't tell me. I'm just the old flunky, not some hotshot investigator. Nobody ever tells me anything."

"It's probably not important."

"He said it was. Said he couldn't talk about it on the air."

Rhodes wondered what Andy could've found out. "Have him meet me at the Dairy Queen."

"You gettin' yourself a Blizzard? 'Cause a Blizzard's got a lot of calories in it if a man's watching his weight."

"I'm not watching my weight."

"Maybe you oughta be, then."

"I get plenty of exercise."

"Like what?"

"Climbing trees to avoid being trampled by hogs," Rhodes said.

"When was that?"

"I'll tell you later," Rhodes said, and signed off.

It was a little after the lunch hour, and the Dairy Queen wasn't crowded. When Rhodes entered, he saw Andy Shelby sitting in a booth to the left of the door. Unlike a lot of people who wore hats, Andy was old-fashioned and took his off when he was indoors. It sat on the seat beside him.

Rhodes went to the counter, placed his order, paid, and took the little slip with his number on it over to the booth. He slid in across from Andy, who was eating a strip of fried chicken.

"You beat me here," Rhodes said.

Andy put down the chicken strip and wiped his mouth and fingers with a skimpy napkin. Rhodes could remember a time when napkins in the DQ and other fast-food places had been substantial enough to do some good, but those days were long gone.

"I was close by," Andy said. "Did Hack tell you I found something?"

"He did," Rhodes said. "He didn't tell me what it was, though. I think you hurt his feelings."

"It wasn't something I wanted to put on the air. I'm not sure I even want to say it in here."

Rhodes looked around. Nobody was nearby. "I think we're safe enough."

"Let's wait till your food comes. What'd you order?"

"A burger," Rhodes said, feeling a little guilty. He blamed Hack for that. "And a Dr Pepper."

"Which burger?"

"The one with the deep-fried jalapeño strips and pepper jack cheese."

"It have that jalapeño ranch dressing on it, too?"

"That and some lettuce," Rhodes said.

"A well-balanced meal," Andy said, as the woman behind the counter called Rhodes's number.

Rhodes got his food and returned to the booth. When he'd unwrapped his burger and rammed his straw down through the plastic top on the Dr Pepper, he said, "Now you can tell me what you found out."

"I talked to a man named Turner. Brad Turner. You know him?"

"I don't think so."

Rhodes bit into his burger. It might not be as well balanced as Andy had said, but it was satisfying.

"He lives a couple of blocks from the Moore place," Andy said. "In that little shotgun house on the corner. Painted green."

"I know the house," Rhodes said.

"Crotchety old guy, not friendly in the least. Didn't want to talk to me. I could tell he knew something, so I kept after him, but you need to see him. I think he knows more than he's telling."

"He did tell you something, though."

"I think he did it just to get rid of me," Andy said. "After arguing with me for a good while and trying to make me leave, he told me he saw somebody around the Moore place last night."

"Did he say who it was?"

Andy looked around, then leaned across the table and whispered, "He thinks it was Mayor Clement."

"Uh-oh," Rhodes said.

Andy leaned back. "That's putting it mildly."

Rhodes put down his burger. He wasn't feeling hungry anymore. "What else did Turner say?"

"Nothing. He said he'd told me all he knew, but I don't believe him."

Rhodes took a sip of his Dr Pepper, then said, "Why not?"

Andy shrugged. "I can't really say. Kind of a hunch, I guess. A feeling. You know?"

Rhodes knew. After you'd been in law enforcement for a while, you developed a kind of instinct, a little something in the back of your head that sent out a signal when somebody was lying. Maybe there was more to it than that. Body language, tone of voice, a look in the eyes, something that didn't register consciously but that sent out a warning to you.

"There's one other thing," Andy said. "It doesn't have to do with the Moore house, though."

"Tell me anyway," Rhodes said.

"He wears a tinfoil hat," Andy said.

"A tinfoil hat?"

"Sort of. You go and talk to him. You'll see."

Rhodes decided he was hungry after all. He took another bite of his burger. If someone in a tinfoil hat was claiming he saw the mayor, there wasn't a lot to worry about.

"At least he didn't claim it was aliens he saw," Rhodes said after he'd chewed and swallowed.

"This time," Andy said.

"This time?"

"You never know what people might come up with, and I think there's more to it. You need to talk to him."

"As soon as I finish this burger," Rhodes said, and he took another bite.

The narrow green house was in bad need of a new coat of paint, and the yard wasn't kept much better than the one at the Moore place, which hadn't been touched by a mower in many long years.

Rhodes stopped the county car in front of the house and got out. He saw a man sitting on the little front porch in an old recliner that leaned to one side. There was a wooden kitchen chair beside the recliner that also leaned a little. The man didn't get up.

Rhodes got out of the car. There was no sidewalk, but a smooth path had been worn through the grass to the porch. Rhodes stopped at the step and looked at the man in the recliner. He appeared to be about seventy. He wore a pair of faded overalls and some raggedy canvas shoes with the soles about to peel off at the front. The gaps made the shoes look like they had little mouths.

The man's face was deeply creased, and he hadn't shaved in a while. The unshaved look was apparently popular among youngsters, if Rhodes was to judge by what he saw on TV. On an older man, it just seemed careless. To Rhodes, it seemed careless on younger ones, too, but he'd never been in the loop when it came to fashions.

A blue Texas Rangers baseball cap with a red *T* on the front sat on the man's head. The cap wasn't made of tinfoil, but some kind of foil stuck out around the bottom edges, indicating that the cap was lined with it.

"Brad Turner?" Rhodes said.

"That's me," the man said. He made no effort to get out of his chair. "Who're you?"

"Sheriff Dan Rhodes."

"That deputy sent you, I bet. I told him all I know. I don't have anything else to say."

The rickety wooden chair beside the recliner looked as if it might fall over on its own, but Rhodes was willing to give it a try if Turner would let him.

"I'm just here to clarify what you told the deputy," Rhodes said. "Mind if I sit down in that empty chair? It's a hot day, and I could use some shade."

Turner didn't appear to like the idea, but he said, "Okay, come ahead."

Rhodes stepped up on the porch. The old boards creaked, and Rhodes thought that maybe he shouldn't have had that burger for lunch. He eased himself down on the chair. It squealed but didn't collapse, and Rhodes relaxed.

When Rhodes was settled, Turner said, "You talk to your deputy?"

"I did. He said you saw somebody around the Moore house last night."

"We'll get around to that in a minute," Turner said. He touched the baseball cap. "The deputy tell you about my cap?"

Rhodes didn't see any need to lie about it. "He mentioned it."

"I could tell he was eyein' it. He prob'ly thinks I'm crazy. Worried about the gover'ment spies and such."

147

"He didn't say anything about that."

"He was thinkin' it, I bet. Hell, I know better'n to think this cap could keep the gover'ment's eyes off me. The gover'ment's spying on ever'body they can, sure, but they do it with cell phones and computers. I don't have either one of those things, so they can peep on 'em all they want to for all I care. You wanna know why I have this foil in my hat?"

Rhodes didn't know what the right answer to that would be, so he went with "Only if you want to tell me."

"Don't mind tellin' you. Be easier to show you, though." Turner got out of his chair and went out into his overgrown yard. The soles of his shoes flopped as he walked. "Come on over here."

Rhodes got up carefully and joined Turner in the yard. Turner pointed over the roof of his house in the direction of the cemetery. "See that?"

Rhodes saw some fluffy clouds, but he was pretty sure that wasn't what Turner meant.

"Cell phone tower," Turner said, and Rhodes saw it then, or the tip of it. It was quite a distance away. "RF waves."

Rhodes must have looked puzzled, because Turner added, "Radio frequency waves. I decided I'd rather stuff some foil in my cap than get the brain cancer. Be better if I could cover my whole head, but that's not gonna happen. Too damn hot. So the cap'll have to do. Let's go back up on the porch."

When they were seated again, Turner pulled a grimy handkerchief from a pocket of his overalls, took off his cap, and wiped his balding head.

"Damn foil is scratchy and makes me sweat," he said. "Better'n the brain cancer, though."

"Bound to be," Rhodes said.

Turner put the handkerchief away and put the cap back on his head, and Rhodes noticed a worn wedding band on his finger.

"I got some more foil in the house," Turner said. "You want some?"

"No, thanks," Rhodes said. "I'm not going to be here long."

"Your choice. It wasn't always like this around here. Back when I moved in, there weren't such things as cell phone towers. A man was a lot safer in those days."

"What about your wife?" Rhodes asked. "Is she worried about the cell phone tower, too?"

"Betty Jane," Turner said. "That's my wife. Or was. She left me a long time ago. Run off with some fella to live in Arkansas."

"I'm sorry," Rhodes said.

"No need to be. I've got over it. You want to hear about the Moore house?"

"I'd like that."

"Lots of funny things go on there at night. I don't have a TV, so I sit out here on the porch a lot."

Rhodes wasn't surprised that Turner didn't have a TV set. No telling what kind of radiation one of those things gave off.

"Can't sleep too well, either," Turner said, "what with all the radio frequency waves around here, so I'm out on this porch late sometimes. See all kinds of things. Like down at that Moore house."

"What kinds of things?" Rhodes asked.

"Lights, mostly. Cars driving around. That kind of thing."

"See any people?" Rhodes asked, glad that Turner was so talkative. All it took was a little encouragement.

"Not so I could recognize 'em, but I seen a few."

"What about last night?"

"Saw some cars," Turner said. "Heard some noises, might have been gunshots. Didn't think anything of it. I hear things from other people's TVs all the time. Thought that's what it was till the county car showed up with their lights goin'."

"That was me," Rhodes said. "And one of the deputies."

"Couldn't see who it was. Didn't think much about it, really, till that deputy showed up this mornin' and said somebody'd been killed. I thought back about some of the cars that drove by here when he said that, and I remembered that one of 'em belonged to the mayor."

"You sure about that?"

"Pretty dang sure. It was a big Alexis, one of those SUVs. You know anybody else around here who drives an Alexis like that?"

Clifford Clement owned a black Lexus SUV that he was careful to keep polished to a high shine. Rhodes could think of a couple of other people who owned a Lexus, but not an SUV.

"Mayor Clement's not the only one," Rhodes said.

"Maybe not, but I think his is the one I saw. Don't know what he'd be doin' out around here at night."

"You just saw the car, not who was in it?"

"That's right, but it was the mayor's car. He thinks he's a big dog, drivin' that Alexis. Movin' fast, too."

Rhodes wasn't convinced. "What makes you so sure it was the mayor's car since it's not the only one in the county?"

151

"Don't really know. Somethin' about it, though. It was his, all right."

Pretty flimsy, but maybe Turner had some other information. "See any other cars?"

"There was a pickup that roared outa the backyard," Turner said. "This was all after the shots was fired, if it was shots I heard."

"What kind of pickup?" Rhodes asked.

"Can't say. I didn't get much of a look at it."

"Anything else?"

"Nope." When he said it, his eyes shifted. He hadn't been looking at Rhodes. The whole time he'd talked, he'd been looking straight ahead. Now his eyes slid off to the right. "You gonna arrest the mayor?"

"Not just yet," Rhodes said. "I have to have more to go on than what you saw."

"The big dogs always get off," Turner said. "Never spend a minute in the calaboose. Somebody like that, somebody people like, no matter what he does, he gets off scot-free. A nobody like me, he'd be in prison for the rest of his life."

"We don't even know that it was the mayor you saw." Rhodes stood up. "I'll check it out and see what he has to say."

"You should," Turner said. "That Moore place is haunted. You know that?"

"So I've been told," Rhodes said.

"You believe in ghosts?"

Rhodes didn't want Turner to stop talking, so he said, "I keep an open mind."

Turner took off his cap and wiped his head again. "I think they come back to haunt us. Don't do no good to run from 'em. They can find you wherever you are. You take that Moore fella. You prob'ly don't remember him, but he was one mean dude. Shot stray dogs with a pellet gun."

"I heard about that," Rhodes said.

"His own dog ate on him after he died."

Rhodes didn't bother to correct Turner. He didn't think it would do any good.

"Man like that," Turner said, "man that would shoot a dog, he'd do about anything. Don't guess he was any great loss."

"I doubt that he'd agree," Rhodes said.

"You might could ask his ghost about that. I think he's the one making the lights shine down there. Been doin' it for all these years. Mean fellas, they can't rest easy, even if their dyin' was their own fault."

"A heart attack's not necessarily anybody's fault," Rhodes said.

"Brought it on himself by meanness," Turner said. He stood up. "I got to go in now. Time for my nap."

Rhodes stood up, too, and thanked Turner for his help.

"You arrest that mayor," Turner said. "If there was any shootin', he was in on it. You can count on that."

"We'll see," Rhodes said.

CHAPTER 10

Rhodes drove back to the jail. He had a lot of questions about Brad Turner, not to mention the mayor and Ace Gable, but Rhodes knew where to get the answers, or some of them. He didn't need computers to keep up with people in Clearview. He had Hack, who in spite of his complaints that nobody ever told him anything managed to keep up with most of what was going on in town, even though he seldom left his desk. He didn't even have to quiz Rhodes about the murder. He'd already caught up on almost everything.

And then there was Lawton. Whatever Hack didn't know about Clearview, Lawton probably did. All Rhodes had to do was ask. It might take a while to get the answers from them, but eventually the answers would come.

"You gonna enter the bull ridin' at the rodeo this year?" Hack asked when Rhodes walked through the door.

"You been visiting a Web site on county time?" Rhodes asked, sitting at his desk.

"It's part of the job," Hack said. "If people'd just keep me in the loop, I wouldn't have to look. Almost didn't get to find out anything today, since that Web site's been down most of the time. It's back up now, though. You looked just like Sage Barton when you tangled with that bull."

"Let's don't start that Sage Barton stuff," Rhodes said. "Is there anything I need to know about?"

"Heard from the hospital. Earl Foshee's still unconscious. He'll be okay, but it might take him a while to come around."

Rhodes hoped Earl would be all right. He might be a drug dealer, but he didn't deserve to spend his life in a coma. Nobody deserved that. Besides, Rhodes wanted to question him about what had happened at the Moore house.

"Anything else?" Rhodes asked.

Lawton came in from the cellblock about then, but Hack pretended not to notice him.

"Might be one thing," Hack said. "We got a call from Miz Hovey. You know Miz Hovey?"

"Elberta Hovey," Rhodes said. "Lives on the south side of town."

"That's her," Lawton said.

Hack shot him a look. "I'm the one took the call."

"I know it," Lawton said. "I was just lettin' the sheriff know he had the right woman in mind."

"I'm glad I have the right woman in mind," Rhodes said. He knew he was going to have to put up with a certain amount of Hack's and Lawton's contrariness before he could ask them the questions he had, so he might as well get it out of the way. "What happened?"

"You know much about Miz Hovey?" Hack asked. "What her house is like, what her income is, stuff like that?"

Rhodes didn't know where this was going, but he seldom did when Hack and Lawton got started on him. There was no hurrying them.

"She's not rich," he said. "Her husband died about ten years ago. She probably lives on Social Security."

"Prob'ly so," Lawton said, earning another look from Hack.

Rhodes just waited, and after a second or two Hack turned back to him and said, "So you don't think she's got nine million dollars around the house?"

Rhodes had heard stories about people

who didn't trust banks and who kept large sums of money under mattresses, in mason jars buried in the backyard, or in the freezer compartment of the refrigerator. In spite of all the stories, however, Rhodes had never known of an actual occurrence of that sort of thing, and Mrs. Hovey didn't seem a likely candidate to be the first person of his acquaintance who'd hidden money around the house, especially such a huge sum. Even nine hundred dollars would be a stretch for someone in her financial situation. Nine million was an impossibility unless her deceased husband had owned the biggest life insurance policy in Blacklin County.

"I don't think she'd have more than ninety dollars lying around," Rhodes said. "Why?"

"Because she called and said her brother had robbed her," Hack said.

"Got away with the whole nine million," Lawton said.

Hack sighed.

"Well, he did," Lawton said. "Nine million bucks. That's a lot."

"It is," Rhodes said, before Hack could jump on Lawton. "It's even more than I make every year. Did we have the brother arrested for stealing all the money?"

"You want the story or not?" Hack asked.

Rhodes grinned. "I thought I had the

story. Mrs. Hovey. Nine million dollars. Brother stole it."

"You're messin' with me," Hack said.

"Me?" Rhodes said. "Mess with you? I know better than to do that."

"You and Lawton are a real pair of comedians, you know that?"

"I don't see you laughin'," Lawton said.

" 'Cause you ain't funny."

"I thought you said I was a comedian."

Rhodes figured it was time to step in and maybe even find out what was really going on.

"I'd like to know what we're doing about the theft," he said. "Did you send Buddy to investigate?"

"I sent him," Hack said. "It turned out there wasn't any nine million dollars. Her brother didn't steal it, either. It was under the kitchen table. Buddy found it."

"The nine million dollars?" Rhodes said.

"Nope," Lawton said. "What he found was —"

"The lottery ticket," Hack said in a rush before Lawton could finish the sentence. "The jackpot's nine million this weekend, and Miz Hovey was sure she had the winning numbers. Came to her in a dream, she said, so she went right out the next day and bought a ticket. She had it on her kitchen

159

table, under a butter dish, when her brother came over. When he left, it was gone, and she thought he'd taken it. Those two never did get along. Anyway, he hadn't taken it. She'd moved the butter dish or something, and the ticket fell under the table. She was real sorry 'bout causin' trouble for ever'body, but she was sure glad to find that ticket."

"She's gonna be mighty disappointed if she don't win," Lawton said.

"Maybe I'll win," Rhodes said.

"You buy a ticket?" Hack asked.

"Nope."

"Didn't think so. Lawton and I didn't, neither. We're waitin' for one of them really big Powerball deals before we make our investment. Hundred million or so. Then we'll go all in. Maybe buy two tickets."

"Good luck," Rhodes said. "Is that the only big crime of the day?"

"That's it," Hack said. "Pretty quiet otherwise."

"Good. You want to tell me a few things about some of our local residents?"

"If I know anything."

"I'm sure you do, and if you don't, Lawton will."

Hack snorted. "Wouldn't count on it."

"We'll see. Let's start with Ace Gable.

What's the word on him?"

Rhodes had begun with Gable because he was the one Hack and Lawton were likely to know the least about. Since Gable had been in town only about five years, he didn't have much of a history, and he had none at all with the sheriff's department, never having been arrested.

"Bought a muffler from him once," Lawton said. "Seemed like a nice enough fella. Why you askin'?"

"Vicki Patton works for him. She used to be Neil Foshee's girlfriend."

"Don't know him," Hack said. "You want me to check the databases?"

"Good idea," Rhodes said.

Hack had been the first in the office to get computer literate, and Rhodes trusted him to run the database checks. Rhodes had learned a few computer skills, but Hack was still ahead of him, a fact that Hack was quick to remind him of if the occasion arose. If it didn't arise, Hack would sometimes remind him of it anyway.

Hack turned to his computer, and Rhodes said, "What about Brad Turner?"

"Lives up by the graveyard," Lawton said. "Not far from the Moore place. Been around forever. I remember when he worked for the light company. Used to be a meter

161

reader. That was back when we had meter readers, 'fore they put those computerized things on the houses. A man had to go right up to the meter and look at it his ownself. It wasn't easy, what with people havin' dogs in their yards and all. Things have sure changed a lot."

Lawton stopped and looked at Hack, who was busy with the computer and didn't have anything to offer.

"Turner don't have a lot of friends, if any," Lawton continued. "Keeps pretty much to himself. Little bit crazy. Don't like folks much."

Rhodes had pretty much figured that out for himself.

"I hear he wears a tinfoil hat," Lawton said. "That kind of thing puts people off."

"He just lines his baseball cap with tinfoil," Rhodes said. "It's not too noticeable."

Hack turned around in his chair. "You know that it's not tinfoil, don't you? It's aluminum foil." He looked at Lawton. "Some of us here might be old enough to remember when foil was made out of tin, though."

"I ain't as old as you are, you old coot," Lawton said. "Ever'body still calls it tinfoil, no matter what it is."

"Not ever'body," Hack said. "I don't."

"Don't anybody care what you call it."

Things were getting out of hand again, as they so often did when Hack and Lawton were involved. Rhodes wasn't too concerned about Turner anyway, and he especially wasn't concerned about tinfoil.

"Forget about Turner and his hat," Rhodes said. "Here's the big question. What do you know about Mayor Clement?"

Hack was interested enough in the question to look away from Lawton. "You sayin' the mayor might have somethin' to do with killing Foshee?"

"Nope. I'm saying that somebody claims to've seen the mayor's car up by the Moore place last night."

"Drives that big Lexus SUV," Lawton said. "Not many of them around here."

"Dr. Filby's got one," Hack said. "Wonder what Ace Gable drives."

"We'll find out," Rhodes said. "Is there any reason the mayor might've been there last night?"

"You could ask him," Hack said.

"I'd rather not, not just yet. I need more information."

"I got some," Lawton said.

Hack looked chagrined. He didn't like being one-upped by Lawton.

"Tell us," Rhodes said, trying not to smile.

"There's been some talk," Lawton said.

"Don't stall," Rhodes said. "Just the facts."

"Sounds like Joe Friday, don't he?" Lawton said to Hack, who didn't answer. He was still pouting.

Rhodes didn't say anything, either. He just waited.

"You sure are a killjoy lately," Lawton said to him. "Ain't that right, Hack?"

"That's right," Hack said, relenting. "Been sayin' that for a while."

"The mayor," Rhodes said. "Let's don't forget the mayor."

"It ain't the mayor. It's his nephew."

"What about his nephew?" Rhodes asked. He didn't even know that Clement had a nephew.

"College kid," Lawton said. "Been in town a week or so. People say he's nosy. Drives around in the mayor's car. Asks questions he oughtn't be askin'."

Rhodes was a little surprised that no one had called to complain. "What kind of questions?"

"Drugs. Says he's writin' a paper on drugs in small towns."

Rhodes thought it was odd that someone writing a paper on drugs wouldn't ask the sheriff's department about the situation. Why go to the citizens first?

"You think he was lookin' to buy some?" Hack asked.

"Could be," Lawton said. "I don't know much more than that about it."

Rhodes remembered something Clement had said to him that morning that didn't fit with something he'd heard from Hack a few minutes before. No wonder Clement had tried to persuade him that investigating Foshee's death wasn't important. Clement had made a big mistake, and Rhodes was going to call him on it. He had a couple of questions for Lawton first, however.

"Has Andy been by with the evidence from the Moore house?"

"Dropped it off a while ago," Hack said. "He told me you wanted Mika to check for fingerprints. I called her, and she'll be by later on this afternoon."

"Okay. Did you find anything on Ace Gable?"

"He doesn't have much of a record. A couple of speeding tickets and once for assault. From what I can tell, it involved some guy trying to pick up his date."

Rhodes thought about that, then stood up. "I'm going to talk to Mayor Clement to see what I can find out about his nephew. Call me if you need me."

"Don't I always?" Hack said.

■ ■ ■ ■

Alice King's perkiness hadn't waned with the day. If anything, she was even perkier than she'd been that morning.

"Good afternoon, Sheriff," she said when Rhodes entered the office. "This must be my lucky day, you coming by here twice. I don't think that's ever happened before. I hope you've been having a great afternoon."

"Absolutely," Rhodes said. It would never do for Rhodes to tell Alice that he hadn't been having a great day. If he did, she'd try to jolly him up, and he didn't have time for that. For all he knew, it might involve a cheerleading routine. "Is the mayor in?"

"He sure is," Alice said, with a nod to the open door leading to Clement's office. "You can just go right on in."

Rhodes stepped into the office. Clement was at his desk, and his dour face was almost a relief after Alice's relentless perkiness.

"What is it, Sheriff?" Clement asked. "I hope you're not going to bother me about that business at the Moore house again."

"Sorry to disappoint you," Rhodes said, sitting down without waiting for an invitation that might not have been forthcoming.

"That's exactly what I'm here for."

"Well, I don't want to talk about it any-more. I've said my say."

"I think you're wrong about that," Rhodes told him. "This morning you said that you'd found out about the murder of Neil Foshee on Jennifer Loam's Web site. I'd like to know how you managed that, since the site was down all morning."

Clement fell back in his chair as if Rhodes had struck him. "I . . . you must be wrong about that."

"Don't think so. My dispatcher told me about it. I could always call Ms. Loam and ask her, but I don't think I need to. And here's another thing that you might want to explain to me while you're at it. I've been told that your car was seen in the vicinity of the Moore house at the time of Foshee's death. I'd like to know what you were doing there."

"I wasn't there," Clement said, pushing his chair back from the desk as if trying to get away from Rhodes. The chair hit the wall and stopped, so Clement couldn't escape that way. The only way out of the room was through the door, and to get there, Clement would have to pass Rhodes. Rhodes wasn't planning to let him pass.

"Your car was just out for an evening drive

on its own?" Rhodes said.

Clement didn't laugh at the joke. "I didn't say that."

"You said you weren't in it. If you weren't, who was driving? Your wife?"

"No, not my wife." Clement sighed and pulled his chair back to the desk. "It was my nephew."

"I heard he was in town. I don't think I've met him."

"He's my brother's son. My brother lives in Dallas, and Wade, that's his son, goes to school in Denton. He's spending a few weeks with us this summer while his parents go to Europe."

"He have a drug problem?"

"Of course not," Clement said. "He's a clean-living young man."

"Seems he's been asking questions around town about drugs," Rhodes said. "He was seen in the area where a known drug dealer was killed. That doesn't look very good for him."

It also didn't look very good for Clement. If word got out that his nephew had been involved with drugs while cruising around in the mayor's car, Clement might not get reelected. If he didn't get reelected, he wouldn't be able to continue to try bossing Rhodes around. All the fun would be gone from his life.

"It's not what you're thinking," Clement said.

"If it's not," Rhodes said, "you'd better tell me what it is."

Clement sighed again. Rhodes was reminded of something Peppermint Patty had said in a *Peanuts* strip, something like "Don't hassle me with your sighs, Chuck." Clement probably wasn't a fan of *Peanuts*.

"Wade's majoring in criminal justice," Clements said. "He and I were talking a little bit about the drug problem in small towns like ours, and he got interested. He thought he could get some firsthand information and write a paper for one of his classes next fall. Wanted to impress some professor."

"Why not send him to me?" Rhodes asked. "I'm the sheriff, or maybe you'd forgotten that."

Clement didn't answer, but Rhodes thought he knew why Wade hadn't consulted him. Clement didn't like Rhodes, didn't think he was doing a good job, and might even have thought that some college student could do a better one. Especially one majoring in criminology at a big state university. He might even have told Wade that.

"There's another little thing, too," Rhodes said. "If your nephew knew that Neil Foshee was shot, he should've reported it to the sheriff's department."

"Just hold on there," Clement said. "He did report it. He called it in anonymously. He didn't know that Foshee was dead. He heard the shots in the house just as he got out of his car. He got back in the car and left immediately. Surely you can't blame him for not staying there when shots were being fired."

Rhodes didn't blame him, but he wasn't going to tell Clement that. He said, "There's another thing. You remember our little discussion about implying and inferring?"

Again Clement had nothing to say.

"Well, I remember it," Rhodes said after a second or two. "How do you think it would look if people thought you were trying to shut down a murder investigation because your nephew was involved? Don't bother to tell me I was inferring something, either, because now we both know better."

The office was air-conditioned, but Clement had begun to sweat. "I was wrong to do that. It was a mistake."

Rhodes nodded. "I'm glad we agree on that. Now call your nephew and tell him to get in here so we can all three have a nice little talk."

"He might not want to come. Might not have a way to get here."

"That's okay," Rhodes said. "I can go and get him. I haven't arrested anybody all day, and it's about time I did."

"He can use my wife's car," Clement said, reaching for his phone.

CHAPTER 11

Wade Clement looked like he was about fifteen to Rhodes, who'd noticed that more and more people were looking younger than their years to him. Rhodes had a feeling that wasn't a good sign as far as his own age went.

Wade went in for the same kind of facial stubble that Brad Turner sported, and while it did look careless to Rhodes, it didn't look quite as bad as Turner's. Wade's was also considerably darker than Turner's, which was mostly gray.

Wade had something besides stubble in common with Turner. He wore a baseball cap, a Texas Rangers cap just like the one Turner wore, except newer and minus the tinfoil. Or aluminum foil. Wade, in fact, looked a bit like a baseball player, a second baseman maybe, or a shortstop. Compact but muscular. He had an easy smile, but he seemed a little worried about his situation.

"I guess I'm in trouble, right?" he said.

He was sitting in a chair near his uncle's desk. He'd gotten to the office soon after Clement called him, and while Clement hadn't explained anything over the phone, he'd mentioned to Wade that the sheriff wanted to talk to him.

"Trouble?" Rhodes said. "Maybe not. We'll see. Let's talk about what happened last night."

Wade looked at his uncle. Clement said, "He knows about it."

"I sure do," Rhodes said to Wade. "You were about to visit a known drug dealer when he was shot and killed. You claim you called it in, but your cell phone number is blocked, so we can't be sure it was you. That's for starters. You want to tell me what you were doing there in the first place?"

Wade stiffened. "I didn't know he was killed, not then. I didn't find that out until a little while ago."

"Let's say that's true. We can come back to it if we need to. Just start with what you were doing there."

Wade relaxed a little. "Research. I'm going to do a paper on drug dealing in small towns. I have a professor who's interested in the problem, and I thought it would be good if I could get some firsthand informa-

173

tion about it. Uncle Cliff said it would be okay."

Clement looked as if he'd like to get up and clap a hand over his nephew's mouth, but he sat where he was.

"He told you that, huh?" Rhodes asked.

"Yeah. He said you guys weren't doing much about the drugs here in town and maybe I could help out."

Clement cleared his throat. "I don't believe I put it exactly like that."

Wade shrugged. "Something like that, anyway. I've heard all about how small-town police forces are understaffed and under-funded. You need all the help you can get."

Rhodes nodded. "That's what I always say, but we don't need any help from people who might get themselves killed. You know you could've been the one who was shot last night, don't you?"

"Me?" Wade said. "Why would anybody want to shoot me?"

"People don't always need a reason," Rhodes said.

He'd been asking himself the same question about Neil Foshee. Why would anyone want to shoot him? So far the only person he could think of who might have a reason was Ace Gable.

"I don't think anybody would shoot me,"

Wade said, but he didn't sound so sure of himself now.

"You still haven't told me why you were there," Rhodes said. "Specifically, not generally. You don't drive to a place where a drug dealer's being killed just to help out the poor underfunded sheriff's department."

"I . . . was meeting somebody," Wade said.

"Who would that be?"

"I didn't exactly know."

Rhodes looked at Clement, who just rolled his eyes. By this point the mayor must have been feeling a bit of remorse for some of the things he'd said to his nephew.

"Maybe you'd better explain," Rhodes told Wade.

"Okay, I'll try. I asked around town about drugs. I told everybody I talked to the truth, that I was working on a paper for my college class. I didn't ask any names or anything, and I told everybody I wouldn't mention them in the paper. It took me a while, but I finally talked to a guy who told me about the haunted house and how that's where some drug deals got made. So I thought I'd go by and see."

"You were just going to walk in on a drug deal?"

"Not exactly. This guy I talked to said he'd fix it up so I could meet somebody there, maybe talk to him. Maybe even make a buy from him."

Rhodes couldn't believe that anybody could be so naïve as Wade Clements. Even a college kid should know that a stranger in town didn't go around asking questions about drugs and set up a meeting. That was just crazy, like something from a movie. For that matter, it never turned out well in the movies, either.

"Who were you going to meet?" Rhodes asked.

"No names," Wade said. "Just some guy."

Rhodes didn't roll his eyes the way the mayor had, but he wanted to. "You were going to walk into a possible drug deal with some guy whose name you didn't know in the middle of the night?"

"It sounds kind of crazy when you put it that way."

"That's because it is crazy. Do you own a handgun?"

"Well, sure. Doesn't everybody? I have a CHL, too."

"Did you have the gun with you?"

Wade frowned. "What do you mean? Are you saying I might've shot that guy? I didn't even go in the house."

"Maybe not, but we'll need your handgun to run some ballistics tests. Do you have it with you?"

"No. It's at Uncle Cliff's house."

"I'll see to it that he brings it to the jail," Clement said. "It'll be the one registered to him. I guarantee it."

"I didn't shoot anybody," Wade said. "I didn't even take the gun out of the car."

"Then you don't have anything to worry about," Rhodes said.

He didn't know that they would even have to perform any tests, since he didn't know yet what kind of gun had killed Foshee. The truth was that a little worrying would be a good thing in Wade's case.

"I'll see to it that you get the gun back," Rhodes said. "Eventually. In the meantime, you need to forget about writing a paper on drug deals. Don't ask any more questions, don't try to get involved with police work. Read a book. Watch TV. Play video games on your phone. But don't mess around with the drug stuff. All right?"

Wade looked at his uncle. Clement nodded. "Do what he says. You're in enough trouble already. Besides, the sheriff has too many civilians meddling in his business."

That was just like Clement. He couldn't resist getting in a little dig to remind Rhodes that he knew about Seepy Benton. Rhodes thought Benton was a different case, however. He was meddlesome, true, but he'd proved useful in the past, not that Rhodes was going to tell him that.

Rhodes stood up. "If I'm not at the jail when you bring the gun by, give it to one of the deputies. I'll let you know when you can pick it up."

"So I'm not under arrest?" Wade asked.

"Not yet," Rhodes told him.

Rhodes left the mayor's office, got a sprightly good-bye wave from Alice King, and went outside into the hot late-afternoon sunshine. He turned for a look at the old city hall building. It wasn't what it used to be, but at least it was still standing, unlike so many of the buildings that had once made up Clearview's downtown area. The town's original city jail was on the second floor of the building, and the windows still had the bars on them. Rhodes hadn't been on the second floor in years, so he didn't know what purpose the cells might be serving now, if they served any at all. Storerooms seemed most likely.

Rhodes got into the county car and turned on the air conditioner. He rolled down the windows to let some of the heat escape and called Hack to tell him to run a search to see if Wade Clement had a record and to find out if there was anything that required his attention.

"Nope," Hack said when Rhodes asked. "Just the usual. Somebody called in a copper theft. Len Goolsby complained about a pickup circling the block. Said the driver was prob'ly checkin' out his wife, who was out in the front yard waterin' the flower bed."

"Did you send somebody to take a look?"

"At Len's wife?"

"You know what I mean."

"I sent Andy to check on both things. He's handling the other thing, too."

"What other thing?"

"Bea Ferrell and her husband got into a fight. Well, not a fight. Just lots of yellin' and throwin' the dishes. It was a Facebook thing."

Facebook things were cropping up with way too much regularity lately. Rhodes was afraid somebody was going to be seriously hurt before long.

"Bea says her husband was lookin' up his old girlfriends from high school and friend-in' 'em," Hack continued. "He claims it was them lookin' him up and that it'd be impolite not to friend 'em. Somewhere along in there the yellin' started. Neighbors called it in."

"Everything end peacefully?"

"Guess so. Andy's still there at the Ferrells' place."

"Good. Here's something we need, the gun registrations for Ace Gable, Clifford and Wade Clement, and Vicki Patton. Have Mika look for those."

"You're pilin' it on her."

"She can handle it. Anything else I need to know?"

"Yep, one other thing. You need to go by and see Mikey Burns out at the precinct building."

"Why?"

"Says he has something to tell you about Neil Foshee."

"He say what it was?"

"Nobody ever tells me anything," Hack said. "I don't know if I've mentioned that, but I've been meanin' to."

Rhodes pretended to think it over. "I don't think you've mentioned it."

"You know dadgum well I have, not that it's done any good."

"I'll bring it up at the next meeting," Rhodes said.

"What meeting? When is it?"

"I'll let you know," Rhodes said.

Before going to see Burns, Rhodes drove by

the Moore place. It wasn't too much out of the way, mainly because nothing in Clearview was too much out of the way. In the daylight, the old house didn't look frightening in the least. It just looked run-down and dreary. It wasn't going to last for many more years before it just gave up and sagged down to the ground, too old and tired to stand up any longer.

In spite of its harmless appearance, however, something about the house bothered Rhodes. He couldn't figure out why. Maybe it was the air of decay. He remembered reading "The Fall of the House of Usher" long ago in high school, and if there had been a deep, dark lake nearby for the Moore house to crumble into, it would've been a perfect fit with the story. The Usher place had been home to some odd doings, and so had this one.

Maybe Rhodes was bothered because Neil Foshee had been killed inside the house, but Rhodes had been in any number of places where people had died. The feeling he had now wasn't the same. It was a prickly feeling on the back of his neck, almost as if someone were watching him from inside the house.

Seepy Benton might have said there was a ghost involved, but Rhodes didn't think that was it. He didn't put much stock in ghosts. He thought there was someone in there. He drove around to the back of the house but didn't see a car anywhere. He parked and got out of his own car. He ducked under the crime-scene tape and walked through the backyard. As hot as the day had been, the grass hadn't dried in the shade of the trees.

Rhodes went on into the house and stood in the kitchen. It was quiet except for the occasional creak of an old board, and a musty smell hung in the air. Some of the fast-food wrappers still lay on the floor. The light coming in through the windows showed that the spiderwebs he'd seen the night before were dusty brown. There hadn't been any new ones for a while. It was as if the spiders had decided one day to go and find somewhere else to live.

Rhodes went into the next room, the one where Foshee had been killed. He saw nothing that aroused his suspicions, but the prickly feeling didn't go away. Then he heard something, a skittering and a chittering in the walls. Rats. Or mice, more likely. That must have been what had bothered him, the thought of the mice running around in the house. He had nothing against mice, or even rats, not really. His last encounter with rats had been in an old cotton warehouse that he'd been searching with Buddy. Buddy had told him some story about a man long ago who'd been chased by rats. He'd hidden in a tower, but the rats had found him. They'd whetted their teeth on the stones, Buddy said.

The noise in the walls stopped. Rhodes heard paper rustle in the kitchen and went back in there. A rat crouched in the middle of the floor, looking at him. Not a mouse. A rat. A big gray rat with black eyes and a skinless tail. It wasn't quite as big as a cat, but it was the size of a kitten. It didn't appear to be afraid of Rhodes at all.

Rhodes took a step toward the animal. It sat up on its haunches, sniffed the air, and ran straight at him.

Rhodes hadn't been expecting that. He'd thought the rat might run toward the back door or out another exit, but the rat had different ideas. Rhodes did a quick-step and hopped out of the way as the rat ran into the other room and disappeared.

Rhodes wondered if the rat had been watching him all along. Maybe that accounted for the prickly feeling. The feeling hadn't gone away with the rat's departure, but it seemed to be a little less.

A rat like that could have a bad effect on

anybody. It was awfully big.

Rhodes decided it was time for him to leave. He was almost to the back door when his phone rang. He'd never played basketball, but he had a pretty good vertical leap when startled. He dug out his phone and answered. The caller was Hack.

"You weren't answerin' the radio," Hack said.

"I'm not in the car," Rhodes told him.

"Not in the car? You goin' over to see Mikey Burns, or ain't you?"

"I stopped by the Moore house first," Rhodes said. "To have a look around."

"Well, Mikey says he's gonna leave early today, and he's gettin' antsy."

"I'll go right now," Rhodes said.

He stuck the phone back in his pocket and walked through the yard to the car. He still couldn't shake the feeling that someone was watching him. He looked around, but he didn't see any pale faces peering at him from behind broken or dusty windowpanes. He didn't see the rat, either, so he got in the car and left.

CHAPTER 12

A couple of the other county commissioners had recently built new stone buildings to house their offices. On the inside they had large modern offices and meeting rooms with comfortable chairs.

Mikey Burns hadn't followed their lead as yet. He still had his office in a big metal building with covered bays in the back for road graders and trucks and other county equipment.

Unlike his headquarters, however, Burns himself was flashy. He drove a bright red Pontiac Solstice convertible, which he'd had since it was new. It was on the way to becoming a collectible at this point, but it suited his personality. It was parked in front of the building, and Rhodes parked next to it. He was careful not to let the door of the county car touch the side of the convertible when he got out.

Going inside, Rhodes was greeted by Mrs.

Wilkie, who had changed a good bit since beginning to work for the county and becoming interested in her boss. Her hair was still an unlikely color, but it wasn't the unnatural reddish orange it had been. It was styled, or so Rhodes suspected, by Lonnie Wallace or one of his assistants at the Beauty Shack. She'd recently done away with her glasses for contact lenses, and she even had an occasional kind word for Rhodes, who figured she'd finally forgiven him for marrying Ivy. She wasn't as perky as Alice King, but then nobody was as perky as Alice King.

"Good afternoon, Sheriff," Mrs. Wilkie said when he came into the room. "The commissioner is expecting you. You go right on in."

Rhodes did as instructed. Burns sat behind his battered old desk, and he waved Rhodes to a seat in one of the office's folding chairs. The other furniture consisted of a couple of old green filing cabinets and Burns's desk, atop which were the only fairly new objects in the office, a computer and monitor.

Burns was given to wearing aloha shirts, but the one he had on today wasn't as bright as usual. It was covered with guitars against a black background. He also wore a straw planter's hat. Hack had said he was planning to leave early, and it looked as if he was already on his way.

"We need to talk, Sheriff," Burns said.

"That's what I'm here for," Rhodes said. "You know something about Neil Foshee?"

"Maybe. I'll get to him in a minute. We need to talk about the drug problem in general first. The hog problem, too."

Rhodes wasn't sure what the two problems had to do with each other, but he figured Burns would tell him.

"Okay," Rhodes said. "Let's talk about them. You go first."

"That was my plan." Burns opened the middle drawer of his desk, pulled out a newspaper, and laid it on the desk. He opened it up and tapped it with his finger. "You know what this is?"

Rhodes was tempted to say it was a newspaper, but Burns probably wasn't in the mood for jokes. Rhodes couldn't see the article that Burns was tapping, so he had no idea what was in it. Either Burns thought Rhodes had better eyesight than he actually did or he expected Rhodes to get up and take a look at the paper.

Rhodes got up and looked. He saw a drawing of a circular object with four arms sticking out from its sides. The arms were topped with rotors.

"It's a drone," Rhodes said.

"Exactly," Burns said. "It could be the answer to our problems."

"Which problems?" Rhodes said.

"The ones I just mentioned," Burns said. "The druggies and the wild hogs. You get it?"

Rhodes walked back to the folding chair and sat down. The chair squeaked. Needed some WD-40 or Rhodes needed to lose a little weight. Or both.

"I think I get it," Rhodes said, "but I'm not sure. You'd better clarify it for me."

"It's simple," Burns said. "If we had a couple of drones, we could surveil the whole county without having to leave this building. We'd have a couple of monitors and operators, and those two people could keep up with the whole county. We could spot the meth houses and move right in on them. We'd know who was there and what they were doing. We could find out where the hogs were holed up during the daylight hours and —" He paused. "There's a little problem with the hogs. What we'd need for them is another drone, an armed one. We'd bomb those suckers. Blow 'em up. Scatter pork parts all over the county if we had to, but we'd get rid of 'em."

Offhand Rhodes could come up with only a couple of hundred objections to Burns's cunning plan, but he thought it would be best to start with the obvious one.

"Would the military let us have something like that?"

"Sure they would. The sheriff's department already has one down in Conroe. Lot of places have 'em that don't want it known yet."

"Armed ones?"

"Well, maybe not armed ones, but they have surveillance drones. We're already behind the curve."

"Expensive, aren't they?" Rhodes asked. "Plus you'd have to hire the operators. It takes a lot of training to pilot one of those from a desk."

"Well, sure it does, but the county would benefit a lot. You have to spend money to make money."

Rhodes didn't think any of the other commissioners would agree with anything Burns had said. "Are you going to recommend this?"

"That's where you come in," Burns said. "You're the sheriff. You run all the law enforcement, so you're the expert on what we need. You make the recommendation, and I'll support you."

"I'll have to study on it some first," Rhodes said. "It's a complicated thing to deal with."

Burns would probably forget all about the drone in a few weeks, just as he'd forgotten other things, like the M-16 he'd wanted the county to buy.

"I understand," Burns said. "It's not something you can decide on in just a few minutes. You let me know next week. Now here's something else for you to think about, and it's an even better idea."

Rhodes didn't see how it could be much worse. "What is it?"

"An MRAP."

"A what?

"An MRAP, a Mine Resistant Ambush Protected vehicle, and here's the best part. It won't cost us a penny. The army's giving them away."

"Why on earth would we need a tactical vehicle like that?"

"Think about it," Burns said. "Need to execute a warrant? One of those babies would pretty much take care of any resistance. Got somebody holed up in a house with hostages? One of those babies would take care of that, too."

"One of those babies would take care of a zombie apocalypse," Rhodes said, "but do we really need one? We're just a small sheriff's department, not an invading army. So far nobody's planted any IEDs to try to stop us. We haven't had to break down any concrete walls to get to a fugitive."

Burns ignored him. "We could get one easy. I know of one town a lot smaller than Clearview in this very state that's gotten over three million dollars' worth of equipment from the army, all at no cost to them. They didn't get an MRAP, but they got all kinds of neat stuff. We might even get some grenade launchers. Other places have." He paused, thinking something over. "You know what? We might be able to use the grenade launchers on the hogs if we don't get the drones."

"This will take a lot of study," Rhodes said, hoping it wouldn't take Burns long to forget about it. Rhodes didn't want to be the commander of an army or anything like it.

"You study hard," Burns said. "And fast. Everybody's getting ahead of us. We'll look like a second-class county if we don't get our act together."

"I'll give it a lot of thought," Rhodes said, "and I'll let you know as soon as I can. Right now, I know you're in a hurry to get away, so tell me what you want to say about

Neil Foshee before you have to leave."

Burns leaned back in his chair. "I heard he'd been killed. You know who did it yet?"

"I'm working on it," Rhodes said.

"You talked to Roger Allen?"

Allen sold Chevrolets at the local dealership. As far as Rhodes knew, he had nothing to do with Foshee.

"I didn't know he was connected to Foshee, so I haven't talked to him. Should I?"

"Might be a good idea. He came by here a day or so ago complaining about the drug problem in the county. He said it was personal with him. Not here exactly, but because he had a cousin over in Longview that got hooked on meth and it ruined his life. He went crazy for the stuff. Lost his business, left his wife, wound up getting killed when he tried to break into a house to get drug money. Homeowner killed him with a rifle shot to the head. Anyway, Roger was saying that if something wasn't done soon, he was going to do it himself. He didn't want this county to be overrun with drugs like some of them are and have people breaking into houses and getting killed over drug money."

"He's never complained to my office," Rhodes said. He was starting to feel like

Hack about nobody telling him anything. First Wade Clement and now Roger Allen.

"I don't want you to get the wrong idea about what I told him," Burns said. "I told him this county had less trouble with drugs than just about any county in the state and that was because you and your department were doing such a good job. I told him it was wrong to be thinking about taking the law into his own hands. I don't think he meant he'd really do it. He was just wound up, but he mentioned the Foshee boys by name. Everybody's heard about that big arrest you made on them, and then they bonded out. What got Roger started, though, besides the Foshees being back on the street, was some young guy asking around town about drugs. Seemed to think there was a problem here, and he was going to write it up for some college paper or something."

"Wade Clement," Rhodes said.

"Who?" Burns said.

"The mayor's nephew. That's who talked to Roger. Wade's a college student in town for a visit with his uncle. He's majoring in criminology in college, and he claims he's writing a paper for some class about small-town drug problems. I think he's causing more problems than we had before he got here. I've talked to him about it."

"I hope so. We don't need that kind of thing. You better talk to Roger, too. He's got a temper. I wouldn't put it past him to decide to go after those Foshees on his own, even if I tried to calm him down."

Rhodes stood up. "I'll talk to him."

Burns stood up as well. "I don't think he killed Neil, understand. I just think you need to talk to him."

Rhodes nodded. "Right. That's what I'll do."

"You think about those drones, too. Your recommendation would sell the idea. I'll recommend the MRAP myself. It's free, it's tactical, and it looks great. That thing could drive right over a car if it had to. We could sure use one."

"I'll give it a lot of thought," Rhodes lied, wondering why anybody would want to drive over a car. "You're in a hurry to get away, so I'll go on now and talk to Roger Allen. Thanks for the tip."

"Always glad to help," Burns said.

Rhodes went on out and saw that Mrs. Wilkie was getting her purse out of the bottom drawer of her desk. He wondered if she and Burns were going to leave early together, not that it was any of his business. He gave her a wave and a smile and left.

■ ■ ■ ■

Rhodes thought he had time to visit the Chevy dealership before he went home for dinner, so he drove out the highway toward Walmart where so many of the local businesses had relocated. Clearview's downtown might have died, but businesses all along the highway leading up to Walmart on the east side of town had been thriving.

The Chevy dealership was no exception. It covered a couple of acres of ground, and Rhodes didn't even want to think about the value of the inventory of new and used cars. If Mikey Burns's drone malfunctioned and bombed the dealership instead of a bunch of hogs, the county would never be able to pay off the lawsuit the insurance company would bring against it, and that was if there were no casualties. Burns was the one who needed to do more thinking about what he was asking for, not Rhodes. Rhodes had already made up his mind.

Rhodes wound through the cars situated where people could see them from the highway and parked in front of the dealership's building, which was at least half a block long. The entire front was made up of windows and big glass doors. Cars were parked inside the building as well as outside in front of the windows. Rhodes parked in one of the spots reserved for visitors, and he was barely out of the county car before Roger Allen came bounding out of the building to meet him.

Roger had been a football player for the Clearview Catamounts a good many years before, not long after Rhodes's own inglorious athletic career. Roger had been a lineman, big and fast, as Rhodes recalled, but he hadn't kept in shape. He was still big, but he didn't look fast, and he'd gained some weight that wasn't as well distributed as it might have been. Not that Rhodes hadn't done the same. He was no longer "Will o' the Wisp" Dan Rhodes. Never had been, really, but it had been nice to be thought of that way even for a short time.

"You here about the Tahoes, Sheriff?" Roger asked, sticking out his hand.

Roger had a salesman's jovial tone and a smile to go with it. He was dressed casually in cotton slacks and an open-necked shirt. Although it was late afternoon, he was closely shaved, and not just his face. Roger was completely bald, and his head was shaved as close as his chin.

Rhodes shook hands and said, "What Tahoes?"

"Nobody's told you?" Roger said.

"Nobody ever tells me anything," Rhodes said, knowing he sounded like Hack and not liking it.

"I know the feeling," Roger said. "Come on in. We need to talk."

That was something Rhodes could agree with, so he went inside with Roger. The air-conditioning was turned down to Arctic, but it felt good after the heat of late afternoon. Roger led Rhodes to one of the little desks scattered around the showroom, and they sat down.

By that time Rhodes had figured out what was going on. A few months previously he'd mentioned to Mikey Burns that the county's patrol cars were becoming something of a problem. Because of the ways sedans had changed over the years, there wasn't as much space at the back doors as there once had been, and there wasn't a lot of room in the backseats, either.

If this had been a problem only for the people who were arrested and put into the cars, that would be one thing, and it could've been overlooked. However, it was also a problem for the officers if a prisoner didn't want to get into the car and decided to put up a fight or if someone was impaired by drugs or alcohol and wasn't cooperating.

Something like a Tahoe would be a much better option in those circumstances, besides being more suited for the kind of country the officers had to travel in Blacklin County. A Tahoe would've come in handy, for example, if Rhodes had wanted to chase the Foshees across the pasture in a vehicle that morning.

Rhodes had explained all this to Burns, but Burns hadn't seemed particularly enthusiastic, certainly not as enthusiastic as he was about drones and tactical vehicles. He must've paid attention, though, and actually looked into it.

Roger laid out some brochures on the desk. "This is what I'm thinking of for you. All black or all white, take your pick, and with the county decal on the side in gold it'll look really sharp. Or we could go with those new stealth markings. Man, you can hardly see those things at all, but they're there. You look like an unmarked car but you really aren't."

"Did Mikey Burns talk to you about this?" Rhodes asked without looking at the brochures.

"Yeah. He didn't say it was a done deal or anything, but I'm glad you came by. I told him we could make the county a good deal. You wouldn't have to buy a whole fleet all at one time. You could just transition from the sedans to the Tahoes when one of the sedans was taken out of service. Mikey mentioned that you were kind of hard on sedans."

Rhodes didn't think the damages to his county car were entirely his fault. The county cars were often involved in accidents, and even though he sometimes happened to be driving them when the accidents happened, they were never his fault. Well, not always.

"I hope we can do some business with you," Rhodes said, "but that's not why I'm here."

"It's not?"

"Nope. I came about something else. We need to talk in private."

The showroom was deserted except for a couple of salesmen who were a good distance away, the clerk who took payments for repair work, and two men and a woman in the service department, also a good distance away in the opposite direction.

"We can talk here," Roger said. "Nobody's going to hear us. What's the problem?"

"Neil Foshee," Rhodes said.

Roger got a guarded look. "What about him?"

"Somebody killed him."

199

"Who did it?"

"I don't know," Rhodes said. "I was hoping you could tell me."

CHAPTER 13

"That dang Mikey Burns never could keep his mouth shut," Roger said. "Maybe we'd better not talk here after all. Let's go to the break room."

He got up and started off without waiting for Rhodes. Rhodes trailed along behind him. They went across the showroom and past the pay station, turned left, and went down a hall. At the end of the hall on the left was the break room. No one was inside, and when Rhodes followed him in, Roger shut the door and turned the lock.

Rhodes looked around the room and saw two bridge tables, eight folding chairs, an old couch, a counter with cabinets, and a coffeemaker sitting on the stained countertop. The flashy look of the showroom didn't extend to this part of the building.

Roger pulled out a chair and sat at one of the bridge tables, so Rhodes joined him.

"I should've asked if you want some coffee," Roger said.

"No, thanks," Rhodes said. He didn't like coffee.

"Smart move. The coffee here's terrible. I don't drink it myself. Just as soon drink muddy water." He leaned forward, putting his arms on the table and clasping his hands. "Look, I think you have the wrong idea about me. I went off half-cocked the other day and said a few things to Mikey Burns that I shouldn't have said. He tell you about my cousin?"

"He told me," Rhodes said. "I'm sorry for your loss."

"He was a good friend when we were kids. I haven't seen him much since then, but he didn't deserve to get killed like that. The meth made him crazy."

Rhodes didn't ask how or why the cousin had gotten started on drugs. The stories were always different, but all too often they had the same ending.

"You ought to think about gangs," Roger said. "The Mexican gangs are bringing more and more meth into Texas. That's what the sheriff told me when my cousin was killed. They had enough trouble there with the local meth cookers, but the gangs are bringing it in and pushing out the locals. Some of them have wound up dead. It could be the same with Foshee."

"We don't have that problem here," Rhodes said. "Not yet."

"I met this college boy the other day," Roger said. "He was in Max Schwartz's barbecue place with his uncle having lunch. His uncle's the mayor, and I've been trying to tell him that a Chevy's as good as that Lexus of his any day, so I sat down with them. Kid's name is Wade, and he tells me he's writing a paper on the drug problem. Got me all ticked off, and when I talked to Mikey, I was still feeling it. I shouldn't ever have said anything. I didn't mean anything by it, and I've calmed down now. Been calm ever since I blew off steam with Mikey, in fact. I just wanted to talk to him about the Tahoes, and I don't think we ever even got around to it. You don't think I killed Neil, do you?"

What Rhodes knew was that Roger had talked a lot and talked fast, the way a salesman would trying to close the deal. That didn't mean he was telling the truth.

"I haven't formed an opinion yet," Rhodes said. "Where were you last night around midnight?"

"I get it," Roger said. Little beads of sweat had formed on his bald head. "I know how it is. I can see you have to check up on everything. I watch this TV show, *Dateline,* so I know how it works. You have to rule everybody out, so you want to know if I have an alibi. On *Dateline* it's just about always the husband who did it. You ever watch that show?"

"Life would be easier if all the murders were committed by husbands," Rhodes said. "Foshee wasn't married, though."

He'd had a girlfriend, however, and Rhodes wondered about Vicki. He'd let her off the hook too easily, maybe because she and Ivy had become friends. He'd have to talk to her again.

"I'm married," Roger said. "You know that. Evelyn and I've been married for twenty years. You can ask her about last night. We were at home, watching TV until ten thirty, and then we went to bed. Just like always. You can ask her. She'll tell you."

Husbands didn't just commit all the murders on *Dateline.* If their wives were alive, they always dragged them out for alibis. If Ace Gable had been married, he'd have done the same. What they didn't know was that Rhodes didn't necessarily believe wives when they vouched for their husbands. Sometimes they were telling the truth, sometimes they were doing what they thought was their duty, and sometimes they were planning to use the alibi as blackmail later on. Rhodes didn't know which one of those it would be in the case of Roger's wife, but he'd find out.

"You go talk to Evelyn," Roger said. "She'll tell you."

"I'll do that," Rhodes said.

Rhodes didn't spend much time with Evelyn Allen. As expected, she vouched for Roger's whereabouts and swore up and down that he wouldn't kill a fly, much less a human being, even if the human being was a scum of the earth like Neil Foshee, who probably deserved what he got, even if she shouldn't say so.

Like her husband and the mayor, Evelyn wondered why Rhodes was even wasting his time investigating the death of someone like that when he could've been tracking down copper thieves or identity thieves or perfectly healthy people who parked in handicapped spaces.

Rhodes went on home after talking to her. He didn't put much stock in her backing up Roger's story. Roger might have called her as soon as Rhodes left the Chevy dealership. Probably had, in fact. Roger wasn't going to get off the hook that easily.

"You're home early," Ivy said when

Rhodes came in. "I can't remember the last time you got home early."

Rhodes couldn't remember, either. Even Yancey was surprised, and for a couple of seconds he forgot to show how happy he was. He recovered, though, and began to yip happily. The cats, of course, couldn't have cared less whether Rhodes ever showed up again or not, as long as they got fed.

"I'm glad you're here," Ivy said. "I'm going to fix a special supper for us."

"Sounds good," Rhodes said, instead of asking what she was planning. Ivy had been making healthy meals for too long to suit him, and he wasn't sure he wanted to know.

She told him anyway. "Lasagna rolls. How does that sound?"

It sounded great, but Rhodes figured there was a catch. "Healthy ones?"

"Delicious ones. They'll have a lot of good things in them."

"Such as?"

"Spinach, marinara sauce, cheese, you know?"

"No meat?"

"Well," Ivy said, "sort of."

As far as Rhodes was concerned, there was no such thing as "sort of" meat. He asked Ivy what she meant.

"Tofu," she said. "Lots of protein. Yum."

"Yum," Rhodes said, trying to sound more enthusiastic than he felt. He was glad he'd had the burger at the DQ for lunch, but he wasn't going to mention that to Ivy.

"You go on out and visit with Speedo," Ivy said. "I'll call you when it's ready."

"All right," Rhodes said. "Come on, Yancey."

Rhodes looked around, but he didn't see the little Pomeranian. Then he heard yipping. Yancey was already at the door.

The lasagna rolls weren't bad, Rhodes had to admit. The tofu had been crumbled, so it wasn't as if he had to eat a big bite of it all at once, and the vegetables had been tasty.

While he was helping Ivy clean up the kitchen, Rhodes told her what he'd been doing that day and where he'd gotten on the Foshee murder, which was pretty much nowhere.

"You left out the part about the bull," Ivy said. "I saw it on the Internet. You could've been a rodeo star if you hadn't gone into law enforcement."

"You can't believe everything you read on the Internet," Rhodes told her.

"There was video," Ivy said, "so I didn't just read it. I saw you in action. I thought it was very touching when the family thanked you. I'm sure everyone in town thinks you're a real hero."

"I expect everybody knows better," Rhodes said, putting aluminum foil over the casserole dish that held what was left of the lasagna rolls. "I was just lucky."

"That wasn't lucky," Ivy said. "That was skill, or maybe it was ability. Whatever. Lucky is different. Lucky is when you get through the night without a call from Hack. Maybe this will be one of those nights."

Rhodes put the casserole dish in the refrigerator. Sam, who was sleeping nearby, opened an eye and looked at him, then closed the eye. Jerry, beside Sam, didn't bother to open an eye.

"It would be nice if this was one of those nights when Hack doesn't call," Rhodes said.

But of course it didn't turn out that way.

The phone rang while Rhodes was brushing his teeth. He'd already had a shower, and he was just about ready for bed, so he had no doubt the call was from Hack with some emergency. He was right.

"Ivy's a good bit nicer than you are," Hack said after Rhodes rinsed his mouth and took the phone from Ivy. "She didn't get aggravated with me one bit for callin', but I can tell you are."

"All I've said was 'hello,' " Rhodes said.

"Yeah, but it was the tone you used. You're aggravated, all right. I can always tell by your tone."

"I'm not aggravated yet, but I'm going to be if you don't tell me why you called."

"Well, for one thing the hospital called, and Earl Foshee's doing just fine. You can go in and talk to him tomorrow."

"Good," Rhodes said, "but that's not the real reason you called."

"Nope. The reason's different."

"Then you'd better tell me what it is."

"Got a problem at the Moore place."

"Not more shooting, I hope."

"No shooting, but there's people parked out in front, walkin' around. Somebody called it in, said they looked suspicious. Might try to break in."

Breaking in would be easy enough, though Rhodes couldn't think of why anyone would want to do it. "Can't Ruth handle it?"

"She's down in Thurston. Somebody's stole all the copper out of the Babtist church's air conditioner."

Evelyn Allen would be glad to hear that at least one member of the department was investigating a copper theft, if not to hear about the theft itself.

"You could get Duke," Rhodes said.

"Could, maybe, but this is your case. You're the one's been workin' it."

Rhodes couldn't argue with that. "I'll get dressed."

"Good idea," Hack said. "Wouldn't do for you go to out there in your jammies."

When Rhodes arrived at the Moore house, he saw a white van parked at the curb. Two men stood at the gate looking at something one of them was holding. The headlights of the county car gave Rhodes enough of a look at the two men for him to recognize one of them. It was Seepy Benton, and Rhodes figured that the other one was Harry Harris, Benton's assistant ghost-buster.

Rhodes drove past the van. A sign on the side said CLEARVIEW PARANORMAL INVESTIGATIONS. The *C, P,* and *I* were red, with the other letters in black. Two sheeted ghosts floated at either end of the name. They weren't particularly scary ghosts.

Rhodes parked in front of the van and walked to where Benton and Harris were looking at their equipment. Both men had flashlights, but they weren't turned on.

"Hey, Sheriff," Seepy said. "You probably wonder why we called you here tonight."

"You didn't call me," Rhodes said. "Hack did."

"That was a joke," Seepy said. He was wearing a bright red polo shirt with an odd design on the left side, some sort of logo, Rhodes supposed.

"I see you've noticed the emblem on my shirt," Seepy said. "I designed it myself. It's a Kabbalistic Tree of Life drawn on a Star of David inscribed in a hexagonal cross-section of the Cube of Space. I'm one of the Illuminati."

"Suspicions confirmed," Rhodes said. "Is there a Blacklin County chapter?"

"I'm working on it," Seepy said. "I had a feeling you might show up here tonight. The law never sleeps here in Blacklin County. Harry and I aren't breaking any laws, though, and we haven't crossed your police line. We're just standing here on the side-walk, which is the right of any private citizen."

"Sure it is," Rhodes said. "Occupy Blacklin County. Good evening, Dr. Harris."

The only times Rhodes had dealt with Harry Harris had been at the college, where Harris chaired the English Department. He looked like an English professor should, always wearing a suit and tie. Even his graying goatee seemed right for his profession.

However, he was dressed differently for his night's ghostbusting expedition. He wore jeans and a shirt that Mikey Burns would admire, an orange number covered with white palm trees. He still had the goatee, though.

"Good evening, Sheriff," Harris said. "I hope you don't mind our doing a little investigating here. This house is the perfect place for us to check out our equipment, and it has the reputation of being haunted."

"Reputations don't count for much," Rhodes said. "I doubt that you'll find anything."

"The sheriff's a skeptic," Benton said.

"Ah," Harris said. "Do you know Wordsworth, Sheriff?"

"We were introduced when I was in school, but it was just a brief acquaintance. Had something to do with daffodils. I haven't had much to do with him since."

"There's a poem of his you might like. Not many people read it today. It's not about daffodils. It's called 'The Affliction of Margaret,' and in it a grieving mother says, 'I look for ghosts; but none will force their way to me: 'tis falsely said that there was ever intercourse between the living and the dead.' Intercourse in this instance means —"

"I know what it means," Rhodes said. "I passed that English class, and for what it's worth, I agree with that grieving mother. Ghosts don't do any talking to the living, and that's because there aren't any ghosts."

As soon as he said it, Rhodes felt the prickling on the back of his neck, as if someone were watching him. He shook off the feeling.

"A skeptic, like I said," Seepy told Harris, "but then he hasn't seen this."

"Seen what?" Rhodes asked.

Seepy passed him the device he'd been holding. "It's our EMF meter, and we're getting a high reading. There could be a ghost in that house."

Rhodes grinned. "I should introduce you to Brad Turner. He lives not far from here, and he wears a tinfoil hat."

Seepy looked insulted. "I've never worn a tinfoil hat in my life."

Rhodes eyed Seepy's disreputable straw hat. "It might be an improvement, but you need to understand why Turner wears the tinfoil." Rhodes pointed toward the cell tower. "Look over there. See the flashing red light?"

"It's on the top of a cell tower," Harris said. "We know about it."

"We don't just know about it," Seepy said.

"We've compensated for it. We've stood at both ends of the block and walked toward this gate. The reading goes up no matter which direction we come from. Something in the house is moving the meter."

"The something doesn't have to be a ghost," Rhodes said, handing the EMF meter back.

Seepy took the meter and said, "I know an easy way to find out."

Rhodes put up a hand to stop Seepy from going on. "I know what you're going to say."

"So?" Seepy said. "How about it?"

Rhodes thought it over. What would be the harm in letting Seepy and Harris walk up to the house? They'd see that the reading didn't increase, and they'd go home. That meant he could go home, too, and that he wouldn't have to spend the rest of the night arguing with them.

"All right," Rhodes said. "I'll open the gate, and you can slip under the tape. Just don't go in the house. Let me get my flashlight first."

Benton and Harris high-fived as Rhodes walked to his car. He returned and opened the gate, which gave out a wild *skreeeeek* that seemed to unnerve Benton momentarily. It made the prickle return to the back of Rhodes's neck, too, and this time he couldn't shake it off.

"Ready?" Rhodes asked, trying to ignore the prickly feeling.

Benton and Harris nodded. Rhodes held up the tape for them and followed them into the yard, shining his flashlight along the cracked and overgrown walk.

"Look at this," Seepy said, handing the EMF meter to Harris.

"I've never seen it get that high," Harris said. "Something's in there."

"You need to see this, Sheriff," Seepy said, holding out the meter.

Rhodes looked at the lighted digital read-out. It was well into the teens now. It had been under ten outside the gate.

"We really should go inside," Seepy said.

"There aren't any ghosts inside," Rhodes said. "Mice, yes, and rats. But no ghosts."

"You aren't afraid of rats and mice, are you?" Seepy asked.

"What about ghosts?"

"I ain't afraid of no ghosts."

"Very good," Harris said. "*Ghostbusters* is excellent entertainment, but very unrealistic. We're not expecting to find Gozer the Traveler in the house, just a lonely ghost, purely insubstantial. Nothing to be afraid of at all."

"If there's nothing there, we'll leave,"

Seepy said. "I've been certified by the Citizens' Sheriff's Academy. I know how to deal with a crime scene, and you can keep an eye on Harry to be sure he doesn't mess up."

If it hadn't been for the funny feeling on his neck, Rhodes would've turned him down, but it seemed as if there might be something in the house after all. Not a ghost, and not just a rat, but something.

"Just don't touch anything," Rhodes said. "I'll go first."

He went up on the porch and opened the door, which for some reason opened easily this time. The rainy dampness on the previous night must have made it stick.

As soon as Rhodes crossed the threshold, he felt a chill. Seepy and Harris felt it, too, and it excited them even more than the EMF reading.

"No doubt about it," Seepy said. "This place is haunted. CP Investigations has found its first ghosts!"

"You haven't found anything yet," Rhodes said.

"We will, though," Seepy said, and the door slammed shut behind them, just as it would have in a scene in a bad horror movie.

Rhodes controlled his vertical leap, but Seepy and Harris didn't. Rhodes wasn't impressed. He could take them in a contest any day. They hardly cleared the floor.

"We're trapped," Seepy said.

"No, we're not," Rhodes said. "There's a back door. Besides, we can open this one."

He went over to prove his point and tugged on the knob, but he couldn't budge the door. It was tightly stuck.

"Trapped," Seepy said again. "It's like *House on Haunted Hill.*"

Rhodes was beginning to wonder if Seepy was cut out for the ghost-hunting business. "We're not trapped. Remember what I said about the back door?"

As he spoke, something scuttled past them on the floor. Rhodes turned the flashlight downward and saw a rat the size of a kitten. It surely couldn't be the same one he had seen that morning. All rats looked alike, so this had to be another one.

The rat ran up the stairs toward the second floor, and Harris said, "Follow that rat."

"Why?" Rhodes asked.

"Because animals are more sensitive to the paranormal than we are. The rat might be trying to tell us something."

Rhodes didn't think so. He didn't have a high opinion of a rat's ability to communicate with humans. He didn't see the harm in following the rat, though. He already knew there was nothing on the second floor.

"Go ahead," he said.

"You first," Seepy said. "You're the sheriff."

Rhodes laughed and went up the stairs, lighting the way with his flashlight. Seepy and Harris had turned on their own lights, but they stayed close to him. At the top of the stairs Rhodes looked around for the rat, but he didn't see it.

Benton and Harris were interested in the bedrooms, but they found nothing that Rhodes hadn't seen the night before. They did get a higher reading on their meter, but it was about the same in every room.

"No ghosts," Rhodes said after they'd investigated all the bedrooms. "Not even any rats. Time for us to leave."

Seepy and Harris were reluctant, but they didn't have any good arguments in favor of staying. All three of them went back out into the hallway and were about to go back down the stairs when they heard an agitated squeaking noise.

Rhodes shined his light on the stairs to the attic. The rat sat hunched on the top step. Its body shook with the effort it took to squeak so loudly, and its eyes seemed demonically red in the flashlight's beam.

"Rats don't usually vocalize," Seepy said. He sounded as if he knew what he was talking about, but then he always did. "It's trying to tell us something. Where do those steps lead?"

"The attic," Rhodes said. "Or I think they do."

"You didn't check it out?"

"Look at the dust on those stairs. Nobody's used them in years."

"Ghosts don't disturb the dust," Harris said.

"We need to see what's up there," Seepy said. "If we can get past the rat."

"The rat's as scared of you as you are of him," Rhodes said.

"I'm not scared. I just don't want to force an encounter that won't end well for the rat. You go first."

Once again Rhodes couldn't think of a good reason not to do what Seepy wanted. In fact, he wished now that he'd taken a look into the attic when he was in the house before. He turned his light on the stairs. Now that he looked at them closely, he could see that the dust had been disturbed by little rat tracks, but that was all. He started up the stairs.

Dust puffed out from beneath his feet with

each step. The old boards creaked. The noise didn't appear to bother the rat, which waited for Rhodes at the top of the stairs, but when Rhodes was a couple of steps away from the top, the rat flattened its ears and ran past him. Harris maintained his composure, but Seepy nearly fell back down the stairs as he jumped out of the rat's path. Harris reached out a hand and grabbed Seepy's arm to steady him.

"You all right?" Rhodes asked.

"I'm fine," Seepy said. "I must have put my foot wrong and slipped."

Rhodes grinned. "Right. It could happen to anybody. You sure you want to go into the attic?"

"I'm sure."

Rhodes thought the door might be locked. If it was, they'd just have to leave it that way. He didn't intend to break it down.

It wasn't locked, however. The knob didn't turn easily, but it turned, and the door swung open with a *skreeeek* to rival the gate.

Rhodes stepped into the attic. The ceiling was high enough for him to stand, and he shined the light around. Seepy and Harris waited outside. Maybe they wanted to be sure there wasn't an army of rats in there, sharpening their teeth on some handy stones.

Rhodes didn't see any stones, however, and he didn't see any rats. What he saw was cobwebs, lots of them, thick and dusty. Eight or ten old cardboard boxes sat well away from the attic windows, which were all intact. Dust lay thick on the boxes. Just past them near the rear of the attic was a rectangular wooden structure, a closet for storing things not to be left out in the open room.

"See?" Rhodes said. "No ghosts. Just dust."

The ghost hunters looked disappointed until a sudden chill settled over the attic. Rhodes thought the temperature must have dropped at least five degrees, instantly.

"They're here!" Benton said.

"Where?" Harris said.

"I don't see them, but they're here. Look at this meter."

Rhodes couldn't see the meter, but from the excitement in Seepy's voice, he judged that the reading had risen as fast as the attic had cooled.

"The boxes," Harris said, and he and Seepy hustled over to look at them, dust pluming around their feet.

Rhodes went along, too. The boxes didn't crumble when Benton and Harris touched them, but they were so dry and stiff that it was a near thing. Benton and Harris looked into all of them. Inside were what appeared to be old schoolbooks and papers. No ghosts.

Seepy and Harris were clearly disappointed. While they pawed through the dusty books and papers, looking for some trace of the paranormal, Rhodes looked at the closet. He'd check it out, but he didn't expect to find anything other than more old papers and books.

He went past the boxes and took hold of the knob on the closet door. It was covered with dust. The rusty mechanism squeaked when Rhodes turned the knob. He pulled the door open, and two rats even bigger than the one on the stairs jumped out and ran across the dusty floor and through the doorway.

Rhodes shined his light into the closet and saw just one thing: a human skeleton.

CHAPTER 14

There was more than just a skeleton, but not much more. Some bits of what appeared to be dried flesh clung to it, but the rats had done away with most of it over the years. Or something had. Natural decomposition, maybe. Rhodes shined the light around the closet, but he saw nothing else other than dust and rat droppings. Small pieces of what might have once been clothing lay on the floor. And there was something else.

Rhodes turned around to see Harris and Seepy standing there.

"The EMF meter's going crazy," Seepy said. "What's in the closet?"

"Take a look," Rhodes said. "Don't touch anything."

Seepy stepped past him and directed his own beam into the closet. "Good grief! That looks like a skeleton."

"It *is* a skeleton," Rhodes said.

Seepy backed away, but he had out his phone and was taking pictures.

"Look at this," Harris said to them.

He handed the EMF meter to Rhodes. The reading had dropped well below ten.

"Have you noticed that it's warmer in here now?" Harris asked.

Rhodes nodded. The house did seem warmer, but they were on an upper floor that still held more of the heat of the day than the lower levels. The prickly feeling at the back of his neck was gone, too, but he didn't try to explain that to himself. He didn't try to explain the rat, either. It was just a rat, after all.

Seepy joined them and looked at the meter. "The ghost is gone now, that's all." He sounded relieved. "It served its purpose. It was calling to us so we'd find this skeleton." He paused. "A skeleton in a closet. Our first success is a cliché, but I'll take it. How would a skeleton get here?"

"Good question," Rhodes said.

"Are you certain it's even real?"

"It looks real enough. I'll find out for sure."

It was always possible that the skeleton wasn't real, or that if it was, it had been put into the closet years ago as some kind of bizarre practical joke. Who would the joke be on, though? How long had the skeleton lain there undiscovered?

"What will you do when you find out if it's real?" Harris asked.

"I'll think of something," Rhodes said, hoping that he would.

"You need to find out whose skeleton it is," Seepy said. "Or was. Whatever."

"I don't know if we can do that."

"Maybe Harry and I can. We haven't really thought about communicating with the spirits of the dead, but we could try."

"The spirit is gone," Harris said. "It led us here, and then it was free. Wordsworth was wrong. This ghost forced its way to us. It wanted us to find the skeleton. We've done what it wanted, and it's gone."

"We may have found the skeleton," Rhodes said, "but there's a lot more to do."

"Who you gonna call?" Seepy asked.

"Not the Ghostbusters," Rhodes said, "and not CPI. This is going to be a criminal investigation, not a paranormal investigation."

"If it hadn't been for the paranormal investigation," Seepy said, "you wouldn't even have found the skeleton. You didn't even look in the attic. Not that I'm going to point that out to anybody."

Rhodes hated to admit it, but Seepy had a

point. However, he also thought that he'd eventually have investigated the attic on his own. He just hadn't gotten around to it yet, not that there was any use in telling that to Seepy. He'd never believe it.

"You've been a big help," Rhodes said, "but now you need to drop out of the picture. There aren't any more ghosts for you to find. Your own EMF meter tells you that."

"He's right," Harris said. "It's not showing anything unusual at all."

Rhodes didn't believe that ghosts were the cause of the EMF meter reading, but he was glad that Benton and Harris seemed to if it made it easier to convince them to leave.

"You two go on home," he said. "If I need any paranormal help, you'll be the first ones I'll call."

"How about an endorsement," Seepy said. "Something for our ads. We're going to have them starting tomorrow on Jennifer Loam's Web site. We could put, 'Sheriff Dan Rhodes says he'll take care of the normal investigations and leave the paranormal to us.' That's what you said, isn't it?"

"More or less, but I'm not giving you permission to use my name. As a county official, I can't give out endorsements."

"We could just say 'Certain county officials who must remain nameless.' "

"Don't," Rhodes said. "Just go home."

"Okay, but how about this: I'll leak the story to Jennifer Loam. 'Intrepid paranormal investigators aid sheriff in finding skeleton in closet.' We could reenact it right now. I could do a video on my phone while Harry lights it with his flashlight. Very spooky and thrilling. You need to act surprised when you see the skeleton, but I know you can do it."

"Maybe I can, but I won't."

"The story's going to get out. You might as well make the most of it."

"You mean *you* might as well make the most of it."

"Well, it would help get our business off to a great start. We'll be getting calls from all over the county. The state, too. The nation."

"Tomorrow, the world," Rhodes said.

Seepy smiled. "Why not?"

"Does the phrase 'delusions of grandeur' ring a bell?"

"We'll see," Seepy said. "We'll see."

"I hope you can sleep tonight," Rhodes said. "Your head might be too big for your pillow. Now go on home."

Seepy and Harris lingered for a few seconds, but they didn't argue anymore. Before they left, however, Seepy had one more thing to say. "That's the skeleton of a woman, by the way. You can tell by the pelvic structure."

Rhodes didn't argue, and Benton and Harris went back downstairs, leaving Rhodes alone with the skeleton. He shined his light on it and wondered how long it had been there and who it had once inhabited. He was going to need more help than the county could provide to get the answers he was looking for. Dr. White was fine for autopsies, but he wasn't a forensic scientist. The skeleton would have to go to the state lab for testing.

Rhodes considered calling Hack and having him send the EMTs to get the skeleton, but he thought better of it. He got out his phone. He'd make the call himself. Hack would ask too many questions.

After making the call, Rhodes examined the skeleton more closely. He could see that the skeleton was really just a collection of bones, not anything that was likely to get up and dance around like one of the skeletons in *Jason and the Argonauts.* While it looked intact lying on the floor of the closet, there was nothing to hold the bones together. The ligaments had decomposed or been eaten by rats. Rhodes couldn't tell by the light of the flashlight, but the state lab would be able to tell whether the bones had been gnawed.

Rhodes didn't need the lab to tell him the cause of death. Taking a closer look, he saw that the skull was indented and cracked as if it had been struck with something. Maybe the state lab could come up with an answer on what the something had been, or maybe it would just be called a blunt instrument if the lab folks liked to stick with the classics.

Rhodes took photos of the skeleton, and when he was finished, he got an evidence bag from his car for the scraps of cloth. Once they were bagged, he looked around the attic again. He didn't find anything of interest. The boxes weren't going to be of any help, but they'd all have to be examined more closely anyway. Rhodes would have someone pick them up the next day.

When the EMTs arrived, Rhodes went down to explain the situation to them. They weren't used to dealing with skeletons, but he wanted them to take the bones to Ballinger's Funeral Home, to be prepared for transportation to the state lab. They'd be better at handling the bones than Rhodes would.

The bones were loaded into the ambulance, and Rhodes followed it to the funeral home, which had once been a mansion owned by one of Clearview's prominent families. The family was now pretty much forgotten, and only the older people in town or the younger ones interested in the community's history knew that the old mansion had once been home to a family at all. For more than sixty years now it had been a funeral home, and most people thought it always had been. Rhodes wondered if there was some kind of moral there, but he couldn't think of one.

Clyde Ballinger lived in a small brick building in back that had been the servants' quarters when the mansion was built. Clyde was a bachelor, and the little two-story building had all the room he needed.

Rhodes knew Ballinger would have been alerted by the EMTs about the arrival of the bones. Sure enough, he greeted the ambulance and directed their proper storage. Then he joined Rhodes, who was waiting for him in the apartment.

"Read any good books lately?" Rhodes asked, nodding at the stack of paperbacks on the desk.

"A few," Ballinger said. "I quit reading on the tablet. It just wasn't the same. I missed holding the books. I even missed the smell of them."

Ballinger's taste ran to older books, preferably crime novels with lurid covers and titles like *You'll Die Next!* The books had become harder and harder to find, but Ballinger had discovered that many of them were being republished in electronic form, so he'd been reading on a tablet computer.

"Here's the thing," Ballinger said. "It's not as much fun buying the books online as it was finding them at garage sales, but at least they're real books. You know?"

Rhodes didn't know, not being addicted to books himself, but he agreed with Ballinger that you couldn't beat the real thing.

"You take skeletons," Ballinger said, reaching into his pile of books. "Back in the old days, they liked to put skeletons on the covers of books. Like this one."

He handed Rhodes a copy of a book called *The Skeleton in the Clock* by someone named Carter Dickson. On the cover a young woman wearing a green blouse and a skirt with what looked to Rhodes like a sixteen-inch waist was staring at a grandfather clock that contained a skeleton. The skeleton was intact and standing inside the clock. It looked nothing like the skeleton Rhodes had found in the closet at the Moore house, and Rhodes's waist looked nothing like the woman's.

Rhodes passed the book back to Ballinger. "Maybe I should read it. It might help me solve my own skeleton problem."

"I doubt it," Ballinger said, putting the book back in the stack. "It's a complicated story. Not my usual kind of thing. It's like your problem in a way, though, since it has to do with a bet about spending a night in an old prison where a lot of executions took place. Not exactly a haunted house, but close enough, I guess."

"The skeleton I found was in a closet," Rhodes said, "not a clock."

"Still close enough. Any idea whose skeleton you found?"

"Not a one. I hope the state lab can help me out. I'll call them tomorrow, and we'll work out transportation. What about Neil Foshee? Did Dr. White come in and do the autopsy?"

"Came in this afternoon," Ballinger said. He opened a desk drawer and took out some papers. "Here's the report."

Rhodes glanced through the report but didn't see anything unexpected. Cause of death was a bullet to the heart. Dr. White had extracted the slug, a .38, which he'd bagged. The bag was attached to the report.

"Any idea who killed him?" Ballinger asked.

"Not yet," Rhodes said. "I'm working on it."

"Does it have anything to do with that skeleton?"

"I don't see how," Rhodes said.

Rhodes stopped by the jail after leaving the funeral home. He wanted to write up the report on the skeleton. He wasn't surprised when he found Jennifer Loam waiting for him. He put the bag of scraps in the evidence room and then greeted Jennifer.

"Seepy Benton called you, I guess," Rhodes said.

"He did," Jennifer said, "but he told me I'd have to talk to you before the story could be released. I knew you'd come in to write a report, so I stopped in to wait." She glanced at Hack. "I filled Mr. Jensen in on things. He claims that nobody around here ever tells him anything."

"Dang right, they don't," Hack said. "I might've found out next week or next month or whenever you put it on the Internet, but that's the only way."

Rhodes didn't bother to contradict him.

"I want to be sure I have the details right before I run anything," Jennifer said. "It's too bad there's no video."

Rhodes didn't think it was too bad at all,

but he didn't mention that. He said, "Tell me what you know. I'll correct you if you're wrong."

Jennifer went through the story, reading from notes on a tablet computer. Seepy had been thorough, and of course he'd thrown in a lot of details about how he and Harris had been investigating the paranormal aspects of the Moore house and how their EMF meter had revealed the presence of a restless spirit inside, a restless spirit that had led them to the skeleton in the closet. He'd made it sound as if Rhodes had asked for the assistance of the intrepid investigators of CPI, and Rhodes let that stand. It made it appear that he knew what he was doing instead of having neglected to search the closet in the first place.

"That sounds about right," he said when Jennifer had finished. "There's a lot of emphasis on a ghost, though. I didn't see any ghost. Nobody else did, either. All I saw was some rats. If Seepy wants to believe that a ghost led us to the skeleton, that's all right, but don't say that I believed it."

"You ought to," Hack said. "What about all that gettin' cold and then warm? What about that meter thing? Sounds like a ghost to me."

Rhodes didn't say anything about the

prickly feeling on the back of his neck or about the slamming door. He didn't want to encourage Hack, not that he needed any encouragement.

"It wasn't a ghost," Rhodes said, but by this point he was beginning to wonder. "When Andy comes in tomorrow, have him go over to the house and look through those boxes in the attic. Did Mika come by this afternoon?"

"Yeah, she was here. Did some work on the bags, lookin' for prints. She wrote up a report for you. It don't say much. All the prints were smeared because of all the grease on the bags and the fingers of whoever touched 'em. She got one or two that might do to look for a match with."

"We'll have her check them against the prints of the Foshee boys first," Rhodes said. "They're probably the ones who were eating that stuff. Did Wade Clement bring by his sidearm?"

"Sure did. It's a Glock automatic. Nine millimeter."

Since Foshee had been killed with a .38, that would seem to let Wade off the hook, but Rhodes wasn't going to rule him out.

"We'll hang on to it for a while," Rhodes said. "Tell Mika to check the registration along with those others I asked for. Tell her that I want her to examine the cloth in the evidence bag I brought in, too. Maybe she can tell what it is or give a guess as to how old it is. After that she can go through the records for the past forty years and look for missing persons reports."

"We don't have a lot of folks goin' missin'," Hack said. "I could probably tell you most of 'em myself."

He probably could, Rhodes thought. "What about any around the time when Ralph Moore died?"

Hack thought it over. "Nothin' comes to me. It'd be a big deal if somebody disappeared. In the papers and all over town. I'll think about it tonight and see if I can come up with anything."

"Ask Lawton, too."

"Lawton? Why'd I ask him? He can't even remember his own phone number, much less his birthday. I'm surprised he can find his way here. He —"

"Ask him anyway," Rhodes said.

Hack didn't respond, unhappy at being cut off in midrant, but Rhodes knew he'd talk to Lawton about it.

"Do you have any suspects in Neil Foshee's murder, Sheriff?" Jennifer asked.

"None that I can talk about," Rhodes said.

"That's how he is," Hack said. "Won't tell

you anything. Close-mouthed, just like I was tellin' you."

"Just doing my job," Rhodes said. "Now if you'll excuse me, I'm going to write up my report on the skeleton and then go home and try to get some sleep."

"Good luck with that," Hack said.

Rhodes's sleep for the rest of the night wasn't interrupted by any calls from the jail, but Rhodes was restless because he couldn't stop thinking about Foshee's death and how it might have come about.

Ace Gable just might be temperamental enough to try to do something about Foshee after he'd come into the store and pestered Vicki. He did have a record for assault on someone who'd bothered his date. The incident was long ago, but it was still an indicator of a temper.

Vicki herself didn't seem to be a killer, but Rhodes knew better than to rule anybody out of an investigation. He'd learned that most people were capable of just about anything, given the right circumstances. Vicki might well have wanted to get Foshee out of her life forever. He was a bad memory she didn't need to have hanging around.

Wade Clement couldn't be ruled out, either. He might have lied about the meeting with Foshee. Instead of hearing gunshots, Wade might have been the one who fired them. He'd said he didn't go inside the house, but that wasn't necessarily true. Bringing in the Glock didn't mean anything. It might be registered to him, but he could've used another gun.

Of all the people he'd talked to, Roger Allen seemed the least likely to have killed Neil. He was still upset about his cousin, but Neil hadn't been involved directly in that death. Roger just wanted to sell the county a Tahoe or two, and Rhodes hoped Mikey Burns would let the deal go through.

After an hour or so of tossing, turning, and wondering, Rhodes finally went to sleep. It was a restless sleep, because for the rest of the night he dreamed about skeletons.

The next morning Rhodes filled Ivy in on the night's events. She'd been asleep when Rhodes came in, and even Yancey's yips hadn't waked her.

"The skeleton story was better than anything you've told me for quite awhile," she said. "I like ghost stories, and this is a real one."

"Except that there was no ghost," Rhodes said.

"I think it was a ghost," she told him. They were sitting at the kitchen table with a breakfast of reduced-calorie orange juice, turkey bacon, and Egg Beaters. "It was trying to find a resting place for those bones, and now after all these years they're going to have a proper place."

"I wouldn't call the state crime lab a proper place," Rhodes said.

He crunched a piece of turkey bacon between his teeth. It was okay. Not good, but okay. Yancy yipped softly under the table, and Rhodes slipped him a bit of the bacon. The cats slept by the refrigerator, as still and quiet as if they were just stuffed toys. They didn't care for turkey bacon.

"The lab will return the bones to you, and you can see to it that they're buried properly," Ivy said. "You'll put a name with them, too."

"You sound pretty sure of yourself."

"I am. I know you. You don't quit until you find what you're looking for."

Rhodes washed some bacon down with orange juice. "Sometimes it takes a while."

"The ghost has waited a long time," Ivy said. "It can wait a little longer."

"I didn't see any ghost," Rhodes said, "so there wasn't a ghost."

" 'There are more things in heaven and

earth, Horatio . . .' "

"Everybody's quoting literature to me," Rhodes said. He'd already mentioned Harris's quotation from Wordsworth to Ivy.

"Sometimes literature is where the answers are."

"I liked Harry's quote better."

"I think mine's closer to the truth."

"If I'm remembering the play correctly," Rhodes said, "Hamlet would've been better off if he hadn't paid any attention to that so-called ghost."

Ivy smiled. "Things didn't work out very well, I have to admit."

Rhodes didn't want to push the argument any further. He just returned Ivy's smile and finished his breakfast.

The Blacklin County hospital had grown considerably in the last few years with the addition of two new buildings. Rhodes wasn't sure about the reason for the growth, but he had some theories. One was that the population of the county was aging and needed more medical care. Young people didn't stay around the rural counties in Texas anymore after they graduated from high school. They went to college, or if they didn't go to college, they went to the cities, which was where the jobs were.

Long ago, there had been jobs in Blacklin County, too, but many of those jobs no longer existed. Even longer ago than that, there had been cotton farms all over the county, and every little town had a cotton gin. A lot of families had made their living by farming. Not anymore. Farming was too uncertain, and it no longer paid. Rhodes hadn't seen a cotton crop since he was a boy. The gins were gone, with nothing left of them but a few stray bricks.

So the youngsters left, the population got older, and more medical care was a necessity. Clyde Ballinger's funeral home wasn't likely to be lacking in business for years, either. Rhodes didn't even want to think what might happen to the county in fifty years. There might not be anybody left.

This early in the day the hospital parking lot had plenty of empty spaces. Rhodes parked and went inside, stopping at the reception desk to ask where to find Earl Foshee. He got the room number and went down a hallway to the room. He hadn't posted a guard on the room because he didn't have enough deputies to put one there and because he didn't think he needed one. Earl wasn't going to slip away, and if he did, Rhodes would just bring him back, not that they'd had much luck in locating

Louie so far.

The hospital smelled like every other hospital Rhodes had been in. He didn't know what it was, but it always reminded him of sickness and death, or injuries, like the one Earl had suffered, or worse. Rhodes had spent enough time in hospital beds not to want to do any more time in one.

Rhodes went into Earl's room and found Earl sitting up in bed and eating breakfast. He had bacon, eggs, and orange juice, all of which reminded Rhodes of his own breakfast, except that he supposed the bacon was pork, the eggs were real, and the orange juice was full of sugar. Earl didn't look any the less healthy for it.

Earl was just about finished eating when Rhodes came in, and Rhodes told him go to ahead.

Earl nodded and kept on eating. Rhodes pushed a blood pressure monitor out of the way and sat in the visitor's chair. He wondered why chairs in hospitals were so uncomfortable. He didn't think they were cheap. Maybe hospitals didn't want visitors to linger.

After a few minutes Earl wiped his mouth with his napkin, tossed it onto his plate, and leaned back against the elevated mattress. Rhodes got up and pulled the folding table away from the bed.

"Good breakfast?" he asked.

"Pretty decent for a hospital," Earl said.

"How's the head?"

Earl touched his head, which had a bandage stuck where the hog had kicked him. His hair was shaved all around the bandage. It made his mullet look even worse, which Rhodes wouldn't have thought was possible.

"Hurts a little," Earl said. "They told me I got a bad concussion. Need to stay here a day or so. Might hurt myself if I move around too much. The doctor said it was maybe a grade three concussion, whatever that means. I can't remember how I got it, and he says that's not a good sign."

"Hogs ran over you," Rhodes said, sitting back down.

"Yeah, that's what the doctor said. I got bruises all over me, so I can sure believe it. I don't remember any of it, though, not after I got out of the pickup and went in the woods. The doctor says that happens sometimes."

"What *do* you remember?"

"I remember you chasing me. You were after me and Louie, but we got away."

Rhodes looked around the room with its institutional green walls. The window looked out on the parking lot and street.

"I wouldn't call this getting away," he said. "When you're discharged, you'll have to go to jail."

"I didn't mean to run. Louie made me."

"Why would he do that?"

Earl looked out the window as if there might be something interesting outside, but there wasn't.

"Earl?" Rhodes said.

"I saw a squirrel out in the parking lot this morning," Earl said, still looking out the window. "Lots of squirrels around these days. Didn't use to be squirrels in town, but they're all over the place now."

"We weren't talking about squirrels. Why did Louie make you run?"

"I don't want to talk about it."

"You might as well. Sooner or later you're going to have to."

Earl turned his eyes back to Rhodes. "I don't know anything for sure anyway."

"That's okay. You don't have to be sure. Just tell me about Louie."

Earl looked back out the window and didn't say anything for a few seconds. Rhodes waited.

"The thing is," Earl said, "Louie was with Neil the other night. At that house."

"I knew somebody was," Rhodes said. "Neil had to get there some way or other, and there was no transportation around."

Earl stared at the ceiling. "A man ought not to speak against his brother."

"Family's important," Rhodes said. "I know that."

"That's what Louie says."

Rhodes didn't know where the conversation was going, but it seemed promising. He wanted to keep Earl talking.

"Neil was your family," Rhodes said, "but it's the law's job to find out who killed him. Not yours or Louie's. Louie should know that."

"Louie don't care about that. That was all just talk. Anyway, that's kinda what worries me."

"You don't have to worry. I'll find the one who killed Neil. You need to tell me where Louie might be so I can find him before he gets in real trouble."

"I think he's in real trouble already," Earl said.

"Running away was bad," Rhodes said, "but he's already in worse trouble than that."

"I don't mean cooking meth," Earl said.

"What do you mean, then?"

Earl sighed. "I mean I think Louie's the one that killed Neil."

CHAPTER 15

Rhodes sat quietly for a while and let Earl's comment sink in.

"You hear what I said, Sheriff?" Earl asked.

"I heard you," Rhodes said. "I was thinking it over. Why would Louie do a thing like that? Kill his cousin, I mean."

"He thought Neil was gonna sell us out."

An orderly came in to pick up Earl's breakfast tray at that point. He was another person who looked about fifteen years old to Rhodes. Maybe there was something in the water they drank. Or maybe it was vitamins.

"How was breakfast?" the orderly asked.

"It was pretty good," Earl said. "I like sausage better than bacon, though."

"I'll see what I can do for you tomorrow," the orderly said.

"I like the patties," Earl said, "not the links."

"I think they have those," the orderly said, and he carried the tray out of the room.

The last sausage Rhodes had eaten had been turkey sausage. Maybe being in the hospital wasn't as bad as he remembered it.

The door closed and Rhodes said, "Who was Neil supposed to be selling you out to?"

"There was this kid going around town asking questions. Neil was gonna talk to him."

"I know about him," Rhodes said. "Wade Clement. He's harmless."

"Yeah, Louie said that's what he wants people to think. Said he was working on some college paper. Louie thinks he was some undercover DEA agent."

Louie might just be paranoid enough to believe that, but it still didn't make any sense to Rhodes. The Foshees were out of jail only because they'd posted bond. Rhodes thought it was a cinch that they'd be convicted on any number of fairly serious charges when they went to trial. Or maybe they'd take a plea bargain. They'd get jail time whichever way things went, so the Foshees were already in so much trouble that Neil couldn't sell them out. He didn't have anything to sell.

Rhodes explained that to Earl, but Earl said, "What it was, was Louie thought Neil would try to make some kind of deal with the DEA. Testify against me and him for a lighter sentence or maybe immunity. My guess is they got into an argument about it, and Louie shot Neil."

"Had Louie talked to Neil about it?"

"Sure, but Neil just laughed at him. Said there wasn't any DEA agent around here, that this was just some college kid he was going to talk to. Louie got mad about it. One reason Louie was suspicious was that the one who set it up was Colby Lane. Louie knows that Colby's one of your snitches."

Rhodes looked at Earl in disbelief. Colby Lane was a shade-tree mechanic who'd been employed by the Chevy dealership until he became too unreliable because of his drinking. He'd been in jail a few times, usually for alcohol-related offenses, but other than that Rhodes hardly knew him.

"What gave Louie that idea?" he asked.

"Louie says anybody's been in jail and out as much as Lane must have something going on with the sheriff, so it figures he's your snitch."

"Who would he snitch on?" Rhodes asked.

Earl looked blank. He didn't have an answer for that one.

Rhodes stood up. "Louie's wrong about

Lane, and he's wrong about Wade Clement. Lane has a drinking problem, and Wade Clement's just a college kid. Are you sure Louie killed Neil?"

"I didn't say I was sure, but I think that's what happened. Louie was pretty upset when he got back to the house last night. He wouldn't talk about what happened or anything except to tell me that Neil was dead. When your deputy drove up today, Louie told me not to say anything, just follow along with him, so that's what I done."

It was just crazy enough for Rhodes to believe it was the truth, and Louie had known Neil was dead. He'd been at the Moore house, no question about that. Now it was more urgent than ever to find Louie.

"Do I really have to go back to jail, Sheriff?" Earl asked. "I paid my bond."

"You paid it, and then you ran," Rhodes said, "so you really do have to go back to jail. We'll try to make you comfortable."

"I bet you will," Earl said.

"It might help if you'd tell me where Louie is. I can get you a cell with a window so you can watch the squirrels."

"You ain't funny, Sheriff."

People told Rhodes that all the time. He didn't let it bother him.

"If Louie killed Neil, you could be considered an accomplice. Tell me where he is, and I'll be sure that's on the record."

"I don't know where he is."

"You must have some idea. Just give me your best guess. You don't want Louie sneaking back into town and coming after you, do you? If he finds out you've been talking to me, he might decide he needs to handle you the way he handled Neil. After all, you really *did* sell him out."

Earl's mouth dropped open. He plainly hadn't thought about it that way.

"Somebody else might get hurt, too," Rhodes said. "Nurses, doctors, other patients. You don't want that on your record."

"He might be at the lake," Earl said after a few seconds.

"Which one?" Rhodes asked. There were three big lakes in the county, and all of them had cabins and houses around them.

"Merritt's Lake," Earl said.

That wasn't one of the three big ones. It was a small lake, what northeners would call a pond, on private land that had once belonged to the Merritt family. It had gone through a number of owners since then, but the old name had stuck. Rhodes had been fishing there a time or two back in the days when he still had time to fish. It had been a while, but he remembered that there was an old tumbledown house on the property not too far from the lake. It wouldn't do to live in, but someone could hide out there for a while. There were houses like it all over the county on properties that had once been farmland but were now used for grazing cattle or not used at all. The Foshees would know where all those houses were, having used more than one of them to cook up a little meth in.

"I'll take a look," Rhodes said.

Earl sat up straight in the bed. "I was supposed to meet him there. If you find him, don't tell him you talked to me."

"Don't worry about that," Rhodes said. "I won't say a word."

Mika Blackfield was already at the jail when Rhodes got there, and she'd apparently been there a while. She and Hack were talking about something when Rhodes walked in. Rhodes said good morning, and Hack told him that the sheriff from Bates County had called.

"What about?" Rhodes asked.

" 'Bout Neil Foshee. You wanted him to notify the next of kin, but there ain't none in his county. Last one died early this year. Speakin' of kin, here's somethin' else. Mika looked into the Moore house owners, and all Moore's kin are dead now. Won't be any more tax payments on that place. You might could buy it cheap if you wanted it."

"I don't want to buy a house," Rhodes said. "Especially that one."

"Don't blame you," Hack said. "It's got ghosts. I read it on the Internet, so it must be true. Ain't that right, Mika?"

Mika was short and slim with very black hair and eyes and a warm smile. Hack had begun trying to enlist her into his efforts to drive Rhodes crazy ever since her first day on the job. So far she hadn't gone along with him, at least not completely.

"We Japanese believe that all people have a spirit or soul," Mika said. "It's called the *reikon*. If someone dies violently or if proper rites aren't performed, or if the spirit is somehow driven by a strong emotion, like revenge, the *reikon* can become a *yurei*. That's a spirit that can come into our world."

This wasn't exactly what Rhodes had hoped to hear.

"The *yurei* stays here in our world," Mika continued, "until certain things have been taken care of, until the conflict that brought it here is resolved. So that might be what people call ghosts." She paused. "I've never seen one, however."

252

"I don't think you ever will," Rhodes said, "and things on the Internet aren't always true, either, even if Hack believes them."

"Jennifer Loam's site is usually very accurate," Mika said.

"It sure is," Hack said, "and she mentions ghosts. Seepy Benton says they were there, too."

Rhodes sighed. He was sighing way too much lately. "Mika, did you find any evidence of ghosts in the things we collected from the crime scene?"

"No. I didn't find much else, either. The fast-food bags are so greasy that the prints are all smeared. I got one or two good ones and a lot of partials, but that's all. I haven't checked for matches on AFIS yet."

"See if they match any of the Foshees. We have those prints on file. What about that material from the closet?"

"I looked at that this morning. It's cotton and it's old and rotted. That's about all I can tell you."

That wasn't a lot of help, but Rhodes hadn't expected much. "Hack, what about Wade Clement? He have a record?"

"Not 'less you count speedin' tickets. Ever' college boy has those."

"Any reports on the whereabouts of Louie Foshee?"

"Nope. Not a one."

Rhodes hadn't expected that there would be, but it never hurt to ask.

"What about the gun registrations?"

"I'll check those right now," Mika said.

"You can let me know when I get back. Hack, Call Buddy and have him meet me at Miss Nora Fischer's house in about three-quarters of an hour. I have a lead on Louie, and I'll want backup."

"You think he's hidin' at Miss Fischer's?"

"No, but he might be at Merritt's Lake. Who owns the land now?"

"Frankie Welch," Hack said. "Says he's gonna start leasin' it to deer hunters in the fall, or so I heard."

Welch was the owner of Clearview's only office supply store, which was in the little strip mall a couple of doors down from Ace Gable's parts store.

"Call him up," Rhodes said. "Tell him I'm going out to his place to look for somebody who might be in the old house near the lake. I'm going to talk to Miss Fischer about something else before I go out there."

"You gonna tell me what it is you're gonna talk to her about?"

Rhodes looked at Mika. "He says I never tell him anything."

"He tells me that about you, too," Mika

said. "You shouldn't be mean to him."

She was more on Hack's side than Rhodes had thought, or maybe she was just joshing him. She knew how to keep a straight face, so it was hard to tell.

"You oughta listen to her," Hack said. "We employees like to be treated well, since we don't get paid much."

"I'm going to talk to her about Ralph Moore," Rhodes said. "Anytime you want to know something else, just ask me."

"I ask you all the time, but you don't tell me."

"Maybe I will next time."

"I ain't countin' on it," Hack said.

Nora Fischer had been Rhodes's history teacher in high school. She was around eighty years old now, and she'd lived in Clearview all her life. She knew nearly everyone in town, having taught them or their children or them *and* their children. And grandchildren. She'd remember Ralph Moore.

She was cautious about opening her door, but when she saw who was there, she opened it wide.

"You come right on in, Danny," she said. She'd called him that ever since high school, and he wasn't going to try to change her.

"What are you doing out and about so early in the morning?"

Nora was short, not even five and a half feet tall, and she wore her steely gray hair in a bun. She had on thick glasses, but she'd often assured Rhodes that her eyesight was just fine, thank you very much, when he'd inquired.

"I was hoping to ask you a few questions," Rhodes said. "About Ralph Moore."

"I've heard a little about the sad things going on at his old house," she said. "Come on back to the kitchen, where we can sit down."

Rhodes followed her through the living room and down a short hall to the small, neat kitchen. A newspaper was spread on the table, and a coffee cup and saucer were beside it.

"Would you like some coffee?" Nora asked.

"No, thanks," Rhodes said. "I don't drink it."

"My goodness. How do you get your caffeine?"

"I don't get a lot of it," Rhodes said.

Since he'd stopped drinking Dr Pepper, he got hardly any at all. The lack of it hadn't bothered him.

"I have to have my coffee in the morning," Nora said. "It gets me going."

She sat in the chair nearest the newspaper, and Rhodes sat down opposite her.

"I still like newspapers," Nora said, removing her glasses and laying them next to the saucer. "I know the Internet is where everybody reads the news now, but I'm old-fashioned."

Rhodes was glad to hear it. He didn't want to go into much detail about what had happened at the Moore house, and if Nora hadn't read about the ghost, his job would be easier.

"I just want the newspapers to last as long as I do," Nora said. "I'm planning on twenty more years at the very least."

"I hope you get there," Rhodes said. "I'm not so sure the newspapers will."

"That would be a real shame. You didn't come here to talk about that, though. You asked about Ralph Moore. What did you want to know about him? It's been a long time since I'd thought of him at all."

"I'm not sure what I want to know," Rhodes said. "Just tell me about him."

"He taught chemistry and physics. He was very smart."

"What I'd like to know about is more personal," Rhodes said, "not what he taught."

Nora thought for a while. "Do you remember any stories you heard about him? There used to be so many."

"I remember some of them," Rhodes said.

"A good many of them were true. Students didn't like his classes. They thought he was arbitrary and unfair. He didn't like animals any more than he liked his students, and he chased them off his property, used a pellet gun on them. At school he could be hard to get along with."

Nothing new in any of that.

"What about friends?" Rhodes asked. "Did he have any?"

"Oh, yes, several." Nora took a sip of her coffee and set the cup back in the saucer. "He could be ingratiating when he wanted to be, and he could even be charming if you were a woman."

Rhodes wasn't sure, but he thought Nora might have blushed.

"It's just that he didn't suffer fools gladly," Nora went on. "If you were an intelligent adult, he could get on well with you. If he had doubts about your intelligence, it was a different story."

Rhodes thought that Moore would be depressed if he knew that his house was now a haven for rats and mice.

"You mentioned women," Rhodes said.

"Did he have women friends?"

"I heard rumors, but nothing substantial. No one ever saw him out with a woman. Some women I knew wouldn't have minded going out with him, though."

"Anybody in particular?"

"Lindy Holmes. She taught home ec. Do they still have home ec, I wonder?"

"If they do, it wouldn't be the same kind of course it was back then. What happened to Lindy Holmes?"

Nora laughed. "Dave Hardesty was hired as an assistant coach, and she forgot all about Ralph. She and Dave got married and moved to Dallas. He had a coaching job in one of the big schools there."

So much for the idea that Lindy Holmes might have been the skeleton in the attic.

"Do you remember anyone in town having disappeared around the time Ralph died?" Rhodes asked.

Nora gave Rhodes a quizzical look. "Danny, what are you getting at here? I don't understand."

Rhodes figured he might as well tell her most of the story. It was already on the Internet, and it would be on TV by tonight if it wasn't already, and she'd see it in the paper tomorrow. The big cities couldn't resist a story with murder and a ghost.

After he'd laid out most of the details, Nora said, "I can't imagine Ralph killing anyone." She paused. "I know everyone says that after a mass murderer goes on a rampage, but Ralph was different. He had a sense of humor, and he had empathy. Not with students, necessarily, but with some of the faculty. I remember when Fran Sanderson's husband died. Ralph was so kind to her. He just wasn't the type to kill anyone."

Nora got up from the table and carried her cup and saucer to the sink. She set them in it, ran water in the cup, and returned to the table.

"So you don't think the skeleton in the attic could've been someone he murdered," Rhodes said when she was seated.

"I suppose it could've been, but it's awfully far-fetched. Killing someone? I can't see that. Putting the body in his own attic? I can't see that, either. Anyway, no one disappeared around that time, at least not that I heard of, and I'm sure I'd have heard about it."

"What about a few years before or after Ralph died?"

Nora shook her head. "If it happened, I don't remember it. Could it have been someone who came here, someone from out of town?"

Rhodes should've thought of that. Moore could've had a visitor and gotten into an argument with her, an argument that resulted in her death.

"Did Ralph ever mention a visitor? A friend? A relative?"

"Not that I recall," Nora said. "All his relatives lived out of state. One of them could've come to visit. He wouldn't necessarily have mentioned it. He was a very private person."

"I can believe it," Rhodes said. He stood up. "Thanks for talking to me. You've given me some things to think about. I appreciate the help."

Nora started to stand, but Rhodes said, "I'll see myself out. You finish reading the newspaper. If you think of anything that might help me out, give Hack a call at the jail."

"How is Hack doing these days?" Nora asked.

"Ornery as ever," Rhodes said.

Nora laughed. "I'm not at all surprised."

CHAPTER 16

Rhodes was about halfway down the side-walk in front of Nora Fischer's house when Buddy pulled his county car to the curb. Rhodes walked over to the car, and the window whirred down.

"Hack says you got a line on where Louie's hiding out," Buddy said.

"He could be at that old house at Merritt's Lake," Rhodes said. "That's what Earl told me, for what it's worth."

"Earl oughta know. Be a good place to hide out."

"Maybe. I'll head out there and you can follow me," Rhodes said.

"Check," Buddy said, and the window whirred up.

Merritt's Lake was down past the town of Thurston, to the north of the area of the county usually called the Big Woods. It would take a while to get there, and while he drove, Rhodes thought about the skeleton and the ghost. Although he hadn't admitted it to anybody, and didn't want to admit it even to himself, there was something very strange about all that had happened at the Moore house over the past couple of days.

No matter how hard he tried, Rhodes couldn't explain the behavior of the rat. It was easy enough to say that the feeling he'd had of being watched was just a natural reaction under the circumstances, but that rat had certainly seemed to be up to something. It was almost as if it were leading him to the closet where the skeleton was.

Or that was what it might look like if a person let it. The power of suggestion, that was all it was. Had to be. Rhodes had let himself get a little spooked by the whole haunted house thing, and his imagination had taken over. That was the answer.

The other things, the temperature drop, the slamming door, and the EMF meter readings, didn't have to point to anything unnatural, but they were strange when taken together with everything else. But ghosts? It just wasn't possible. Not that Seepy Benton would agree. He'd be touting his ghost-hunting abilities from now until forever.

The skeleton itself was another problem. Rhodes kept asking himself the same two questions. Where had it come from? How had it gotten into the attic?

Rhodes wondered about what Mika had told him. What was the word she used? *Yurei.* An unquiet spirit, roaming the earth until it had some kind of satisfaction, some rite performed or something settled. Revenge, maybe, or just having its earthly remains buried.

Rhodes shook his head. He didn't want to believe that.

As he was crossing over the river that flowed out of one of the county's larger lakes, something else occurred to him.

Ralph Moore had taught chemistry and physics, subjects that weren't too far removed from biology. Rhodes remembered that the biology teacher was Will Seegers. He'd still been teaching when Rhodes was in school, but somehow Rhodes had managed to avoid biology class. There had been a skeleton used in biology class at one time, though. Rhodes was sure of that even though he hadn't taken the class. He'd seen the skeleton when walking down the hallway past the biology classroom. Rhodes didn't know whether the skeleton was real or plastic, but what if it had been real? If Seegers and Moore had been friends, it wasn't impossible that the skeleton could've been stored in Moore's attic. It was worth checking into.

Seegers had retired and moved away. He now lived down on the coast somewhere, Galveston, maybe. Rhodes would find out and give him a call. It would be quite a relief if the skeleton turned out to be nothing more than a prop for biology lectures. The clothing scraps could have been from something else, and any plastic monofilament holding the skeleton together would have long since decayed. The caved-in skull could've been the result of an accident at school, and it might even explain why the skeleton had been moved out of the biology class. It all made sense, and Rhodes was hopeful that he'd come up with the solution.

He was feeling fairly cheerful as he passed through what was left of Thurston, which wasn't much. At one time, in the days when cotton was king, Thurston had been a thriving community with several cotton gins, grocery stores, a drugstore, a service station, a hardware store, and much more. Now only a few buildings were standing, and the population was dwindling. Rhodes drove by the building that had once housed a store owned by Hod Barrett. It was still a store, but the new owner had made it over into something more resembling a fast-food restaurant. He'd installed a grill in back, and his wife cooked hamburgers and chicken. He sold a few things, but mostly candy and ice cream along with a few staples. And beer. He'd added a cooler, and now residents of Thurston and anybody else who happened by could purchase a six-pack to go if they wanted one. It was the only business left in town.

Driving through didn't take long. Rhodes checked his rearview mirror to be sure that Buddy was still behind him. He was, and Rhodes flipped his blinker light on for a left turn. He left the paved road and drove down a one-lane dirt road that wound among pastures and woods. Trees grew close to the road in a lot of places, and patterns of light and shade flowed over the car. Rhodes hoped he didn't meet another driver on the narrow road. It wasn't likely. Not many people lived out in the country around here.

Rhodes crossed over a wooden bridge at Sand Creek and kept going for several more miles, winding around from one dusty county road to another and passing an occasional isolated house. Only one of them appeared to be occupied.

Something else was nagging at him just

below the level of consciousness, something that didn't fit with everything else, but he couldn't quite bring it to the surface. The more he tried to think what it could be, the farther it slipped down into the dark recesses of his mind. He figured it would make itself apparent eventually, or if it didn't, maybe it wasn't important in the first place.

Rhodes looked down the dusty road in front of him. He wasn't far from Merritt's Lake now. If he hadn't known where he was going, he wouldn't have been able to find it. He was way off the main roads, back in the areas of the county where hardly anyone traveled these days. He saw an iron gate in the fence on his left. A white sign with faded red letters hung on the gate. It said POSTED — KEEP OUT. Rhodes didn't think it applied to him, but just to be sure, he stopped the car in front of the gate and got on the radio to Hack.

"Did you get Frankie Welch on the phone?" he asked.

"Sure did," Hack said. "You can go right ahead and take a look around his place. He said to tell you not to go fishin', though. He's savin' all the big bass in that lake for hisself."

"Seems a little selfish," Rhodes said, not

that Welch had anything to worry about. There had been a time when Rhodes routinely carried fishing gear in the back of his county car, but that time was long past. Rhodes hadn't been fishing in so long, he wasn't even sure he could remember how to cast a lure.

"Can't blame a fella for wantin' those big, fat fish to be at the end of his line and not yours," Hack said.

Rhodes knew Hack was just trying to get a rise out of him, so he signed off, racked the mic, and got out of the car. Buddy was parked right behind him, the window of his car already down.

"We gonna go in hot and fast?" Buddy asked as Rhodes approached.

"Nope. We don't even know that Louie's around, and if he is, we don't want to scare him off. We'll go in as quietly as we can. The way I remember it, the lake's down in a depression just past those oak trees there." Rhodes pointed. "The road winds past them and down to the lake. We'll go about halfway around the lake and then stop. We won't try to go any farther in the cars."

"We need some rugged vehicles," Buddy said. "For bouncing around in pastures and such."

Rhodes thought about the Tahoe that

Roger Allen had mentioned. This would be a good time for it. Or for an MRAP, for that matter. In something like that they could just roll up to the old house and push it over. That would be a bad idea, even though Mikey Burns would probably go for it. It wouldn't be as exciting as blowing pig parts all over the county, but if Louie was in there, it might squash him like a bug. Mikey might even go for that, but it didn't fit with Rhodes's ideas about enforcing the law, and Mikey wouldn't go for the lawsuit that Welch might file if they demolished his house without permission.

"Maybe we'll get some new vehicles soon," Rhodes said. "For now we'll stop and walk. That way maybe we won't alert Louie that we're here, and we won't be bouncing around so much."

"Okay," Buddy said. "Is that gate locked?"

"Never has been," Rhodes said. "Wouldn't do any good. If anybody wanted in, they'd just climb over it."

"You think that's what Louie did?"

"Louie had to walk here, so he probably came across country from the other side. Maybe he'll be tired out and won't give us any trouble."

"Wanna bet?"

"Not a chance," Rhodes said.

269

He went to the gate, which was fastened with a chain with a couple of links hooked on a nail driven into a fence post. Rhodes unhooked one link and let the chain drop. The gate swung open. Rhodes didn't see any cattle in the pasture. He didn't think Welch had any.

"Don't bother to close the gate," Rhodes told Buddy.

He got in his car and drove through the opening. There was no road in the pasture, just ruts worn from the passage of other vehicles over the years. Weeds grew between the ruts, which Rhodes followed up a little rise. He passed by the oak trees and saw the lake in the little depression. The water covered about an acre, though the lake had been larger in years when there was a lot of rain. Lily pads and cattails were thick and green around the edges of the water, and Rhodes was sure that some big bass lurked in the shadows of the lily pads.

The old house stood at the edge of some woods about a quarter of a mile from the lake. Rhodes stopped the car and got out. Buddy stopped practically at the bumper of Rhodes's car.

"We need the heavy artillery?" Buddy asked.

"Shotguns should be enough," Rhodes said.

He barely had room to get to the trunk to get out the weapon and shells. Buddy got the gun from the trunk of his own car, and both of them thumbed shells into the magazines after checking the safeties.

"If Louie's in the house," Rhodes said, "I'll try to talk sense into him. Don't do any shooting unless you absolutely have to."

"You know me," Buddy said.

Rhodes did know Buddy, and that was the problem. What he knew was that Buddy loved to pull his big revolver at any opportunity, and while he'd never shot anybody, there was always the chance that he'd get carried away, especially with the shotgun right there in his hands.

Another problem was that Buddy had a powerful streak of hardheaded Puritanism. He didn't like drugs, and he didn't like drug dealers. Rhodes didn't like them, either, but he didn't have the same strong dislike that Buddy did. Rhodes just wanted to put them in jail. Buddy wouldn't mind exterminating them.

"Kevlar?" Buddy asked.

Rhodes thought about the last time he'd walked up to a house where Louie was. There had been a lot of shooting.

"Kevlar might not be a bad idea," he said. The vests were heavy and hot, and Rhodes didn't even know if Louie had a gun, but he didn't see any need to take chances.

They got the vests and put them on, securing the straps.

"Let's go," Rhodes said when he had his vest adjusted. "Easy does it. We don't want to spook him."

"You think he hasn't heard us by now?"

"He might have. We're still a good way off, though, and the weeds are high enough to screen us a little bit. We'll stick to the ruts and just walk right up to the house."

"Okay," Buddy said. "You think these vests will really stop a bullet?"

"They're guaranteed," Rhodes said, though he had no idea if that was true. "The odds are in our favor."

Buddy nodded, and they started up the hill, each man with his shotgun barrel against his shoulder. When they were within fifty yards of the house, Rhodes stopped and put up a hand. Buddy stopped beside him.

"Not much of a place to hide," Buddy whispered, and Rhodes had to agree. The house looked as if it hadn't been painted since sometime in the Hoover administration. All the windowpanes were missing, and so were the screens, if there'd ever been any.

The roof was caved in over about half the house, and the porch had fallen away.

"If he's here, he couldn't be very comfortable," Rhodes said. He raised his voice. "Louie! Louie Foshee! You in there? This is Sheriff Rhodes."

Rhodes stopped talking and listened. He thought he heard a couple of squirrels arguing back in the trees, but that was all.

"Not there?" Buddy said.

"Not answering if he is," Rhodes said. "Louie! Come on out. We don't want to have to come get you. You might get hurt."

"You might get hurt yourself," Louie called out from inside the house.

"Guess he's in there, all right," Buddy said. "Or maybe the house is haunted."

"Let's not get that started," Rhodes said. "Louie! You know what's going to happen if you don't come on out. Don't make this any harder than it has to be."

Silence. Rhodes and Buddy waited it out. Behind them down at the lake a fish flopped in the water, making quite a splash.

"Big bass," Buddy said. "Wish I had a rod and reel."

"So do I," Rhodes said. "Louie! Come on out."

Louie came to the door. "You caught that damn Earl, didn't you. He told you I was

273

here, didn't he."

"I'm just a good guesser," Rhodes said.

"Yeah, right. You wouldn't have guessed this place in a million years. That damn Earl, letting himself get caught and then ratting me out. I'm gonna tear him a new one."

"You won't be sharing a cell. Anyway, Earl's in the hospital right now. He had a run-in with some hogs."

It was quiet for a while, and then Louie said, "Hogs got him? That's how you caught him?"

"The hogs helped," Rhodes said.

Louie gave a little laugh. "You got anything to eat with you?"

"Nope," Rhodes said, "but I'll see to it that you get a good meal at the jail."

"I got a Snickers in the car," Buddy said. "He can have that if he wants it. Got a bottle of water, too."

Rhodes grinned. "Buddy says he has a Snickers bar if you want it."

"You won't shoot me?" Louie said.

"Just put your hands on your head and come out. We'll give you a Snickers and a bottle of water."

"Okay, but don't shoot," Louie said.

He clasped his hands on his head. He was about to jump to the ground when Rhodes

274

said, "You have a gun, Louie?"

"No. No gun."

"Come ahead, then. Don't fall."

Louie jumped down. He stumbled but didn't fall.

"Walk on down here," Rhodes said. "Take it slow."

Louie took it slow. When he was ten yards from them, Rhodes and Buddy stood aside and let him walk between them on the weedy median between the ruts.

"Stop right there," Rhodes said. "Put your hands behind you."

Louie did as he was told. He was dirty and bedraggled. His mullet was plastered to his head with sweat. Maybe some things were worse than having a thin spot in your hair.

Rhodes said, "Cuff him, Buddy."

Buddy handed Rhodes his shotgun. "He smells kinda bad."

"I ain't had time for a bath," Louie said. "People been chasing me, and that place I was in don't have running water, in case you were wondering."

Buddy cuffed him without comment.

"I'm going to give you your Miranda warning," Rhodes said.

"What for? You're just picking me up for running off. I don't mind admitting it. You caught me. I didn't commit any new crime. I won't try to run again."

"Can't be sure of that," Rhodes said. He laid out the Miranda rights and asked Louie if he understood them.

"Sure. I've heard 'em before. I still don't see why you needed to tell me."

"I don't like to take chances," Rhodes said. "Now spread your legs a little bit."

As he said that the thing that had been itching at the back of Rhodes's brain surfaced. He'd been pretty sure it would come to him.

"Buddy's going to pat you down now," he said.

Louie grimaced. "I told you I don't have a gun."

"We want to make sure you don't have one that you forgot about."

Buddy started the pat-down, and Louie said, "Don't touch me if you don't love me."

Buddy didn't smile. "It's a good thing for you the sheriff doesn't believe in police brutality."

Louie looked up at the sky. "That Snickers is likely gonna be melted in this heat. I bet it's a hundred and twenty in that car."

"You don't have to eat it," Buddy said, continuing the pat-down.

"Just meant it might be messy and all. Get

chocolate all over me."

"Like I said, you don't have to eat it."

"I'll eat it," Louie said.

Buddy straightened up and said, "He's clean." Buddy sniffed. "I mean, he's not clean, but he doesn't have a weapon on him."

"I thought you might have your .38 with you," Rhodes said to Louie.

"I don't have a .38. I don't like 'em. I like an automatic, like a Glock."

Rhodes had a feeling Louie would say something like that. Louie and Earl liked to think of themselves as tough guys, and these days the tough guys used Glocks. The idea that Louie killed Neil with a .38 was what hadn't rung true to Rhodes, although it had taken him a while to realize it. Of course, Louie could have been attempting to mislead him, but Rhodes didn't think that was the case. Louie couldn't think that fast.

"Automatics can jam on you," Buddy said, patting the butt of his .44 Magnum. "A revolver's a lot more reliable."

"Everybody's got his own opinion," Louie said. "Me, I like an automatic. That is, I would if I was gonna use a gun at all, which I'm not. I don't use guns. Don't even own one."

If he didn't, it was because Rhodes and

Andy had confiscated all of them at the meth bust a while back. Rhodes handed Buddy his shotgun.

"Let's go on down and get in the cars and turn on the air," Rhodes said. "It's too hot to stand out here in the sun and debate handguns."

Not only was it hot, but Rhodes was afraid the top of his head would blister if they stood there too long. A matted mullet did have its advantages, even one that looked as bad as Louie's did, and so did a hat.

"You go first, Louie," Rhodes said.

Louie led the way, and when they got to the cars, he stopped and turned to face Rhodes and Buddy. "I can't eat that Snickers with my hands behind me."

"You'll have to do without it, then," Buddy said. "I'm not gonna feed it to you."

"We'll give it to him out here," Rhodes said. "I'll feed him."

"You sure?" Buddy asked.

Rhodes nodded.

"Let's get shed of these vests and shotguns first," Buddy said.

Rhodes thought that was a good idea. His shirt was soaked underneath the heavy Kevlar. Rhodes told Louie to stay where he was. Louie nodded, and Rhodes and Buddy took off their vests and put them and the shotguns in the car trunks. Buddy got the Snickers out of his car and handed it to Rhodes. It was mushy inside its wrapper.

"You were right, Louie," Rhodes said. "This is a mess."

He unwrapped the candy bar, trying to keep from getting chocolate all over his fingers. He left enough of the wrapper on the bar to hold it with and offered it to Louie, who managed to eat it in three or four bites. While Louie was chewing the last bite, Rhodes handed the chocolate-smeared wrapper to Buddy.

"Put it in your litter bag," he said.

Buddy started to protest, but instead he took the wrapper between his thumb and forefinger and put it in his car.

"How 'bout that water?" Louie asked.

Buddy came out of the car with a bottle of water that he pitched to Rhodes, who caught it and unscrewed the cap. He held to bottle to Louie's mouth, which was covered with chocolate, and let him drink. Louie drank the whole bottle, and Rhodes tossed the empty to Buddy.

"Litter bag," he said.

Buddy didn't respond. He just turned to the car and put the bottle somewhere. Rhodes wasn't even sure Buddy had a litter bag.

"Why'd you say that about the .38?" Louie asked.

"Just wondering," Rhodes said.

"Funny thing to be wondering about."

Maybe Louie wasn't as dense as Rhodes had thought. Maybe he could put two and two together and come up with the right answer occasionally. Even a blind hog turns up an acorn now and then.

"Let's put you in the car," Rhodes said.

He opened the back door of the county car, and Buddy came over to assist Louie's entrance, making sure that Louie didn't hit his head on the roof of the car.

"I'll take him on into town," Rhodes said. "You can go ahead and finish your patrol. Might as well look around Thurston while you're down here and see how things are going along."

"Sure thing," Buddy said. "Might stop at that little café in Hod's old store and get me a burger for lunch. I've heard they're mighty good."

"You be sure to let me know," Rhodes said.

CHAPTER 17

On the ride back to Clearview, Rhodes thought about the night Neil had died. Louie said he didn't have a .38, and Rhodes believed him. However, Louie had been at the Moore house when Neil had died, or that was Earl's story. Earl even believed, or suspected, that Louie had killed Neil, which meant that Louie hadn't told him what happened, or if he'd told him, Earl didn't think it was the truth. Or he'd lied for his own purposes. That seemed unlikely. Rhodes didn't think Earl was that creative.

Having given Louie his Miranda warning, Rhodes could talk to him about the murder, and as long as Louie was willing to talk and didn't ask for a lawyer, everything would be fine. If he asked for one, Rhodes would just have to keep quiet. In fact, if he kept quiet to begin with, Louie might start talking.

Buddy backed his car away from the ruts and turned toward the entrance to the pasture. Rhodes did the same and followed Buddy. When they came to the gate, Buddy drove through and pulled his car off the road, halfway into the bar ditch, so that Rhodes could go on by. Rhodes did so and looked in his rearview mirror to see Buddy get out of his car and go to close the gate. The cold air from the car's A/C unit chilled Rhodes's damp shirt, but it felt good after the hot sun.

After he'd wound along for about a mile, Louie broke the silence in the car.

"How long you think you can keep me in jail?" he asked.

"I doubt you'll see the outside again before your trial," Rhodes told him. "Even if we put an ankle bracelet on you, you'd be a threat to run."

"Damn," Louie said. He was quiet from then until they got to Thurston. "We gonna stop for a hamburger like that deputy of yours said he might do?"

"That would be too much trouble," Rhodes said, "and the county might not want to pay for your hamburger. You've been a lot of trouble to us."

"Yeah," Louie said. "I guess I have. Still like a burger, though."

Rhodes wouldn't have minded giving the burgers a try himself, but not with a prisoner that he'd have to feed one to unless he took the cuffs off. He wasn't going to do that. Louie would just have to suffer.

"You should have thought about eating before you ran off," Rhodes said. "Anyway, you had a Snickers. You should be able to make it until we get to Clearview."

"It ain't right to keep me there," Louie said. "In the jail, I mean. A man has things he's gotta do."

"You should've thought of that before you ran off, I guess."

"I had stuff to do. You wouldn't let me."

"You're talking about Neil, right?"

Louie didn't answer. Rhodes didn't prod him, and it was quiet in the car except for the hum of the air-conditioning, which by this time had pretty much dried Rhodes's shirt.

Another mile or so down the road, Louie said, "He's gonna get away with it, ain't he."

"Who are you talking about?" Rhodes asked.

"The one who killed Neil. He's gonna get away with it."

"You're not showing much faith in your local law enforcement agency," Rhodes said. "We caught you and Earl, didn't we?"

"Hogs is what caught Earl, you said."

"I said they ran over him. We'd have

caught up with him, hogs or not, just like we caught up with you."

Louie snorted. "Earl ratted me out is how you got me."

"Just good police work," Rhodes said. "You were there when Neil was killed, weren't you? You didn't do anything about it then."

"That goddamn Earl. He told you that, didn't he. He told you I was there."

Rhodes didn't bother to deny it. Now that Louie was talking, it seemed like a good idea to let him keep right on doing it.

"Earl don't know a thing," Louie said. "He don't know what it was like. He thinks I ran off and left Neil there, but that's not the way it was. Earl don't know squat. He just likes to shoot off his mouth. Only reason he wasn't with us is because he's afraid to go there. Funny things happen in that place. It didn't bother Neil, but it bothered me and Earl. I didn't like to go there much more than Earl did, but I'm not yellow. I went, but it didn't do Neil any good. He's dead anyway."

"Earl didn't tell me anything about what happened at the house," Rhodes said, "and he didn't mention being afraid. What kind of things was he afraid of?"

"I don't like talking about it," Louie said.

"You'll think I'm crazy."

Rhodes thought about what Mika had said. He thought about the rat and all the other things that had happened over the last couple of days. If Louie and Earl had experienced things like that, he couldn't blame them for being a little bit spooked.

"I've been in the house," Rhodes said. "I felt like somebody was watching me. I saw some big rats in there, too."

"Rats don't bother me none," Louie said. "I've lived around rats all my life. It was the other things. What you said about somebody watching you? I felt like that, too, ever' time I was there."

"Were you there often?"

"I ain't saying I was, and if I was there, it wasn't to do anything wrong. Sometimes a fella just likes to get out of the house and have him a hamburger in a private place without anybody to bother him."

Sometimes a fella wanted to run a drug deal, too, and Rhodes was sure that was what had been going on in the house for a while. He didn't expect Louie to admit it, however, at least not immediately. He found it interesting that Louie had also had the feeling of being watched, but it didn't prove that there were any ghosts lurking about. Anybody might feel that way in a creepy old house with a bad reputation. It was only natural.

"How did Neil feel about being there?" Rhodes asked.

"Didn't bother him a bit. He said he liked ghosts because they weren't like people. They were just spirits, he said. They couldn't shoot you or run a knife in you, he said, but look what happened to him."

"It wasn't a ghost that killed him," Rhodes said. "It was somebody with a gun."

Or maybe it was a *yurei* with a gun. That is, if a *yurei* could or would use a gun. What would Moore's ghost have to worry about, anyway? He'd been buried properly, as far as Rhodes knew. Of course, the skeleton hadn't. If there was a ghost in the Moore house, it was more likely to be the ghost of whoever the skeleton had belonged to. Not that Rhodes believed even for a second that there was a ghost.

Then Rhodes remembered the bullet hole in the windshield of the Foshees' truck, and he started putting a little theory together. He thought he'd try it out on Louie, who didn't seem inclined to ask for a lawyer at the moment.

"You didn't go in with Neil because you didn't like the place," Rhodes said. "Neil wasn't worried. He was just going to talk to some college kid, so he didn't need to have you with him. That about right?"

"That goddamn Earl. He told you that."

Earl had implied some of it, but Rhodes wasn't going to tell Louie that. He said, "I think I know what happened next, too, and Earl couldn't have told it to me."

"If you're so smart, lay it out there," Louie said.

"You were waiting in the pickup. You were a little nervous because you felt somebody or something was watching you. How am I doing so far?"

"Anybody could've figured that out. Sure, I was nervous. I just didn't like that place. It seemed like it was okay when we first went there. Kind of peaceful, you know? An old place where nobody'd been for a long time. After we'd been there a time or two, though, it got different. It made me nervous, like you said. It was just a bad feeling, like something in there had been asleep and then it had woke up and started to watch us."

The pastureland on both sides of the road slipped by. The grass was greener than it had been, thanks to the recent rain, but it could've used more water. Rhodes thought it might have rained a bit more down this way than at the Moore house. Someone had put new fencing up for the pastures along both sides of the road. It must have been expensive, but it looked good.

"I don't know what was watching you," Rhodes said, "but I know that ghosts don't use guns. Somebody shot Neil and then came out to shoot you. I saw the bullet hole in the windshield of your pickup."

"Damn near had a bullet hole in me, too," Louie said. "That thing came through the windshield and buzzed right by my ear like a wasp. Went right on through the back window, too. Scared me more than a ghost."

Louie had been more than bothered, and Rhodes knew it. A nervous man, someone shooting at him from a haunted house? There was just one natural reaction.

"You got out of there," Rhodes said. "Fast."

Rhodes looked at Louie in the rearview mirror. Louie was staring out the window. There wasn't much to look at other than the pastures and the new fences, but Rhodes had a feeling Louie wasn't seeing them anyway.

"Can't blame you," Rhodes said. "You knew it wasn't Neil shooting at you, so he had to be dead. You'd be dead, too, if that bullet hadn't missed you."

"You don't know about Neil and us,"

Louie said, turning to stare straight ahead. "If it wasn't for him, me and Earl'd probably have jobs somewhere, maybe not good ones, but jobs. It was Neil told us we could make easy money cooking meth. He said it was dangerous, but it'd be worth it. He was right about it being dangerous, but it was you and your deputy that like to killed us, not the meth. If you're careful, you won't get hurt, he said, and we was always careful. We never used, neither. That was another thing Neil told us. He said that meth was bad stuff, and that if he caught us using, he'd shoot us. Me and Earl believed him, and we stayed off it. The money came in, just like he said it would, and it was good money. Here I am, though, handcuffed in a cop car, and Earl's in the hospital, been run over by hogs."

Louie stopped and looked out the window again. Rhodes was tempted to say something like *Crime does not pay* or *You can't blame somebody else for all your troubles,* but he knew Louie wouldn't appreciate it.

"I shoulda stayed to help Neil," Louie said after a while. "Or at least shot back, but I didn't, and now me and Earl are in trouble again, all for nothing we did. Earl's been run over by hogs, and I've been hiding in a broken-down dump that don't have more'n half a roof."

"Earl's going to be okay," Rhodes said. "He's just a little banged up. You two won't be in prison too long. You're young enough to do something with yourselves when you get out if you can give up dealing."

"You talk like it's a cinch we're going to the pen."

"It is a cinch," Rhodes said. "Count on it. Even at that, you're better off than Neil. He's dead."

"That damn college kid killed him," Louie said. "Except he wasn't no college kid. He was working for the DEA. I tried to tell Neil, but he just laughed, said I didn't know what I was talking about. He thought the kid was lying about some class thing he was going to do. He thought the kid just wanted to make a buy. I guess he was wrong about it, though. Otherwise, he'd still be alive."

They were getting close to Clearview, so Rhodes eased up on the accelerator and slowed the car. He had a feeling Louie wouldn't talk much once they got to the jail.

"You sure it was the college kid that shot at you?" he asked.

"Damn right. He was waiting for Neil in there. I don't know what happened, but he must've given himself away. College kid, my ass. He was DEA from the git-go. You can't ever trust anybody looks like that."

"Looks like what?"

"Like a kid. Can't trust anybody looks old, either."

Life as a meth cooker had turned Louie into a cynic, if he hadn't been one before.

"So you got out of there and went back to the house," Rhodes said. "Talked to Earl. Got your stories straight."

"We thought you'd show up," Louie said, "you being like you are and all. We were gonna bluff it out, but I could tell you didn't believe us."

"It wasn't what I'd call award-winning acting."

"Yeah, I guess not. We weren't in the drama club at school."

Rhodes doubted that Louie and Earl had been in any clubs. He doubted that they'd even been in school for any longer than the state required them to be.

"So you ran."

"Yeah. So we ran."

"And we caught you. You should've just leveled with me to begin with."

Louie leaned back in the seat and didn't bother to say anything about leveling. That would've been the last thing to enter his mind where the law was concerned.

As they drove into Clearview, Rhodes thought that it at least looked a bit better than Thurston. He could see signs of life. The college building, Max Schwartz's barbecue place, the strip center with its florist shop, the new motel. It was only going back into town and to the jail that the decay became obvious. Still, some of the downtown was coming back to life, and new businesses were restoring a few of the old buildings that were left and moving into them. The town wasn't dead yet.

At the jail Rhodes got Louie booked, and Lawton took him off to get him installed in a cell.

"Sheriff told me I'd get something to eat," Louie said.

"I'll see what I can find," Lawton said, and they went out into the cellblock.

Instead of asking Hack about things he needed to know, which could have led to all kinds of digressions, Rhodes asked Mika about the gun registrations.

"What I'm wondering about is .38s," he said. "Wade Clement own one?"

"If he does," Mika said, "it's not registered in his name. Ace Gable owns one, though."

Ace could've gone to the house as easily as Wade could have. If Wade's story was true, Ace would've been the one waiting there when Neil arrived.

"Vicki Patton doesn't own a gun, or at least not one that's registered," Mika went on. "That doesn't mean she doesn't have one or access to one."

Like Ace Gable's. He would've let her borrow it without asking too many questions, but Rhodes found it hard to believe she'd kill Neil. She'd broken it off with him, and there was no danger she'd ever go back. If Neil had forced the issue, she might've done something about it, but Rhodes liked to think she'd have come to him and let the law take care of it. He'd like to think that, and he almost did. Almost, but not quite. In fact, she'd probably have gone to Ace, which led right back to that .38.

"Getting back to the Clements," Mika said, "the mayor owns a Glock nine, like the one his nephew brought in. The nephew was telling the truth about that one. It's his, and he has a CHL."

Rhodes had been hoping that the mayor or Wade owned a .38. It would have made things easier, at least if Louie was right about Wade.

"Thanks," Rhodes told Mika. "That helps to narrow it down."

"That's not all," Mika said.

"The sheriff, he's kind of a sexist," Hack

said, looking happy to work his way into the conversation.

"I don't think that's it," Mika said.

"It ain't that he means to be," Hack said. "It's just that when he was raised, things were different, and he has a trouble adjustin' to the times we live in now."

Lawton came in as Hack was talking about adjusting to the times, and he joined right in, too.

"You're a fine one to talk," he said to Hack. "Back when you were raised, cars still had cranks on 'em."

"Now you know that ain't so," Hack said. "They might've had runnin' boards, but they sure didn't have cranks. The only old crank I've ever seen is you."

"I had a sweet little '40 Chevy with runnin' boards," Lawton said, ignoring the insult. "It was old when I got it, but it still ran like a sewin' machine."

"Had an engine 'bout as powerful as a sewin' machine motor, too, I'll bet," Hack said. "You prob'ly bought it new off the showroom floor, you being as old as you are."

Rhodes often wondered how topics of conversations with Hack and Lawton could get so far off the track, going in such a short time from .38s to sewing machine motors.

294

They had a gift for it.

"Let's get back to how I'm a sexist," Rhodes said. "And how it has anything to do with what we're supposed to be talking about."

"Tell him, Mika," Hack said.

Mika smiled at Hack. "I think what you must mean is that the sheriff didn't let me finish my report on the Clements."

"I apologize," Rhodes said. "I thought I had. Please go on."

"See what I mean?" Hack said. "He thought he'd let you finish, but you hadn't mentioned somebody he'd plumb forgot. Sexist, like I said."

Rhodes finally caught on. "Mrs. Clement. She has a .38."

"A Colt Detective Special," Mika said.

Rhodes nodded. A little snubnose. Not much good for distance work, but not a bad weapon for personal defense.

"That whole family's licensed to carry," Hack said. "Can't blame 'em. They live in one of the best houses in town, drive a big, fine car. Miz Clement has jewelry, too, and I wouldn't be surprised if they kept a good bit of cash in the house in case of emergency."

"Like the zombie apocalypse," Lawton said. "Gotta be ready for that."

First ghosts, now zombies. It was time for Rhodes to go before it got to werewolves and vampires. He thanked Mika for the information and got out of there.

Once upon a time, long before Rhodes was born, Clearview had been a thriving town, a genuine boomtown, in fact, thanks to the discovery of oil. Most of the oil was long gone now, pumped out and refined and burned in cars long ago. There was some talk that a lot of oil was still under the ground and that modern techniques of drilling could extract it, but so far nothing had come of the talk.

The homes in the part of town where the Clements lived had been built during that boom era, and some of them had been well cared for ever since, including the Clements' big two-story house. The lawn was trimmed so neatly that it looked like someone had gone over it with scissors to be sure that no individual blade stuck up even a millimeter higher than another one. It was like a picture in a fancy magazine, or on the Internet, since magazines were part of the past, like Clearview's glory days. Rhodes didn't envy the Clements, but he did wish his lawn looked a little better. He wondered what their water bill must be and how much they

paid their lawn-care service. He decided that he couldn't afford it unless the commissioners voted him a nice raise, which didn't seem too likely at the moment.

Fran Clement came to the door when Rhodes rang the bell. She was short, almost a foot shorter than Rhodes, with dark, smooth hair. It had been fluffier the last time Rhodes had seen her, and he thought it had been a little lighter color, too. He might have been misremembering, however.

"Well, well," she said. "If it's not the sheriff. Have you come to accuse me of another murder?"

"I don't believe I ever accused you, Mrs. Clement," Rhodes said.

"Please, Sheriff, call me Fran. I feel as if we're old friends. You know all my intimate secrets."

What Rhodes knew was that her husband had been guilty of a bit of hanky-panky that had gotten him involved in a murder investigation, one that had also involved Mrs. Clement. Or Fran.

"Come on in, Sheriff," she said. "No use standing out in the hot sun."

He went inside, and Fran closed the door behind him. He followed her down a hallway to the same room where they'd had their previous little talk about murder. The tile floor was shiny, and the grout was clean. The flat-screen TV was still bigger than anything Rhodes had seen outside the electronics department at Walmart, and the couch covered with buttery leather was still just as comfortable. Rhodes sat on one end of it and Fran sat on the other. He hoped she'd keep her distance. Their last conversation had been awkward enough before she started making passes at him. Or what he'd interpreted as passes. Maybe he'd been doing her an injustice.

"My husband still doesn't understand me," Fran said, inching a little way toward him on the couch.

Or maybe he hadn't done her an injustice after all.

"I don't suppose you care, though," she said.

"It's not any of my business," Rhodes said.

"What *is* your business, then?"

"Guns," Rhodes said. "Murder. Little things like that."

Fran stood up and walked over to the big glass sliding door. She looked out at her back lawn, which was every bit as green and perfect as the front.

"I thought maybe you'd just come to visit," she said, not turning around.

"I don't have a lot of time for visiting,"

Rhodes said. "I need to ask you about your revolver."

Fran turned to look at him. "I have a CHL. I must admit that I didn't do too well on the target shooting, but I passed. The noise made me nervous, and I didn't care for the idea of shooting anything, even a target. I don't think I could shoot a person. I'd be shaking too much. You don't think I shot someone, do you?"

"It's not you I'm worried about," Rhodes said. "It's your .38."

"Cliff bought it for me. We thought it was a good idea for me to have something for protection in this big old house. I haven't used it or even looked at it since the CHL class. I haven't even thought about it, really. Why are you worried about it?"

"Neil Foshee was killed with a .38. I'm sure you've heard all about it."

"Cliff and Wade told me he was killed, but they didn't mention a .38. Wade has a Glock, and he took it to the jail for you to test." She paused. "I don't see why you needed it if a .38 was involved."

"I didn't know it was a .38 that killed him at the time I asked for Wade's gun," Rhodes said, "and I wanted to be sure Wade was in the clear."

Fran ran a hand over her hair. "Then I

don't understand why you're here."

Rhodes stood up. "I'm here because it's not impossible that somebody used your .38 to kill Neil Foshee. I'd like to take a look at it, if you don't mind."

Rhodes hoped she didn't ask for a warrant, because he didn't have one and didn't want to have to get one. He was sure he could get the judge to issue one, but that would take time, and Rhodes didn't want to wait.

"It's in the gun safe," Fran said. "In the bedroom."

"Why don't we take a look."

Fran hesitated, but not for long. "Why not? The bedroom's upstairs."

She walked past Rhodes and back to the hallway where the staircase was located. He followed her up to the second floor, and she led him into a large bedroom with a king-size bed, a walnut dresser, an armoire, and a large jewelry cabinet. She opened the closet, which impressed Rhodes with its organization and neatness. He wouldn't want anybody to look in his closet.

"The gun safe's on the shelf," Fran said. "Now where's that stool?"

She reached behind some blouses hanging from a low bar and pulled out a small stool. Standing on it, she punched the combination keys of the gun safe. Nothing happened.

"It's been a while since I opened this thing," she said.

Rhodes waited, and after another few seconds of thought, Fran keyed the combination into the safe. She opened it and reached inside.

"Oh, dear," she said.

"What's the matter?" Rhodes asked.

"My gun's not here," she said.

CHAPTER 18

Fran searched the closet with Rhodes watching, but the revolver wasn't there. Rhodes didn't think it would be. It couldn't have gotten out of the safe without the help of someone who knew the correct combination for the keypad, and if Fran hadn't taken it, the list of suspects was very short.

"Clifford must have taken it," Fran said, naming one of them. "I don't know why he'd have wanted it."

"You don't have the combination written down anywhere, do you?" Rhodes asked.

"Well," Fran said. "That's an embarrassing question."

"You want to answer it?"

"You saw that I had trouble remembering the combination. It's not like I open the safe often. So, yes, I have it written down."

"Where?" Rhodes asked.

"It's on a piece of paper in my dresser drawer," she said.

She came out of the closet and into the bedroom. She went to the dresser, pulled open one of the top drawers, and brought out a piece of paper.

"Here it is," she said, and handed the paper to Rhodes.

Rhodes took the paper but handed it back without looking to see what was written on it. He didn't doubt that the combination was there. If Wade knew the .38 was in the gun safe, he wouldn't have had any trouble locating the combination.

"You know where Wade and your husband are right now?" he asked.

"Cliff said he was going to his office at the city hall," Fran said. "I don't know about Wade. He borrowed my car and didn't say where he was going."

Fran didn't drive an SUV like her husband. She had a more modest Lexus, the smaller ES model. It was black, like the SUV. It would be easy to spot, but it would have to be where someone could see it.

"He didn't even give you a hint?" Rhodes asked.

"He's Cliff's nephew, not mine. He comes here and visits, and it's like he's on his own. Cliff doesn't tell him what to do, and I don't think it's my place to do it. If he wants to borrow a car, I give him the keys and send him on his way. It's the middle of the afternoon. How much trouble could he get into?"

"If he has a gun?" Rhodes said. "Plenty."

Rhodes wished he'd stopped in Thurston for that hamburger as Louie had suggested, because now it seemed as if he might miss lunch, an all too frequent occurrence. Nevertheless, he had to try to find Wade Clement.

The first thing Rhodes did was to call Hack and have him alert the deputies on patrol to look for Fran's car.

"Why?" Hack asked. "She gone missing?"

"Wade Clement's driving it. He's the one I'm looking for. He might be armed, so be sure to mention that."

"You think he's dangerous?"

"I'm not sure. Just tell them to be careful."

When he had to, Hack could be serious and do his job. He didn't try to get Rhodes into a discussion. He just said he'd take care of things.

Rhodes signed off and drove by the city hall. He saw Clement's SUV parked in his allotted space by the side of the building, but there was no sign of Fran's ES. Rhodes parked and went to the mayor's office.

"Well, well," Alice King said when he got to the door. "What a pleasure to see you again so soon, Sheriff. I'll bet you didn't come to see me, though. You're probably here on business."

"I'm always happy to see you," Rhodes said, "but I admit that I'm looking for the mayor."

"Then you're in luck, because he's here, doing the will of the people."

Clement came to the door of his office before Rhodes could ask what the will of the people was today. He scowled at Rhodes, making it clear that he wasn't feeling nearly as perky as Alice and that he wasn't nearly as happy to see Rhodes as she seemed to be. Sometimes Rhodes thought she was only pretending, but maybe she really was happy to see him. Not Clement. He wasn't pretending. He wasn't happy in the least to see Rhodes standing there.

"You again," Clement said. "What's the problem now?"

"I'm looking for your nephew," Rhodes said.

"He's a grown man. I don't keep up with him."

"What about your wife's .38? Do you keep up with that?"

Clement glanced at Alice, who was trying

to look as if she couldn't hear a word that was being said. She wasn't very successful at it, but Rhodes had to give her credit for trying.

"I don't know what you're talking about," Clement said.

"The gun's missing, and so is Wade," Rhodes told him.

Clement was no longer scowling. He looked puzzled instead. "I don't understand," he said.

Rhodes laid it out for him. "Wade didn't mind bringing in his Glock, and it's no wonder. I found out that Foshee was killed with a .38. Your wife has a .38, but it's missing. So is Wade. If you don't have the .38, then I think he does."

Clement's scowl deepened. "That doesn't sound good."

"It's *not* good," Rhodes said. "That's why I'm looking for him. Did he say anything today that might give me a hint as to where he's gone?"

"He hasn't said a lot since you talked to him yesterday." Clement shook his head. "I can't believe he has Fran's gun. He had his own gun. Why not use that one?"

"If you're going to shoot somebody," Rhodes said, "it's a good idea not to use a gun that can be traced to you, especially if there's another one handy. He could use your wife's gun, put it back in the safe, and who'd be the wiser?"

"You're telling me he didn't put it back, though," Clement said. "Do you think he's crazy?"

"What makes you say that?"

"It seems as if he might have killed Neil Foshee with Fran's gun. Isn't that what you're saying? He must think he's some vigilante in the movies, shooting down drug dealers to clean up the city."

Clement was getting carried away. Rhodes started to give him another little lecture on implying and inferring, but the time didn't seem right for it.

"We don't know that he's killed anybody," Rhodes said. "I just want to find out about that gun."

"There's something else you should know," Clement said. "The only thing he's mentioned since yesterday also sounds crazy. He told me that just being outside the Moore house gave him the creeps. It was like he was being watched."

"There's nothing crazy about that," Rhodes said, trying not to sound defensive. "Anybody might get a feeling like that."

Clement looked doubtful. "I don't know. Sounds crazy to me." He scratched his beard. "You think he might have gone back to that house?"

Rhodes hadn't considered it, but it made sense in a way, especially if Wade had experienced the same sensation that Rhodes had. He might have thought someone had seen him with Foshee and hoped to find some kind of clue in the house. He wouldn't, however. Rhodes was sure that he and Ruth and Andy had found anything that was there to be found.

"Maybe that's where he went," Rhodes said. "I'll go take a look."

"Are you going to arrest him?"

Clement sounded concerned. Rhodes wondered if he was worried about his nephew or about how the arrest of a relative might affect his chances for reelection.

"Well?" Clement said. "Are you?"

"We'll just have to wait and see," Rhodes told him.

Rhodes found the Lexus ES parked in back of the Moore house. He stopped beside it and got Hack on the radio.

"Send me some backup to the Moore house," he said. "Wade Clement might be inside."

"Buddy's closest, out in Milsby. Take him a little while to get there."

"I'll be careful," Rhodes said. "Just tell him to come on."

"Will do," Hack said.

Rhodes got out of the car. It was shady in the yard, but heat and humidity seemed to rise up out of the weeds and hang in the air. There was no breeze to stir the leaves on the trees. Rhodes stopped by the old pickup with the puny hackberry tree sticking up through it near the radiator, or where the radiator would've been had it not rusted almost away.

Standing near the front fender of the nearly fossilized Dodge, Rhodes realized he had no sensation of being watched. He looked at the house and listened for any sound from inside it. All he heard was the sound of a car on a street a few blocks away. He bent over and got the Kel-Tec from the ankle holster. He checked the clip and started toward the house.

He stopped at the back door and listened again. He could hear faint noises, as if someone might be moving around, but not nearby. Rhodes debated with himself about whether to wait for Buddy to arrive. He decided that he could handle Wade on his own, so he pushed up the crime-scene tape that crossed the door and went inside.

It was cooler in the old house, but Rhodes

didn't feel any sense of relief from the heat outside. The afternoon sunlight came in through the broken windowpanes, and dust motes floated in the air. Rhodes went carefully from room to room, being as quiet as he could and hoping that the dust wouldn't make him sneeze. It hadn't before, so he figured he would be all right.

Rhodes didn't find Wade in any of the rooms. He didn't encounter any rats, either, so he had that going for him. Occasionally he heard a noise from above, as if someone, probably Wade, were searching the second floor. Or the rats were moving around. Rhodes didn't think rats would have parked the Lexus in the yard, however.

Rhodes went up the stairway and was again impressed by the fact that the steps didn't squeak. He looked through each of the rooms and found no one. There was no sound from the attic, either, but if Wade was in the house, that was where he had to be.

Sure enough, the door at the top of the attic stairway was open. Rhodes went on up the stairs, stopped at the top, and looked inside the attic. He didn't see anybody, so he stuck his head around the corner and looked toward the closet.

Wade Clement stood in front of the empty enclosure, peering into it. Unlike the closet,

Wade's hand wasn't empty. He was holding a revolver.

Rhodes didn't want to scare him. A frightened person could be even more dangerous than a calm one. A calm person acted with deliberation. A frightened one might shoot at a shadow, or even at a sheriff.

Rhodes stepped back and down a couple of steps. He trained the Kel-Tec on the doorway and said, "Wade Clement, this is Sheriff Rhodes. Put your weapon on the floor and shove it away from you with your foot."

"Sheriff Rhodes? What are you doing here?"

"The question is, what are *you* doing here, Wade. You crossed a police line. That's illegal, you know."

"I was looking for something," Wade said. "I thought it would be all right if I didn't bother anything."

"Did you leave something here the other night?" Rhodes asked.

"I don't know what you're talking about."

"You must have left something when you were here to meet Neil Foshee. That's the only time you would have been here."

Rhodes moved up one step. He could see into the attic, but he couldn't see Wade, who was still off to the side near the closet.

"I told you I wasn't here," Wade said.

"You told me the Glock was your gun, but I see you have another one."

"How can you see it?"

Rhodes thought he might as well mess with Wade's mind a little bit. He said, "I have ways of seeing things like that."

"I don't believe you. This house is crazy, though. There's something in it. Did you know that?"

"There's nothing here anymore," Rhodes said. "The house is empty. Put your gun on the floor and shove it away from you. Let me hear you do it. Then we can talk."

"You must think I killed Neil Foshee," Wade said. "I didn't do it. Somebody else did. Or something else. It's not here anymore, though. You're right about that."

"Put the gun on the floor," Rhodes said.

For a while Wade didn't say anything. Then Rhodes heard the clunk of something solid hitting the floor.

"Did you hear that?" Wade asked. "That was the pistol. I'm going to push it away from me."

Rhodes heard a scraping noise.

"Put your hands on your head and stand facing the door," Rhodes said.

"All right," Wade said. "I'm doing it."

Rhodes decided to take a chance that

Wade was telling the truth. He went up the last step and through the door, his pistol gripped in both hands and extended in front of him.

Wade Clement stood facing him, hands on his head, just as he'd been instructed. The revolver lay on the floor a few feet away.

"I guess I shouldn't have come here," Wade said.

"You guess right," Rhodes said. "Turn around and walk into the closet."

Wade glanced behind him. "I really don't want to do that."

Rhodes didn't much blame him, but he said, "Do it."

"I won't do anything," Wade said. "I promise."

Rhodes gestured with his pistol. "Turn around and walk into the closet."

"You won't shut the door, will you?"

"I won't shut the door. Now go on."

Wade turned and walked into the closet. He stood facing the back wall, and Rhodes picked up the revolver. He sniffed it. It didn't smell as if it had been fired in years, and there was no odor of Hoppe's cleaning solvent, either. It was as if the gun had been in the safe in Fran Clement's closet for a long time. Rhodes stuck the gun in his back pocket.

"Why'd you have the gun with you?" he asked.

"I was afraid to come here without it," Wade said.

"What were you scared of?"

"Ghosts," Wade said, his voice echoing off the wall.

CHAPTER 19

Rhodes marched Wade down the two flights of stairs and out of the house into the backyard, stopping him beside the abandoned pickup. Buddy drove up at that moment, and he stepped out of the county car with his .44 Magnum pointed at Wade.

"This the fella that killed Neil Foshee?" Buddy asked.

"I never killed anybody," Wade said. "I want a lawyer."

"We have some good ones here in Clearview," Rhodes said, "but you're not under arrest, so you don't really need one. You can put your hands down now."

"You sure about that, Sheriff?" Buddy asked. "Want me to cuff him? He looks dangerous to me. Looks like he might run." Buddy grinned. "Nobody can outrun a bullet, though."

Rhodes lowered his own gun. "You can put your sidearm away, Buddy, and don't bother with the cuffs. Wade's not going to run. Are you, Wade?"

Wade let his hands fall to his sides. "No, sir. I'm not going anywhere if I'm not under arrest. You did say I wasn't under arrest, didn't you?"

"That's what I said."

Rhodes took the .38 from his back pocket and handed it to Buddy. "Bag that and take it to the jail. Ask Mika to test it to see if it's been fired recently."

Buddy holstered his Magnum and took the .38. "You sure you'll be okay here?"

"I'll be fine," Rhodes said.

Buddy bagged the .38. When that was done, he got in the car, gave a little wave, and left. Once he was gone, Rhodes leaned over and returned the Kel-Tec to the ankle holster. Rhodes was glad to be out of the house. He was grateful for the shade of the trees, too. He didn't have to worry about his head blistering.

"Let's talk a little bit," he said to Wade. "You mentioned ghosts."

"Yeah. I guess I shouldn't have. I know it sounds crazy."

Rhodes wished people would quit saying that.

"It's not crazy, but I'd like to hear why you thought about ghosts."

"Because this place is weird. That night when the man was shot, I was outside in the car, and I felt like someone was watching me, or maybe wanting me to come inside. All I wanted to do was get away. I don't think I'd have gone in even if I hadn't heard the shots. It was the weirdest feeling I ever had about anything."

"Why were you in the attic today?"

"That's crazy, too. I didn't really want to come back here, but most of the day yesterday I had the feeling that I should. I thought I needed to look around, to find something. I'd been over the rest of the house and was just getting to the attic when you showed up."

"You didn't find anything, though."

"No. Whatever it was that was there before, it's gone now."

"You said the feeling was gone, too."

"Yeah. I didn't want to mention it to you yesterday. It sounded —"

"Crazy. You mentioned that. What you don't know is that yesterday we found a skeleton in the attic."

"A skeleton? A real one?"

"It could be just something from a high school biology class, but it's real enough. We're still trying to figure out how it got there."

"You believe in ghosts, Sheriff?"

"No," Rhodes said. "I don't. Some people do, though. They believe a person's spirit can linger around after death looking for revenge or something."

Not Seepy Benton, however. He had a different take on things, which was no surprise.

"Other people have a much more complicated idea about ghosts," Rhodes said. "They can even make ghosts sound like a scientific possibility."

"I wouldn't know about that," Wade said.

Rhodes was afraid that Wade might ask for an explanation that Rhodes couldn't give him, but he didn't.

"All I know," Wade said, "is that I felt something watching me, something that wanted me in that house. So I came back, to look around to see if I could find out what it was that wanted me there. That's all. I didn't kill anybody, Sheriff. I'm guilty of crossing your police line, but not anything else. Are you going to arrest me now?"

Rhodes thought it over. A night in jail might do Wade some good, but it didn't seem likely.

"Not if you stay out of trouble for the rest of your visit," Rhodes said. "I want you to go by your uncle's office and explain to him what you were doing and why you had the gun. Be sure to apologize to your aunt for sneaking it out of the house. Stay away from this place, too. All right?"

"Sure," Wade said. "I didn't want to come back here anyway, and I don't care if I ever see it again, even if the ghosts are gone."

"There weren't any ghosts," Rhodes said.

Wade nodded. "Whatever you say. Can I go now?"

"You can go," Rhodes said. "Drive carefully. Your aunt might be even more upset with you if you scratched her car."

"You don't have to worry about that," Wade said.

He got in the car and left. Rhodes watched him go, then looked back at the house. Something moved low on the ground by the back steps, and Rhodes went over to see what it was. At first he didn't see anything, but then he noticed a small box turtle that had retreated into its shell. It sat there unmoving, waiting for Rhodes to go away and leave it alone. It might live under the old house, or it could have just arrived from somewhere else. There would be plenty of snails and worms for it to eat under the house, though, so it would make a good home.

Rhodes wondered if the yellow markings on the turtle's shell were some kind of occult code that held the answer to the questions about the skeleton. Not likely.

Rhodes left the turtle where it was and went to his car. He thought it was odd that while he didn't believe in ghosts, he'd come to believe that turtles might be some kind of good luck symbol for him. He was more superstitious than he wanted to admit. In another day or so, he'd be admitting that the Moore house was haunted. Or had been.

Rhodes stood by the county car and tried to see if the turtle had moved. If it was still hiding in the grass, he couldn't see it. Rhodes thought about why he no longer felt a presence in the house and why Wade didn't, either. If the presence — all right, the ghost, the *yurei,* whatever — had left, then it must have accomplished whatever its mission had been. So what was the mission? Revenge? Setting some old wrong to rights? Nothing like that had happened. Rhodes had found a skeleton, or to be honest Seepy Benton and his ghostbusting pal had found a skeleton. That was the end of it.

Maybe that was enough. The *yurei* had stayed until its conflict was resolved. The skeleton had been found, and that was the end of the story.

Except that it wasn't the end of the story. Whose bones were they, and how had they gotten into that closet? Rhodes wasn't even close to having the answers to those two questions. More urgent was the question of who'd killed Neil Foshee. Rhodes had eliminated Louie Foshee and Wade Clement as suspects. He believed they were telling the truth. Who did that leave?

Something tickled the back of Rhodes's mind. He looked for the turtle again, thinking he could use a bit of luck, but the turtle wasn't in sight. It was still unmoving or had gone under the house by now, unless it was on its way to some other place that a turtle would be going.

Rhodes considered Ace Gable and Vicki Patton. They were as unlikely to have killed Neil as Wade. Although he could assign them motive easily enough, it wasn't a strong motive, hardly worth killing a man for.

Then Rhodes thought about Earl Foshee, who'd implicated his own brother. He'd pretended to be reluctant to do it, but maybe that had been his plan all along. Get Neil and Louie out of the way, and Earl would be the drug lord. Not that it was any great position in Blacklin County, but Earl might not look at it that way.

Rhodes was afraid he'd underestimated both the Foshees. He'd have to stop by the hospital and see how Earl was doing. Have a little talk with him. See if he'd confess. It was worth a try.

"Gone?" Rhodes said. He was in Earl Foshee's hospital room, talking to Sue Thornton, the nurse who'd met him in the hallway when he'd gone looking for someone to explain why the room was empty. "I thought he had a severe concussion."

"He wasn't discharged," Sue said. She was tall and thin, and her hair was clipped close to her head. "He slipped out. I came in to check on him about ten minutes ago, and he was gone. So are his clothes. I let Dr. Reese know. I'm sure he's had someone call your office by now."

Not putting a guard on Earl had been a big mistake. Rhodes had been wrong about him. He was shrewd, and he might be a killer. The commissioners weren't going to be happy, and neither was the mayor.

Rhodes thanked the nurse and left the hospital building. He looked around the parking lot. There was no way to know if Earl had stolen a car, but it was a possibility.

It was also possible that Earl hadn't stolen a car, so Rhodes looked around for escape routes that a man on foot might have taken.

Nothing looked promising. Rhodes got into the county car and got Hack on the radio.

"I know all about it," Hack said before Rhodes could tell him anything. "Dr. Reese called and said Earl's gone AWOL. You know the commissioners are gonna jump on you about not puttin' a guard on the door, don't you?"

"I hope they do," Rhodes said. "I'll jump on them about not having enough deputies to do the jobs this county requires. Get Buddy to go out to that house where Louie and Earl were staying. I'm going to look around here in town."

"You think Earl's gonna stay around? I bet he's halfway to Mexico by now."

"Not if he's on foot. Even if he stole a car, he'll need some things from home. You get Buddy out there."

"I sent him as soon as the doctor called," Hack said. "I'm always ahead of the curve."

"Did you tell Buddy not to shoot him?"

"I didn't figger that was my job."

Rhodes hoped Buddy would show a little restraint. It wasn't a case of bringing Earl in dead or alive.

"Let me know if Buddy needs help," Rhodes said, and signed off.

The sun had dropped down behind a cloud bank, but Rhodes didn't feel much cooler. If Earl was on foot, he was going to be going slow, not just because it was hot but because of the concussion. Which way would he have gone?

The Clearview City Park was across the street from the hospital, and it didn't offer much shelter. The hospital itself took up a couple of blocks, so if Earl had gone back north toward town along the sidewalk, he'd have been easy to spot when Rhodes drove up. The road south didn't have anything to recommend it. It was open all the way. Would somebody pick up Earl if he was hitchhiking? Not likely. That left the west side of the hospital. There were houses on that side, and yards with trees. Earl could make his way to the railroad tracks and walk along beside them to the highway, but it would still be tricky for him to get out of town. He'd have to get a ride somehow.

Rhodes got in the county car and drove down toward the tracks. He didn't spot Earl sneaking through any of the yards he passed, but someone or something was moving along in the shadow between a couple of boxcars and an old brick building that a wholesaler used for storage. Rhodes turned off the street and drove beside the tracks until he came to the boxcars. He stopped the car and got out.

Earl would have heard him drive up, if indeed it had been Earl that he'd seen. Rhodes still wasn't sure. He walked along the side of the boxcars opposite the side the man he'd seen had been on. When he reached the end, he bent over and looked underneath the cars. He didn't see any sign of Earl or anyone else.

He went around the end of the cars and looked at the vacant lot behind the brick building. The lot wasn't really vacant. It had plenty of weeds on it, many of them several feet tall, and there were some signs of a structure that had once stood there. Rhodes couldn't remember what it had been. It had been gone a long time. Across the street from the lot were some old vacant buildings. Rhodes didn't think Earl had managed to get that far. He was probably hunkered down in the weeds.

That is, if the person Rhodes had seen was Earl. It might have been just someone who happened to be walking along the tracks. However, Rhodes didn't think that someone out for a stroll would simply disappear into a weedy lot.

Glancing along the edge of the lot, Rhodes noticed a spot where some of the weeds were mashed down. He walked over. Sure enough, someone or something had made a path through the weeds. Rhodes got out the Kel-Tec and followed the path, wading through weeds that reached up to his armpits.

He came to a spot where a concrete foundation of some kind still remained. It was cracked and broken, and the trail ended at the edge of it. Several large concrete blocks lay around, all of them almost hidden from sight by the high weeds.

"You here, Earl?" Rhodes asked.

He didn't get an answer, but he hadn't expected one. A car drove past on the street but didn't slow down to see what the sheriff was doing standing up to his armpits in weeds. Probably too busy texting or talking on his cell phone to notice that there was anybody around.

"Last chance, Earl," Rhodes said. "Show yourself and I'll get you back to the hospital, where you can get the kind of medical care you need. That concussion is too dangerous for you to take any chances."

The weeds on the other side of the little foundation began to shake. Rhodes couldn't feel any breeze, and he didn't think there was a snake big enough to make the weeds wave like that. He walked across the concrete and followed the movement. The weeds ended at a narrow driveway that led to the back of the brick building. The movement stopped.

Rhodes stopped, too.

Earl, and it was bound to be Earl, had a couple of choices. He could try to get across the driveway and into some more weeds, or he could give himself up. Neither choice was a good one, and Earl hadn't been very bright to put himself in such a situation. Rhodes hadn't underestimated Earl's intelligence after all.

He had, however, underestimated Earl's desperation. Instead of taking one of the two options Rhodes believed he had, Earl jumped straight up and charged headlong at Rhodes, windmilling his arms with the weeds whipping all around him.

Rhodes didn't want to shoot Earl. He didn't even want to hit him with his fist, because of the concussion, but he had to stop him somehow.

The weeds slowed Earl down enough so that Rhodes had a second to get ready for him. He waited until Earl was nearly on him, then simply dropped down into the weeds on his left. Earl went right on by.

Rhodes got up as Earl was coming to a stop, walked up behind him, and said, "Stand right there, Earl. I don't want to shoot you, but I will if you don't settle down."

"You wouldn't shoot me in the back," Earl said.

"Sure I would. Not in the head, maybe, but in the leg. Down around the knee joint would be a good place, I think. I'm so close I can't miss."

"I'd sue the county if you do."

"You might even win. Want to put it to the test?"

"You really think I might win?"

"No," Rhodes said. "I don't. You'd be able to predict when it was going to rain, though, by the pains in your knee when the weather starts to change. You think it's worth it?"

Earl's shoulders slumped. "I guess not."

"Good answer. Now put your hands on top of your head and we'll walk to the car. When we get there, I can slip the cuffs on."

"You don't have to do that. I won't give you any trouble."

"You might find this hard to believe, Earl, but I don't trust you."

Earl sighed and put his hands on his head. "Did you get Louie?"

"I did," Rhodes said. "He's in the jail already. Got him a nice, comfortable cell. Not as comfortable as the hospital room you had, but better than that shack at

Merritt's Lake where he was holed up."

"Used to be some good fish in that lake," Earl said. "I caught me a big bass there when I was a kid."

"You're not a kid anymore," Rhodes said. "Let's go to the car."

They started walking through the weeds. Earl said, "Louie's gonna be really mad at me. I shouldn't have ratted him out."

"I don't think he'll mind," Rhodes said. "He's not the one who killed Neil."

"Who is, then?"

"You are," Rhodes said.

CHAPTER 20

Earl protested his innocence all the way back to the jail, which was only to be expected. He was so vehement, however, that Rhodes almost believed him.

"Why would I do it?" Earl whined. "I never wanted to get in trouble with the law, much less kill anybody. I didn't want to be a meth cooker. I just wanted to be left alone. It was Louie and Neil that got me into this mess to start with. Neil said it would be easy. Good money, not much work, that's what he said. He didn't say about how dangerous it was and how we could get blown up. He didn't say about how the law would be after us all the time and put us in jail."

Earl was like a lot of criminals and all-around lowlifes Rhodes had encountered. Nothing was ever their fault. They'd always been lured by bad companions into committing crimes, or they'd been too drunk to know what they were doing, or their teachers or parents had mistreated them. It was always something.

"That must be why you shot him," Rhodes said. "Because he got you into the drug business and got you arrested."

"I didn't shoot him. I told you that already. I wasn't even there when he got shot. Louie was there. Don't you remember what I said?"

"I remember, all right. You ratted Louie out and claimed he was the one who shot Neil. Louie says that's not so. He says you were the shooter."

Earl kicked the back of the seat, jarring Rhodes a little.

"That damn Louie!" Earl said. "He's trying to put the blame on me so he won't be the one going to trial for killing Neil. He's the one did it!"

"Don't kick the seat again," Rhodes said.

"I didn't mean to," Earl said, lowering his voice. If he was trying to sound contrite, he didn't quite succeed. "You got me all stirred up."

Rhodes didn't have anything to say to that. He'd started thinking again, and he wondered why Louie hadn't turned on Earl. It would seem natural for him to do it, but he hadn't even bothered to suggest that Earl might be the killer. Why hadn't he done that? Could it be because he didn't think Earl was guilty?

There was still the problem with the gun, too. Earl wasn't any more likely to use a .38 than Louie was. Even if he had used a .38, where was it?

Rhodes would have to worry about those things later. Right now he needed to stop by the hospital and see what Dr. Reese had to say about Earl.

Dr. Reese cleared Earl for a stay at the jail.

"We're too crowded to have someone in a bed if he doesn't need to be here," the doctor told Rhodes after examining Earl. "If he's feeling well enough to run away and if he didn't suffer any ill effects from crawling around in that weed patch you caught him in, then he might as well be resting in a bed in the jail as in one of ours."

"You're sure he'll be all right?" Rhodes asked.

"I'm never certain about something like that. He should be, though, if he doesn't bang his head on something."

"I'll be careful with him," Rhodes said.

"You do that," Reese said. "Now take him out of here."

"I'll be glad to," Rhodes said.

■ ■ ■ ■

Rhodes got Earl stashed in a cell with a minimum of fuss from Hack, but he knew Hack was merely waiting for a good opportunity to get a few words in. When Lawton returned from the cellblock, Hack got started.

"How many people you goin' to arrest for killin' Neil Foshee?" he asked.

"As many as I have to," Rhodes said, "but so far I haven't arrested anybody for that particular crime."

That was true. Louie and Earl were in jail for a different reason, though they could be charged with the killing at any time if it became necessary.

"Maybe you ain't charged anybody," Hack said, "but you got two men in jail back there you think might've done it, and you went after that Clement kid, too."

"Narrowin' the field," Lawton said. "That's the way to go about it. Cast a wide net. Arrest enough of 'em, and sooner or later you're bound to land on the right one."

"I guess that's it," Hack said. "He's arrested just about ever'body that's ever been close to that Moore house except the mouse."

333

"What mouse?" Lawton asked.

"You know. That one he ran across the first night. Like to've executed him right there on the spot, is what Ruth told me."

Rhodes didn't think Ruth had told him any such thing, but he wished she hadn't mentioned the mouse at all. Hack was never going to forget about it. It was a good thing Hack didn't know about the rat. No telling what he'd make of that.

"Executed him without a trial?" Lawton asked. "Is that legal?"

"Is for a mouse," Hack said. "People do it all the time. They got what they call humane traps now, but people still use the other kind."

"Sounds like a hard life," Lawton said. "Glad I'm not a mouse."

"I hate to interrupt this intellectual discussion," Rhodes said, "but have we heard anything that might be of help in the case and that doesn't involve mice?"

"Guess it depends on what interests you," Hack said. "Mika left you a report, but I can tell you she said that Clement kid's .38 hadn't been fired in about twenty years."

"Wasn't his .38," Lawton said. "Was Miz Clement's."

Hack squirmed around in his chair so he could give Lawton a glare. "I don't need you to tell me whose .38 it was. I know it was hers, but the kid's the one had it in his possession."

"That ain't what you said."

"It's what I *meant,* though, and the sheriff knows it. Ain't that right, Sheriff?"

Rhodes wasn't going to be tricked into taking sides when Hack and Lawton went at it. He'd been dumb enough to do it in years past, but he'd learned his lesson.

"I didn't hear what you were talking about," Rhodes said. "I was thinking."

"What about?"

"About Earl and Louie," Rhodes said.

"That's a sorry subject to think about," Lawton said. "You ought to think about somethin' better."

"What were you thinkin' about 'em?" Hack asked.

"That maybe they didn't kill Neil after all."

"If it wasn't one of them, who was it?" Hack asked.

"Somebody else," Rhodes told him.

"That's a good one," Lawton said with a laugh. "You should've figgered that one out for yourself, Hack. If it wasn't Louie and it wasn't Earl, it just about had to be some-body else."

"The sheriff ain't funny," Hack said. "He

just thinks he is, and you ain't funny, either. Anyway, if it wasn't Louie or Earl, what it's lookin' like to me is that the mouse is gonna take the fall."

"Other people have been involved with Neil," Rhodes said. "Not just the mouse."

"You talkin' about that redheaded woman?" Hack asked. " 'Cause if you are, you're on the wrong track. She wouldn't kill anybody."

"How do you know that?" Lawton asked. "You ain't seen her more than a time or two."

"I ain't seen as much of her as the sheriff has," Hack said, "and that's the truth."

Both of them got a laugh out of that, though Rhodes didn't. He was still a bit embarrassed by the incident in the picnic area, though it had worked out all right. That is, it had worked out if Vicki Patton hadn't killed Neil.

"One more thing," Hack said, "before I forget it. Your friend Seepy Benton came by. He said to tell you to be sure and check out Jennifer Loam's Web site for all the news about the haunted house. That's what he called it, the haunted house. He says there was for sure a ghost there and that it led him to a *corpus delicti*. That's what he called it, but even I know a skeleton ain't a *corpus delicti.* It was a skeleton."

Rhodes didn't bother to explain how a skeleton could be a *corpus delicti.*

"Did you look at the Web site?" Rhodes asked.

"Sure did," Hack said. "Really nice write-up about how Seepy and that Harris fella led you to the skeleton, thanks to their advanced ghost-huntin' techniques. That's the exact words. There was a picture of the skeleton, too. You didn't come off lookin' like Sage Barton this time. Mostly it was all about Seepy and those advanced techniques. He did mention that the whole thing was official, though. I think he said something about how he was assistin' the sheriff in his duties. Had a big ad for his business right on the page, too. Prob'ly half the people in the county are callin' him right now so he'll come run the ghosts out of their houses."

"It was a good ad," Lawton said. " 'We open the doorway between the living and the dead,' is what it said."

"They stole part of that line from William Wordsworth," Rhodes said.

"Poet, ain't he?" Hack asked.

"That's the one," Rhodes said.

"Dead a long time," Hack said. "So he won't sue 'em."

"Not a chance," Rhodes said, but he wasn't thinking about William Wordsworth or Seepy. He was thinking about the skeleton. It was too soon for any information to have come back from the state crime lab. It would take weeks for that, or months. They wouldn't be in any hurry since the skeleton was so obviously old, but Rhodes would like to know more about it. What he'd especially like was to identify it. That didn't seem likely to happen, but the ghost . . . He stopped to remind himself that he didn't believe in ghosts. Whether he believed or not, however, the odd happenings had ceased when the skeleton was found. Why would that be? If some purpose had been accomplished, Rhodes couldn't for the life of him figure out what it was.

He was missing something, and he knew it. He just didn't know what he was missing.

He knew the answer would come to him, though, and not because some rat or ghost led him to it. He wouldn't mind if the rat or a ghost led him to whoever killed Neil Foshee, but that wasn't going to happen.

Neil's ghost wasn't going to be any help, either. It seemed to be happy to remain quiet. Not that there was any ghost, but if there was, it wasn't seeking revenge or anything else, not at the moment.

Rhodes stood up. "I'm going to lunch. Try not to call me for at least half an hour."

"Lunch?" Hack said. "It's nearly five o'clock. That's a mighty late lunch."

Rhodes hadn't realized it had gotten that late. "All right, then, I'm going home and have dinner. Don't call me at all unless it's an emergency."

"Have I ever called you when it wasn't an emergency?"

"All the time," Rhodes said.

Ivy hadn't arrived when Rhodes got home, so he took Yancey out to the backyard for a romp with Speedo. It was still too hot for Rhodes to want to do any romping himself, but it was shady on the back steps where he sat.

The dogs didn't seem to mind the heat. They tussled over the squeaky ball and chased each other all over the yard. After a while they ran over by Speedo's igloo and laid down in the shade to pant. Rhodes had always heard that dogs panted to cool down. He didn't know if that was true, but there were times when he'd felt like panting himself.

After he'd sat on the steps for about fifteen minutes, thinking about skeletons and meth dealers, Ivy came out of the house and sat beside him.

"Hard day?" she asked.

"About the usual," Rhodes said. "You?"

"Insurance is boring. I'd rather hear whether you've caught any killers or found any more skeletons."

Rhodes told her about all that he'd done that day and admitted that he wasn't any closer to finding Neil Foshee's killer.

"I thought it was Louie," he said, "and then I thought it might be Wade Clement. After that, I had a hunch it could be Earl. Now I don't think it's any of them. I'm sort of at a loss."

"What about the ghost?" Ivy asked.

"There wasn't any ghost."

"Let's pretend there was."

"Let's don't. What about your new friend Vicki Patton? Do you think she'd kill anybody?"

Ivy shrugged. "Haven't you told me that anybody is capable of killing somebody, given the right circumstances?"

"I might have," Rhodes said, "but we're talking about somebody you know. Somebody you like. What kind of circumstances would there have to be?"

"I can't think of any," Ivy said. "I'll tell you one thing, though. I don't think she'd go to a haunted house at night and kill anybody. If somebody attacked her, that would be different. How would she even know that Neil would be in that house?"

"I don't know," Rhodes said. "The same goes for Ace Gable. How would he know?"

Speedo had recovered from his romp, and he came running over with the ball, wanting Rhodes to play with him. Yancey came, too. His legs were too short for him to keep up with the black-and-white collie, but he didn't get discouraged.

Rhodes ignored both of them, waiting to see if Ivy had an answer for him. She didn't, but she did have something to say about Gable.

"I think he's perfectly capable of killing somebody," she said. "He's big, and he's kind of pushy. I've dealt with him a few times at the insurance office. I don't mean that he's a bully, but he likes to get his way, and he can be intimidating."

Rhodes thought that someone as big and forceful as Gable was more likely to get his revenge on somebody by using his ability to intimidate, and if that didn't work, to use his fists. At any rate, finding a motive for Gable wasn't easy.

"Has Vicki ever said anything about him?" Rhodes asked.

"She likes him," Ivy said. "She says he's not at all intimidating to her."

Rhodes wasn't sure that meant anything. After all, Vicki had liked Neil Foshee at one time.

Rhodes reached for the ball in Speedo's mouth and got it on the first try because he'd taken the dog by surprise. Usually it was hard to get the ball, even though Speedo wanted him to have it. Rhodes threw the ball across the yard, and the dogs took off at a run.

"Does it ever bother you that you're suspicious of everybody?" Ivy asked.

"I'm not suspicious of everybody," Rhodes said. "Just the people who might've done something wrong. I'm not suspicious of most people."

Somehow Yancey had wrestled the ball away from Speedo. Speedo watched as Yancey raced back toward Rhodes. When Yancey was about halfway there, Speedo took off, caught the smaller dog, snatched the ball away, and ran off. Yancey went after him.

"You have to look on the darker side of things all the time," Ivy told Rhodes.

"Not really. I can always see a little bit of light. We have more good people in this county than bad ones."

"Sometimes I wonder."

Yancey got the ball again and ran away from Speedo, who pretended he didn't care and went off to pant beside the igloo.

"You can take my word for it," Rhodes said. "Nobody's all good, but nobody's all bad, either. It's all mixed up in most people. Even the Foshees are just a little bit away from being good folks."

"It might be a little bit, but it makes a big difference," Ivy said.

"Sure it does, but usually the ones who are a little bit away from being bad manage not to cross the line too often. If they didn't, I'd need a few hundred new deputies."

"What you really need," Ivy said, "is a good night's sleep. Everything will be clearer in the morning."

Rhodes wasn't so sure. "I keep thinking I've been going about this the wrong way. It's like a puzzle with a piece missing."

"If it's missing, you'll find it."

"I hope so," Rhodes said. He stood up. "Come on, Yancey. Time to go in."

Yancey dropped the ball and ran to the house.

Ivy suggested that they have dinner at a restaurant, so they went to Max Schwartz's barbecue place. It wasn't Saturday night, which was why Rhodes agreed to go. He knew there was no danger of Seepy Benton performing. Seepy had been replaced a few months before by a barbershop quartet called the Next Edition, but the quartet had broken up when their tenor moved out of state. The tenor's move out had allowed Seepy to move back in, and he was again providing the alleged entertainment on Saturday nights.

"He's not that bad," Ivy said, when Rhodes mentioned Seepy's singing.

"He's not that good, either," Rhodes said.

"I think his songs are funny," Ivy said.

So did Rhodes, though he thought they were funny only in the sense that they were odd, not that they were amusing. Rhodes hoped that the ghost hunting would keep Seepy busy and maybe even keep him out of Rhodes's hair for a while.

Rhodes felt better after a Seepy-free evening of lean brisket smoked over a mesquite fire. The potato salad and coleslaw were good, too. Rhodes was in an optimistic mood by the time he got home, but then he dreamed about skeletons again, all night long.

CHAPTER 21

The dreams had Rhodes feeling out of sorts the next morning, even though he couldn't quite remember exactly what they'd been about other than the skeletons. He went out to feed Speedo and to spend a few minutes playing with him and Yancey. Yancey, unlike Rhodes, was feeling peppy, and when they went back inside, the little Pomeranian even ran over and yipped at the cats.

Jerry opened one eye and looked at him. Sam didn't open his eyes, but he reached out and swiped at Yancey with one clawed paw. He missed, but even the miss was enough for Yancey, who ran yipping from the room. He'd hide under the bed for a while, but then he'd be all right.

Rhodes had shredded wheat for breakfast instead of turkey bacon, and while he liked shredded wheat just fine, it would've been better with whole milk. Ivy preferred skim milk, which Rhodes thought was really just

345

slightly off-color water, no matter what anybody said.

When he got to the jail, he asked Hack if there was anything that needed his attention.

"Nope," Hack said. "I'll bet you hoped Louie or Earl would call somebody back to the cellblock durin' the night and confess to killin' Neil. Didn't happen, though."

"No emergencies?" Rhodes asked.

"Nope. I'd've called you if we'd had one, even if I had to wake you up. Worst I can tell you is that there was some speeders and some copper thieves. Just the usual."

What was unusual at the moment was that Hack didn't have any long, involved tales to tell. His partner in crime wasn't around, so that could've been the reason.

"Lawton and me got to talkin' last night," Hack said.

Rhodes suppressed a sigh. He'd been wrong about the long, involved stories. Hack was going to start up, all right, even without Lawton being there to help him out.

"You wanna know what we talked about?" Hack asked when Rhodes didn't respond.

"Do I have a choice?"

"You know what?" Hack said. "I'll tell you what. One of these days you're gonna hurt my feelin's, that's what."

"I apologize," Rhodes said, knowing he'd have to listen now. "Please tell me what you and Lawton were talking about."

"Not sure I want to," Hack said.

"We're getting to be like an old married couple," Rhodes said. "Either tell me or don't tell me."

"Now you're gettin' snappish. Lawton's always sayin' how snappish you're gettin'."

It was Hack who was always saying that, but Rhodes didn't bother to point it out.

"I apologize again," he said.

"I accept. What we was talkin' about was that skeleton and how it must've got there in the house. You know how we told you that people didn't disappear around here?"

"I remember," Rhodes said.

"Well, Mika looked, and we don't even have a missing persons file. If you don't count a few runaway kids, that is, and the thing about the kids is that none of 'em's run away in years, not since you been in office. That ain't all, either. The ones that did run away was all found. Any disappearances, such as there was, they've all been cleared up."

"So did you and Lawton come to any conclusions about where the skeleton came from?"

"First thing we thought of was aliens. Like

347

in that Area Fifty-one. You know about that?"

"That's where the government is supposed to have the carcass of the alien that crash-landed in Roswell, right?"

"Right. I didn't think you believed in stuff like that."

"I don't," Rhodes said.

"Well," Hack said, "you can believe it or not, but that's the idea that we come up with. An alien."

"You didn't stick with that one?"

"Couldn't think of any flyin' saucer crashes around here. There was a big flyin' saucer scare back in the fifties, people saw a bunch of 'em. As far as Lawton and me could remember, though, none of 'em crashed."

"I guess that lets out the aliens, then."

"Not necessarily. We tried to think of some other answer, but we couldn't come up with one. So it might be an alien."

"If it is, what should I do about it?" Rhodes asked.

"You might oughta check with the air force, or whoever it is that keeps records on that kinda thing. They could tell you if there was some UFOs that we didn't know about."

"Judging from what I've heard," Rhodes

said, "they don't give out that kind of information to just anybody."

"You ain't just anybody. You're the high sheriff. They oughta tell you."

"Let's wait until we get a report back from the state. That skeleton looked human to me."

"Like you'd know an alien if you saw one."

"I think I'd know," Rhodes said.

"If it wasn't an alien, then what was it?" Hack asked.

"Just somebody like you and me."

"If it was somebody like that, who was it, then?"

"I don't know," Rhodes said, "but I'm going to find out. If you need me, I'll be at the Moore place."

"Gonna check with the ghost about the skeleton?" Hack asked.

"Something like that," Rhodes said.

Rhodes looked around for the turtle before he went inside the Moore house, but he didn't see it. It might have moved on, or it might be under the house or in another part of the yard. Or maybe it hadn't been there at all. Rhodes was starting to think he'd imagined at least a few of the things that had happened lately. Not the skeleton, however. That was real enough.

He went inside and stood in the room where Neil Foshee had died. Because the house was so old, the rooms were big, and the ceilings were high. It had been around a long time, and it had quite a history. It was just the kind of house that would have a ghost in it if there were such a thing as a ghost.

Rhodes waited for a full five minutes, hoping he'd notice a ghostly presence or experience the feeling of being watched. After the five minutes had passed, all he felt was foolish. What had he expected? He knew ghosts didn't exist.

He looked around the room and at the spot where Neil Foshee's body had lain. This must also have been the room where Ralph Moore had died. Two deaths in the same room. Did that make the house more likely to be haunted? Would Neil's death add to the legend?

Rhodes went up to the attic. The stairs still didn't squeak. The closet was empty, of course. Rhodes wondered why he'd even come up there. Had he really planned to ask the ghost anything? He heard a stirring in the walls. He'd disturbed the mice, he supposed. This was their place now, for good and all, as far as Rhodes was concerned.

He went back down the stairs and outside. The turtle was waiting for him. Well, not really. He knew that. It just happened to be there. For all Rhodes knew, it wasn't even the same turtle he'd seen before. The markings on the shell might've been the same, or they might not. Rhodes couldn't tell.

He went on to the county car, and a little breeze rippled through the weeds. The temperature in the yard dropped, although the sun was still shining through the trees. Rhodes turned to look at the house. He saw nothing unusual, but when he turned back to the car, he knew what he'd been missing all along. It was as if he'd known the whole time, and maybe he had. It had just taken this long for it to bubble to the surface of his mind.

He'd been treating all the crimes — Foshee's death, Moore's death, the drug dealing, the disappearance that wasn't a disappearance, and the death of the person who'd left only a skeleton — as if they had nothing to do with one another, as if they were all separate. But they weren't. They were all connected, and now Rhodes knew how. He might even be able to prove it.

Thinking about it now, Rhodes knew it could've been something Hack said that had made all the pieces come together. He wasn't sure he'd mention that to Hack.

The breeze died away, and Rhodes got in his car. He knew where to go now, and what to do.

Brad Turner sat on his porch in the same battered recliner he'd been in when Rhodes had talked to him before. He was wearing the same baseball cap and the same clothes. He looked as if he might not have moved at all.

Rhodes stopped the county car in the same place he'd parked before and got out. Turner didn't get up, but Rhodes didn't expect him to. Rhodes went up on the porch and sat in the wobbly wooden chair he'd sat in, but this time he didn't bother to ask permission. The chair still creaked when he sat in it.

"Hey, Sheriff," Turner said. "Sure is a hot day."

"It is," Rhodes said. "Might get hotter by afternoon."

"Usually does," Turner said. "You ever lock up the mayor?"

"No, that didn't happen."

"Didn't figger it would. The big dogs always get away with anything they want to."

"Sometimes the little dogs do, too,"

Rhodes said. "For a while, anyway."

"Not usually, though," Turner said.

He leaned forward, took off his baseball cap, and wiped his head, and Rhodes noticed that the tinfoil was gone.

"Not afraid of the brain cancer anymore?" Rhodes asked.

"Them radio waves have stopped botherin' me for some reason," Turner said, leaning back. "Don't know why. Maybe the phone company's found a way to make 'em safer."

Rhodes didn't think that was it, not at all. He had a feeling that something else had been bothering Turner's head, but it was gone now.

"Did the tinfoil really help any?" Rhodes asked.

"Sometimes," Turner said, putting his cap back on. "Not a whole lot, though."

"Tell me some more about your wife," Rhodes said. "Betty Jane, I think her name was. Ran off and left you, right?"

"That's it. Ran off to Arkansas."

"What was the name of the fella she ran off with?"

"Can't remember," Turner said. "It was a long time ago."

"How'd you know she went to Arkansas? She leave you a note?"

"She might've. Or she might've called me. Can't recall now. Long time ago, like I said."

"You ever bother to divorce her?"

"Didn't think about it. Figgered it didn't matter."

"I don't guess it did," Rhodes said, "considering that she never got any farther than the Moore house."

Turner twitched a little at that.

"I found her in a closet in the attic," Rhodes said. "Right where you put her."

"I never," Turner said.

"The way I see it," Rhodes said, "the fella she was thinking about running off with was Ralph Moore. You decided to put a stop to it and killed them."

"Way I remember the story, Moore died of a heart attack."

"He had some bruises on him. Might have been in a fight or a struggle that triggered the heart attack. Maybe he was trying to keep you from killing Betty Jane. We'll be getting the DNA tests back on her in a day or so. That will pretty much cinch it."

The DNA wouldn't come back for weeks or longer, but Rhodes didn't think Turner would know that. For that matter, he might not even know what DNA was since he didn't have a TV set.

Turner sighed. "Didn't happen like that,

Sheriff. You got it all wrong."

"You might as well tell me what did happen, then. Before you do, though, I want to tell you that you're not under arrest, but I'm going to tell you what your rights are, anyway."

Rhodes gave him the Miranda warning. "You understand all that?"

"Sure do. Not too hard even for an old guy like me."

"Good. Why are you going to tell me what happened now? You got away with it for a long time, but you must have known somebody would find out sooner or later. Why didn't you just admit what you'd done?"

Turner scrunched down a little farther in his recliner. "Thought I'd be arrested the next day. When that didn't happen, I thought it'd be pretty soon, so I just waited. Before long, I'd waited a year or more. Figgered I'd just keep waitin'." He paused and took a deep breath. "I guess the wait's over."

Rhodes tried to imagine what had happened. It was easy enough. When Moore was found dead of a heart attack, no one had seen a need to search the rest of the house. Nobody knew Betty Jane Turner was missing, because if anyone asked Turner about her, he just said she'd run off to Arkansas with some other man. People in those days were willing to accept that kind of explanation. Probably still were. The Moore relatives never cared about the house and just left it closed up until people broke in and pretty much cleaned it out. Nobody had gone into the attic, or if they had, they hadn't told about the skeleton because they didn't want anybody to know they'd been looting the place. So the years just went by.

"Been a long time," Rhodes said. "Forty years or so. What really happened up there?"

"We had a dog," Turner said. "Betty Jane and I did. Name was Rover. Lots of folks called a dog that back in those days. Don't know if they still do. Anyway, Moore, he didn't like dogs, and he called us a time or two about Rover gettin' in his yard. Then he shot him with his BB gun. Betty Jane went to tell him off, but I guess she didn't. He sweet-talked her, maybe. 'Fore long, she was goin' up there all the time. Took me a while to catch on, but I finally did. I got my pistol and went up there. I was plannin' to shoot Moore. Betty Jane, too. Didn't care what happened to me after I did it. Funny thing, though, I didn't shoot either one of 'em. We got to arguin', and I shoved Betty Jane down. Shoved her hard. She hit her head on the sharp end of a coffee table and caved it in. Her head, I mean. Made an awful sound. Killed her right then and there, I think. Moore jumped me, and I hit him a time or two. Not in the face or anything. He started stumblin' around and tryin' to get his breath. Fell down in the floor not far from Betty Jane, and there they were, both of 'em dead as doornails."

"You didn't try to help either one of them?" Rhodes asked.

"Nope. Knew they were dead. Figgered it was good riddance. Took Betty Jane up to the attic. She wasn't very big, but it was a strain on me, you can bet. Stuck her in that closet and went home and went right on as if nothin' had happened. Went to work, came home, waited for the laws to come and get me. They never did." He looked at Rhodes from under the brim of his baseball cap. "Not till today."

"If you hadn't shot Neil Foshee, I wouldn't have come at all," Rhodes said.

"Yeah, I guess not, but he was calling too much attention to that house. I just wanted to talk to him, get him to go somewhere else before you and your deputies started lookin' too close at that place. I went up there to wait for him two or three nights, but he didn't show up. When he did, I was nice to him. I told him that he needed to find somewhere else to do his deals because

357

this was a quiet neighborhood and we didn't want him around."

"He didn't listen, did he," Rhodes said.

"Laughed at me, is what he did. Called me an old man. I had my pistol with me, knowin' how those drug dealers are, and sure enough, he had one, too. Pulled it on me. So I had to shoot him. He dropped down just like old Moore did that time. I took his pistol and his phone and got out of there."

"Did you really think I'd arrest the mayor for killing him?"

"Thought you might. The mayor was there. I saw that Alexis of his, just like I told you. He was probably gonna buy some drugs."

"No," Rhodes said. "It wasn't even the mayor."

"Sure looked like that big Alexis of his."

Rhodes didn't see any need to explain about the mayor's Lexus. He said, "You must have known we'd investigate Foshee's death. Maybe even find Betty Jane."

"Wasn't too sure you would. That other sheriff didn't find her. It's a funny thing, though."

"What's funny?"

"I been bothered for years by them radio waves, and a day or so ago, they just stopped." Turner touched his baseball cap. "Best I've felt in years."

"I don't think it was radio waves," Rhodes said, thinking of the electromagnetic waves measured by Seepy Benton and Harry Harris.

"What was it, then?" Turner asked.

"Do you believe in ghosts?" Rhodes asked.

Turner gave a short laugh. "Not me. Once you cross over, you don't come back. Ain't that right?"

"I used to think so," Rhodes said. "Now I'm not so sure."

CHAPTER 22

Rhodes arrested Turner, took him to jail, and got him booked without any problems. Turner was compliant and resigned, which made it easy. The problems started after the booking, when Jennifer Loam came in.

"I heard on the scanner that you were bringing in a prisoner, Sheriff," she said. "I thought I'd come by and see if you had a scoop for me."

"He sure does," Hack said before Rhodes had a chance to open his mouth. "Not only did he bring in the man who shot Neil Foshee, but he's solved a murder that nobody's even known about for forty years and found a missin' person that nobody even knew was missin'. I'd like to see Sage Barton do that. He might have a matched pair of pistols, but he ain't ever managed to do anything close to what the sheriff just did."

"Amazing," Jennifer said. "Is all that true, Sheriff?"

"Well," Rhodes said.

"Sure it's true," Hack said, "and that's just what happened. I got a mind like a steel trap, and not a bit of rust on it."

Jennifer brought out her little video camera and aimed it at Rhodes. "I'd like to get a statement from you, Sheriff. Tell me a little about what you've done."

"He can't tell it as good as I can," Hack said.

"He's right," Rhodes said. "I can't. Turn that thing on him. He'll fill you in."

"Durn right I will," Hack said, but he was prevented from telling the story when the phone rang. Hack answered it, and Jennifer smiled at Rhodes.

"Looks like it's up to you," she said.

Rhodes couldn't see any way to get out of it, so he told the story as succinctly as he could. He didn't make any mention of the strangeness he'd felt in the old house, and he didn't say that Brad Turner no longer needed to line his hat with tinfoil. He certainly didn't mention ghosts.

Jennifer didn't let him get away with it. "Dr. Benton and Dr. Harris, our local version of the Ghostbusters, claim that you were led to the skeleton of Mrs. Turner by her ghost. Do you have any comment on that?"

Rhodes thought it over. "I didn't see a ghost," he said.

"They said that their instruments showed a ghostly presence."

"I'm not an expert on those instruments," Rhodes said. "I'll have to leave that interpretation up to the good doctors."

"Would you endorse their services?" Jennifer asked.

"As a county official, I can't give endorsements."

"You'll have to admit that it was unusual for you to find a skeleton that had been undiscovered for forty or more years, won't you?"

"I don't think anybody else ever looked," Rhodes said. "There was no reason to."

Hack was motioning for Rhodes to pick up the phone, so he excused himself from the interview and did so. Wade Clement was on the line.

"I called to ask if it would be all right for me to leave town today, Sheriff," Wade said. "Your dispatcher's been filling me in on what's happened, so I guess I can go. Is that right?"

"That's right," Rhodes said. "The Foshee case is closed."

"I'm glad to hear it. The whole thing was a lot more complicated than I thought it would be. In fact, small-town law enforcement is a lot more complicated than I thought it would be. I'm going to write that paper I told you about, but I have a whole new perspective now. I want to thank you for that."

"We're here to help," Rhodes said.

"Yes, I guess you are, and I appreciate that now. Thanks again."

Rhodes hung up thinking that Wade was probably going to turn out all right. He wouldn't be messing around in police business anymore, no matter where he was. Not for a while, anyway.

After Rhodes got off the phone, Jennifer Loam asked him another couple of questions and then left.

"Oughta be a good story on her Web site later today," Hack said. "Would've been better if I'd got to tell it, though."

"I don't doubt it," Rhodes said.

"I'd've put the ghosts in it."

"That might've been too scary for her readers."

"Shows what you know," Hack said. "I'm one of her readers. We ain't afraid of no ghosts."

The rest of the day went by without anything strange or stressful happening. Rhodes even got to have lunch.

He got home that afternoon before Ivy did. He fed the cats, then took Yancey out back for some fun with Speedo. When Ivy came home, they went out for dinner, this time to the Jolly Tamale for Mexican food. It was a good day all the way around.

That evening when they were getting ready for bed, the telephone rang.

"It's Hack," Ivy said. "I know it is."

Rhodes answered the phone, and of course Ivy was right.

"Got a problem," Hack said.

"Why am I not surprised?" Rhodes said.

"Don't try to tell me you were asleep," Hack said. "It's not even ten o'clock yet."

"Just tell me the problem."

"Vernell's goats," Hack said.

Vernell Lindsey was a local romance writer, and she had three pet goats named Shirley, Goodness, and Mercy. Sometimes they caused problems.

"What's the matter with the goats?" Rhodes asked.

"They got out again. One of 'em's already butted in the side of a car. I called Alton Boyd, and he said he'd meet you at the jail. You better come on down."

"Why me?"

"He says he can't corral those goats all by

himself. Gotta have a helper. All the deputies are busy, so you're elected."

"All right," Rhodes said. "I'll be there in fifteen minutes."

He hung up and told Ivy what the trouble was.

"Are you sure you want to go after those goats in the dark? If one of them butts you, you could get hurt."

Rhodes started to say something, opened his mouth, and then closed it.

"What is it?" Ivy asked.

Rhodes grinned. "I ain't afraid of no goats," he said.

ABOUT THE AUTHOR

Bill Crider is the winner of two Anthony Awards and an Edgar Award finalist. An English college professor for many years, he's published more than seventy-five crime, Western, and horror novels, including *Compound Murder, Murder of a Beauty Shop Queen, Wild Hog Murder* and *Murder in the Air*. In 2010, he was inducted into the Texas Literary Hall of Fame. He lives with his wife in Alvin, Texas.

The employees of Thorndike Press hope you have enjoyed this Large Print book. All our Thorndike, Wheeler, and Kennebec Large Print titles are designed for easy reading, and all our books are made to last. Other Thorndike Press Large Print books are available at your library, through selected bookstores, or directly from us.

For information about titles, please call:
  (800) 223-1244

or visit our Web site at:
  http://gale.cengage.com/thorndike

To share your comments, please write:
Publisher
Thorndike Press
10 Water St., Suite 310
Waterville, ME 04901